Puck

Other Twisted Lit books you may enjoy
Exposure
Tempestuous
Anyone But You

Puck

By Kim Askew and Amy Helmes

Doublet Press

Published by Doublet Press

Trade Paperback ISBN: 978-0-9981613-0-3
eISBN: 978-0-9981613-2-7
Doublet Press Publishing

Printed in the United States of America

Cover design by Eric Wilder.

www.twistedlitbooks.com

ACKNOWLEDGMENTS

"We know what we are, but know not what we may be."
— William Shakespeare, *Hamlet*

Many friends, colleagues and loved ones have played an ongoing part in reminding us of what we are truly capable. For their invaluable feedback and eye for detail we thank our early readers, including Ruth Horne, Richard Simms, Phyllis Helmes, Marianna Fowler, and our literary fairy godmother, Nicki Richesin. Thank you to Jennifer Au, for your unwavering belief in our writing, to Victoria Koch for shedding new light on the process and to our it-girl social media expert, Jannet Kang.

Thank you to our biggest fans and trusted sounding boards, Amy's husband, Mike, and Kim's partner, Eric. And last, but not least, thank you to our parents for being there, then and now. We love you.

Come away, O human child!
To the waters and the wild
With a faery, hand in hand,
For the world's more full of weeping than you can understand.
—William Butler Yeats, "The Stolen Child"

CHAPTER 1

And Though She Be but Little, She Is Fierce

"Get up, Robin," the voice repeats, hacking at my tranquil sleep like a dull meat cleaver. "Up and at 'em, let's go." Before I can fully fathom what's going on, someone yanks back my faded floral comforter. Never mind that it's the middle of the night, and I'm only wearing a ratty Rude Mechanicals concert T-shirt and underwear. The overhead light casts a sick, whitish glow, and unfamiliar faces surround my bed as I scramble into a seated position, ready to bite, scratch, scream—whatever it takes. But then my street sense kicks in, and I remember: never show fear. If they get a whiff of it—even for a second—you'll lose, end of story. I adjust my features into a "see if I care" sneer.

"Get off me, you ass," I yell at the schlubby dude with a white-guy Afro who's just grabbed me by the elbow and hoisted me to my feet. I wriggle free and lunge toward the door, only to be blocked at the end of the bed by a tall, skinny praying mantis of a woman. She and the guy are both wearing maroon polo shirts: Thing One and Thing Two. They clamp on to my arms, but I pick my feet up off the ground and kick like Bruce Lee until they're forced to slowly lower my butt to the floor.

Leaving a family has always been routinely calm, with some harried case worker driving me and my neatly packed suitcase back to the Center. This, on the other hand, feels like a military raid. An abduction. It's starting to register: this (whatever *this* is) is really happening. My stomach drops, and I react with more thrashing and kicking. Sure, they have me outnumbered, but why should I make it easy for them? When has anyone *ever* made it easy for me?

"There's no sense in fighting us, Robin," says the woman who's strong-arming me. Her streaky blonde hair is asymmetrically close-cropped, and her pale green eyes emit zero sympathy—she may as well be some alien life-form anxious to harvest my organs.

"What are you, lady, some sort of exterminator? '*Pest Control: Ridding homes of inconvenient kids since 1998!*'"

I can't even laugh at my own joke, because the truth has hit me like a sucker punch. The awful truth. I'm being thrown out again like garbage, only this time no one's even pretending they care what happens to me. It's like I'm nothing. The last thing I want is for these assholes to see me cry, but the tears are streaming down my face anyway, and the worst part is I can't even wipe them away because my arms are still pinned.

"Who *are* you people? Where's Paula?" I shout, still flailing on the hardwood floor.

"I'm right here, baby." Her face appears in the doorway, and a catch triggers in my throat at the sight of her. She's bawling, too, but so what? No. I won't feel sorry for her, and I'm not buying the tears. She's the one allowing this. She's giving up, and that's far worse than messing up. "I didn't know what else to do," Paula says. "These people are going to—"

"Ma'am, sorry to interrupt, but the less you speak, the better," says the 'fro-sporting pack mule who practically has me in a half nelson. I'm guessing he's supposed to be more "muscle" and less "mouth," because the evil space-alien lady throws him the sort of stinkeye that says she's in charge.

"Nick, let me handle it." Before she can say anything more, Paula approaches her.

"I'm uncomfortable with this, Barb. Can't we just talk to her first?"

"This is the protocol. If rational conversations were all she needed, we wouldn't be here."

"But she's terrified!"

"And that's *okay.* We've already discussed this. Just because she cries doesn't mean you cave. It's not going to work like that anymore." Paula turns away, defeated.

"Paula, *please*!" I shout at her retreating back. My chest feels as though it might implode.

Thing One and Thing Two escort me to the bathroom to pee. Despite my strong protestations, Thing Two, the chick, chaperones the entire operation, as if I'm going to sneak out the second-story window or try hanging myself with Charmin two-ply. After I get dressed, they zip-tie my hands in front of me. (Overkill, by the way. I barely meet the height and weight requirements for a thrill ride at Castles N' Coasters.) Then the body snatchers drag me out the front door toward a big white van with tinted windows that's idling at the curb. It's the kind that might deliver carpets, and at the rate things are going, I'll soon be rolled up inside of one, dead, for all I know. Paula trails behind me, sounding like some ineffective hostage negotiator as she tries to reassure me.

"Do everything they say and you'll be just fine," she says. "Then you'll be home before you know it."

But home isn't here anymore. Not after this. Not

after…I pause at the sidewalk and turn to face her.

"Did Ted put you up to this? Don't you see what he is?"

"This isn't about Ted. This is about you. Getting you on the right road."

"I thought he was finally gone for good, that lech." I can hear my voice wuss out, and I silently curse myself for letting her hear how upset I am. "Instead, I'm the little mess you need to clear out of your life before you can marry and live happily ever after. I get it."

"That's not fair, not after what we've both been through with you. Please, for once in your life, just let someone help you."

If this is her idea of help, I'd been totally and completely wrong about her. And that's what's got my stomach all in knots as I take one last look at her. Her dark brown eyes look wrecked, but she's otherwise completely presentable, wearing the same olive green cardigan and khaki pants she was wearing yesterday when she got home from work, her arms laden with grocery bags. She never went to bed. She knew last night, smiling wearily at me from the sofa and wishing me sweet dreams. How could I have been so stupid? How could I have trusted her? I know I'm no saint, but I actually thought we were okay—just the two of us again. Clearly, I'm wrong. She's made her choice, and I'm not it.

The sky is sapphire, and there are still a few stars overhead. I feel a rush as the dry summer air fills my lungs, and I barely resist the urge to scream a loud "EFF YOU" into the night. Instead, I say nothing. My silence will hurt her more. I step onto the van's running board and slip through the open sliding passenger door, where my manhandlers converge to buckle me in.

When the blindfold goes on, I let loose a string of profanities. The chick running this 4:00-a.m. raid—Paula had called her "Barb"—is sitting next to me on the bench seat in the van's second row, invading my personal space. Her breath smells like coffee. My stomach churns.

"Just as I suspected," she says. "Meryl Streep waterworks around 'Mommy,' but the minute we turn the corner it's bye-bye tears and hello eff-bombs."

"Paula is *not* my mom."

"Okay, Nick, never mind, let's just change the subject," Barb says, but I refuse to let his insult go unchecked.

"You mean screw up her chances of marrying her Prince *Alarming*? Please. She should be *thanking* me." I reach toward the blindfold with my zip-tied hands. I can tell we're on a freeway. "I get bad motion sickness," I say. "I need to take this thing off so I can see."

"Touch it, and we'll have to restrain your arms *behind* your back. We've got a lot more driving to do, and I suspect you won't be comfortable sitting on your hands the rest of the way."

"About as comfortable as you'll be when I throw up in your lap."

"Do you think you're the first kid to try to vomit your way out of this?"

"What is 'this,' if you don't mind me asking? Human trafficking? A trip to the psych ward? I'm a lot of things, but I'm not nuts. Oh, god—" I move my jaw as if chewing rancid gum, puckering my lips in disgust. "My gag reflex is in full effect. Fair warning, lady, it's coming." She sighs and, despite her bravado, slips off my blindfold, wisely not willing to call my bluff where a puke threat is concerned.

"It's always the littlest ones who have the biggest mouths on them, eh, Barb?" says her male comrade from the driver's seat.

"Okay, Nick, never mind, let's just change the subject." Barb sighs. Me? I'm not about to let his insult go unchecked.

"If we're talking big mouths, then you and your giant donkey teeth have the market cornered, Nick." I say. "Your overbite deserves its own zip code."

"Consequences," he replies. I glance at Barb, guessing she'll elaborate. Her type always does.

"There are consequences to your words and actions," she explains. "You'll get a better understanding of what that means when we get to camp. It's a fair guess you will not enjoy them, so I suggest you take that as my one and final warning."

Some kids are enraged by power-tripping authority figures. Me? I get a giddy rush of adrenaline whenever I encounter adults who think they can break me. What they don't understand is that I'm already broken, which means I don't have much to lose. It's almost a game to me—a challenge. I enjoy pushing morons like this off their axes when they least expect it.

"By 'camp,' are you talking weenie roasts, or something more Nazi Germany in feel?"

"I won't dignify those words with a response, Robin."

"Stop calling me that. It's not my name."

"Really? Because I have a binder full of government paperwork that indicates it is."

"Whatever. I won't answer to it. Not even Paula calls me that."

"Well," Barb says, "campers don't get to dictate the terms of their stay with us, but if it is within reason, then I suppose—"

"My name is Puck," I say in a helpful tone. "Rhymes with—"

"Say one more word, and the blindfold goes back on." Her voice is eerily tranquil.

"One. More. Word." (See what I did there? Sometimes I'm my own worst enemy.)

* * *

The road trip from hell is punctuated by pit stops at fully disgusting gas-station bathrooms and revolting homemade cheese sandwiches eaten by them (refused by me) in the van for lunch. My ears keep popping during the drive, but somewhere along the way I nod off and dream that I'm safe in my toddler bed with its Tinker Bell sheets. (Don't judge me: I was, like, four.) I wake up to discover I'm actually leaning against that Barb chick's shoulder like it's a pillow, and I am so disgusted with myself that I completely lose it, yelling and arching against my seat belt. I want to make these assholes as miserable as they're making me, but they both seem bored by my display— amused, even. I can already tell I'm going to have to resort to some new tactical extremes, and when I do, they won't know what hit them. God, do I want a cigarette.

She's removed the blindfold now. Pointless, really, seeing as how there's nothing out the van window but an ugly stretch of wasted universe. Just flat, beige *bland*scape and desert weeds. We eventually turn onto a private drive.

"Say goodbye to your old life, Puck." Barb unbuckles her seat belt as the van rolls to a stop outside a nondescript building made of yellow-painted cinder blocks. (At least she's finally ditched the stupid name my birth mom saddled me with, but I've been around headshrinkers like her long enough to spot a patronizing attempt to "connect.")

I jump down from the van, happy to stretch my stiff legs, and Nick, "The Hick," cuts me free of my zip ties.

"Welcome to DreamRoads," he says, breathing in the air like some demented yogi. "This is the closest thing to paradise on earth, Puck. You'll see." His toothy grin and the way his eyes squint against the descending sun make me unsure if he's being cynical or if he's just plain stupid.

"This blows bagpipes." I sigh, glancing around at my surroundings. Apart from the building, some auxiliary sheds, and a couple of old school buses, the place is all dirt and scrub brush, like God gave up on trying to create anything cool out here, abandoning it to go get a beer instead. Everything is so hard and dry. Barren. Barbed. Giant, rust-colored rock formations frown from a distance, as if they're "incredibly disappointed" in me for blowing some cosmic curfew. Surprisingly, I can't see any fences or gates; only a smattering of large cacti stand sentry, so there's nothing to stop me from bolting when the time is right, which doesn't quite add up. The van has Utah plates, so I'm guessing that's where we are now, given how long we've driven from Flagstaff. Utah, great—the land of uptight religion and high-sodium lakes. My gut still feels iffy from the ride. "I don't suppose I could get a smoke before you inevitably strip me of every basic human right?"

"Well, you've got the strip part right," says Barb. She gestures toward a freckle-faced girl approaching me with an already-irritating smile and clipboard in hand. "Here's Mia. She'll get you set up with new clothes. Then you can join our other campers for the evening meal. You'll be assigned a bed, but don't get too comfortable. It's only for one night."

"The hell?! You mean there's more driving tomorrow?"

"Not exactly."

"Then what? *Exactly*?"

"Don't worry about that right now. We explain things here on a need-to-know basis."

"Well, maybe *I* 'need to know' the name of a decent

child-welfare lawyer so I can sue you and your hippie commune back into the 1970s where you belong."

"I understand that you're feeling frustrated and angry, but—"

"And maybe *you* 'need to know' the only real reason I'm here. It's because my foster mom's beloved fiancé, Ted, tried to get with me in the Biblical sense. Me! A fifteen-year-old! Paula wants to keep me off the grid here, to punish me, I guess, for blowing the whistle on his attempted rape."

I watch and wait for the grenade I just lobbed to send some noticeable aftershock across Barb's face, but she doesn't flinch. "Don't believe me? He was arrested. Look it up."

"I'm aware of the 'Ted' situation," she says, emphasizing every other syllable as if mocking me. The wind picks up, sweeping a mini cyclone of dust across the gravel driveway, and I involuntarily shiver. It's cold out here for early June.

Pissed at myself for bringing up the topic in the first place, I transfer my bitterness toward Ted to a more immediate target.

"Of course. What do you people care so long as you're getting paid? This whole thing's a joke, if you ask me. An epic swindle."

"No one's asking, and this isn't the appropriate time or place," Barb responds. "You'll have plenty of opportunity to discuss your feelings and personal history during our group sessions."

"Oh, counseling, whoop-dee-doo," I practically laugh as the Mia chick leads me by the elbow toward the building. Before I enter through the doorway I yell back over my shoulder, "I wouldn't spill my guts to you people even if you waterboarded me!"

I follow Mia down a long hallway, stepping over the extended legs of two guys my age. They're sitting casually with their backs against the wall, the way my friends and I used to when we'd hang out and smoke weed on the curb behind Goodfellows Pizza. Mia has stopped to root through a cabinet in the hallway, so I offer the guys a "whaddup" nod to acknowledge that they are my brothers from another mother. Evidently the feeling is not mutual.

"Damn, Peabo, check out the new hostage," drawls the hawkish boy with a close-cropped Afro and deep-set black eyes while stabbing his middle finger in my direction. As he sizes me up, his scowl gives way to a broad grin that is more menacing than friendly. A five-pointed crown is tattooed on the side of his neck. Translation: gangbanger. "It looks like a pit bull crossbred with a Muppet!" he adds.

"Fo shizzle," replies the lanky, drowned rat of a sidekick sitting next to him. He's got hair like dirty dishwater and the sort of pasty skin that reminds me of skim milk. Bad acne and a puny porn-star mustache do little in the way of improvements. "Yo, baby girl, can you tell me how to get to Sesame Street—*freak*? Wait, is that a 'she' or a 'he'? Ain't got no rack."

"Does it matter, dude? You strike me as an equal-opportunity horn dog," answers gang-boy, still leering at me, "though I'm pretty sure the only *real* action you've ever seen comes courtesy of the five-knuckle shuffle." He wiggles his fingers then facepalms his cohort, who immediately scrambles to his knees and cocks his arm back to throw a punch. Before he can unleash, Mia closes the cabinet door and glances in their direction.

"Ronnie, Peabo—*consequences*." At her soft-spoken words, Peabo—what kind of dumbass name is that?—freezes with his fist hanging in midair. He raises both eyebrows at Mia with the beginnings of an eff-you expression but then obediently returns to his seated position. Ronnie slides three body lengths away from him to make it clear they're playing nice. Damn. Either mild-mannered Mia is the world's most chill-looking badass ever, or *consequences* is a code word for bodily torture with hacksaws and pliers.

14

"Impressive," I say to Mia when she ushers me into a small office and closes the door.

"What?"

"In the hallway. Those dudes are scared shitless of you."

For about two seconds Mia giggles—straight-up *giggles*—at this. Then she clears her throat and glances at me as sternly as she possibly can. (Which isn't very.)

"There's no swearing allowed here," she says. I eyeball her. She can't be any older than twenty-five, and with the freckles and shiny red ponytail, she looks exactly like the "healthy, natural, fun girl!" in a tampon commercial. "Anyway, we're not trying to scare anyone," she continues with a shrug. "We sincerely want to help you." Seemingly at sharp odds with what she's just said, Mia reaches for a toolbox on a nearby desk and pulls out a pair of—I kid you not—needle-nose pliers. My eyes bug out of their sockets.

"What the hell do you need *those* for!"

"Language," she reminds me once more, pointing the tool in the direction of my face. "Your jewelry. It needs to come out. *All* of it."

I work her for five minutes or so; I'm not giving up any of it without a fight. My piercings are as much a part of me as my hair and my teeth—"It's not fair! What did my nose ring ever do to anyone?"—but Mia doesn't budge. *Fine.* I accept the pliers, finding it a little weird that she trusts me with them. I mean, I could gouge her eyeballs out if I wanted to.

"The tongue ring, too?" Ignoring my puppy-dog eyes, she nods, placing a small mirror in front of me.

"You can get them back when you leave, but first, we're getting you back to *you*. The *real* you. Adornments need to go." Her tone is kind, but firm—sort of like Paula's. I brush away the unwelcome thought.

I'm in the process of grudgingly removing a stud from my right eyebrow when there's a knock on the door and a male voice asks, "Everybody decent in there?"

The speaker pokes his head in, and I see he's wearing the same style of maroon "staff" polo shirt as Mia.

"Hey, you! Come on in!" Mia smiles and glides her rolling chair out of the way to make room for him. "This is Puck, by the way. Puck, this is Xander."

"Awesome," he says with a maddening lack of irony. The dude has "hipster douche bag" written all over him, complete with scraggly blond beard, shoulder-length bed-head hair, and Windex blue eyes (though to be fair, I suppose he has no control over his eye color). In any case, he looks like he should be serving vegan soy lattes at some fair-trade coffee shop. "You're in luck, Puck. We're celebrating your arrival tonight with Sloppy Fauxs."

"Sloppy whos?" I ask.

"Meatless Sloppy Joes," Mia explains. (Can I read people or what?)

"Just came in to grab some buns. Did I just say that?" Xander shoots Mia a devilish grin before climbing a metal rack and rifling through several bags of bread products in a bin near the top. Ripe for scoping out, his own buns are at eye level. The hem of his polo shirt inches upward to reveal the blue gingham waistband of boxer shorts sticking out the top of his grey cargo pants. I catch a quick glimpse of washboard abs. (Verdict: not bad, I guess, if you're into skinny yoga boys.) Jumping down, he clicks his tongue and shoots Mia one more smile before leaving. Her face turns as deep red as her shirt, and I realize I've just hit pay dirt.

"Somebody call the fire department," I say once he's left the room.

"Excuse me?"

"*Xander.* Oh, come on." I fan my face with my hand. "Scorching." She spins away from me in her swivel chair and pretends to write something down in some folder. "Don't tell me you don't see it," I continue. "Are you kidding me?"

"I don't see anything. No, of course not! He's…

he's…my colleague. Besides," Miss Prim adds hesitantly, "there's no fraternizing at camp. It's forbidden. That goes for students *and* staff. You'll see that when…when you sign the rules pledge, and, and—"

"Mm-hmm. If you say so." I eye her like I'm not buying. I can spot a liar a mile away. The stuttering and shifty eyes are a dead giveaway. "So hypothetically speaking, if you and Xander were ever to hook up, there would be—" I carefully ponder my words, "—*consequences*."

Her mouth forms a shocked O. I've got her.

"I suppose," she says, composing herself and then hastily adding: "Hypothetically speaking." I'm not sure when or how I'll use this interesting scrap of information, but like spare change or Kleenex, it seems a useful thing to keep in my back pocket. When it comes to manipulating adults, knowledge is power. Their weakness is my weapon.

I'm done removing all the jewelry, and my head feels about three pounds lighter, as if I could flit up to the ceiling if I wanted to. Mia reaches for the mirror, then pauses.

"You're not going to see your reflection for a while after this," she says. "You may as well take a good last look."

18

Beats me what she's getting at, but something in her tone of voice convinces me to go along with it. The last thing I need is to meet more of those punks from the hallway with snot hanging out of my nose or something. Apart from all that missing metal, the girl staring back in the glass offers up no surprises. Hair: short and spiky, burnt to within an inch of its life by the flame-red home-dye kits I've been using for the last seven months. Eyes: bleary and raccooned-out with the charcoal liner I didn't wash off last night. Face: Uninteresting…forgettable. My features are tiny and pinched. Grandma used to say I was as cute as a Keebler elf, but I don't see any trace of that little girl in the mirror. She bolted a long time ago, and more power to her. (My situation isn't exactly the sort you'd willingly stick around for.) If Grandma could see me now, she'd say I've got all the makings of a demonic circus clown. Then she'd feel guilty about my having a meth-head for a mom, so she'd end up letting me stay home from school and watch game shows with her all day. You can bet she'd never have sent me to this godforsaken place, no matter how many holes I punched in my face. Grandma was *the* best.

I smooth a wonky eyebrow hair with one of my fingers. I'm feeling like a major scuzzball, and I still feel sick in the pit in my stomach from the ride. At any rate, the image in the mirror is making me feel even worse, so I hand it back to Mia.

"You're our last intake recruit for the summer." Recruit? She makes it sound as if I were picked in the third round of the draft, like I should get an oversize team jersey and an interview with Sports Center. "You're replacing a last-minute dropout. All the other campers have been here for at least a week or two—some even longer than that. They can show you the ropes, but if you have any specific questions or problems, come to me or one of the other counselors, and we'll try to sort you out."

"How long do I have to stay here?"

"DreamRoads is open-ended."

"What about when school starts back up in September?"

"You leave when you successfully graduate from the program—or if your parents decide for some reason to pull you out early."

"I don't have parents. At least, not the kind who can get me out of here." Mia turns red and averts her eyes.

"The fact that you're even here means someone cares about you. A *lot.* So—" she changes the subject (they always do at this point in the conversation), "—what size shoe do you wear?"

"Six and a half. Aren't I entitled to my one phone call

20

or something?"

"Chin up, girl. This isn't prison." She says this almost sympathetically, holding up a pair of khaki camouflage pants to judge whether or not they'll fit me.

"Last rites?"

"It's going to be fine. You'll be amazed at what having a fresh start out here in the high desert can do." I'm not convinced. After six different foster homes and double that many schools, I've about had it with fresh starts. "We're pretty much done here," Mia concludes, "so you can change into these clothes, but first, I've got to make sure you haven't brought anything in with you."

"What, you think I'm clenching a semi-automatic between my butt cheeks or something?"

"If you don't want me to do it, I can always go get Barb and she can—" Aww, *hell* no. I'm not letting her battle axe of a boss anywhere near my naked body, so I wriggle my elbow through the armhole of my shirt.

"Okay, okay, okay," I mumble. "Geez. You could at least buy me a drink first."

CHAPTER 2

A Lion Among Ladies Is a
Most Dreadful Thing

For the record: What happens at dinner is not my fault.
Poking at my applesauce with a plastic spoon and trying
not to inhale the vile stank of Sloppy Fauxs, I keep my
ears peeled and my mouth shut, avoiding eye contact with
the handful of other kids and staff members seated along
the dining room's two metal picnic tables. I'm sitting with
three other girls my age and some overweight dreadlocked
dude they've been calling Snout. It's hard to tell if the
moniker actually bothers him, because he's mostly just
acting like a crazy person, rocking back and forth and
repeating the phrase "Walla Walla, Washington" over and
over. Ronnie and Peabo—the boys who dissed me in the
hallway—are over at the other table, but still close enough
that I can hear more of the off-color remarks they're
lobbing in my direction.

The girl directly across from me has long platinum hair that's a weave, for sure. I know from experience you can't bleach hair that white and still have it so glossy and perfect. Her gums have not stopped flapping since she sat down, and all she's doing is bitching. I mean, I get it. I'm feeling all kinds of aggro myself, but the difference is, she's whining about stupid things, like her ragged cuticles and the "Made in India" tags on the pants and T-shirts they're making us all wear. It's idiotic, like a homeless person complaining about the color of his sleeping bag. What's weird is that she looks familiar to me, but I can't put my finger on where I might have seen her before. God knows I'm not down with the rich-bitch set, although at the moment, I can't decide who annoys me more: this chick, or the two ass-kissing girls on either side of her. Stealing another furtive glance at Slap-Me Barbie, I can't help but think of those plastic toy teeth that you wind up and let clatter across the table. She just won't *shut up.*

"Xander!" she calls out. "How many times do I have to explain that I don't eat gluten products of any kind?" With her plastic spoon, she nudges the top of her sandwich bun off the plate until it's lying faceup on the table. Snout quickly reaches across me to snag it. He holds the bun close to his mouth and sniffs it like a paranoid squirrel, mumbling under his breath. As far as I can tell, this kid's brain has officially derailed.

"Puck! Have you met everybody?" Mia says before sitting down next to me with her dinner tray. She waves to another maroon-shirted girl, who squeezes onto the end of the bench next to us. Like Mia, she seems like she might just as well be pledging a sorority, not presiding over a bunch of teenage castaways. But whereas Mia is all perky and cute, this other counselor reminds me of a deer with long thin arms, high cheekbones, and olive skin. "Puck, this is Ellen," says Mia, making introductions. "Ellen, Puck." A stray wisp of Ellen's precise black bob falls into her face. Tucking it behind her ear, she purses her lips together like maybe she's trying to smile, but instead it comes off like a lopsided frown.

"Wait a minute," says the diva with verbal diarrhea. "The newbie gets to be called Puck? This is so unfair!"

"We've been over this a thousand times, Tonya," says Ellen, unfurling her paper napkin onto her lap. "I don't care what sort of private helicopter you arrived in; you're just a regular person here like everyone else. And you'll be treated as such."

"Regular and rock star don't go together—that's an oxymoron, with the emphasis on *moron*," says one of the girls sitting across from me. She has frizzy ombre-dyed hair and a sizeable gap between her two front teeth.

Catching the eye of the other girl at our table, she says, "You saw her in Vegas, right, Frances?"

"Yeah, the 'Titania Now' tour," replies the other suck-up—or should I say groupie? Because once I hear the name Titania, it becomes instantly clear to me who the bitchy diva is. "I saw you in Vegas *and* Reno. What a great show," the girl named Frances continues, yanking out her ponytail holder and reassembling her wavy auburn hair into a bun. It looks like an atomic bomb is detonating from her head. "I camped out for tickets, and it was totally, *totally* worth it. I bought a bottle of your fragrance, *Immortal*, too."

The celebrated object of the girls' idolatry flips her tresses behind her shoulder.

"See, Frances and Nissa just made my point," she says. "The whole planet knows me as Titania—eleven million self-titled albums, to be precise. So why act like it's some kind of dirty word?"

"Titania is a trademark, some slick music executive's idea of branding," Ellen responds. "It's a label, not a person. It's not *you.*"

"Maybe that's why you're here, Tonya," Mia chimes in. "To figure out who you really are underneath all those false trappings of glamor and fame."

"Not to mention those computer-enhanced vocals!"

shouts a familiar voice from the other table.

"*Nothing* on me is 'enhanced,' Ronnie, so shut your mouth!" Titania yells back.

"If only some voice coach had 'nads enough to tell *you* that, the world would be a better place," he responds, goading her. (He's right, by the way: Titania can't sing for shit. Not that I'm into her brand of bubblegum pop schlock, but I've heard enough to cringe.)

"C'mon, Ronnie, we've talked about this," says another young staffer seated at his table, his voice a slow drawl. (I'm willing to wager the state of Texas is inked somewhere on his body.) "If you want to voice opinions here, please do so with respect."

"But respect has to be earned; isn't that what Barb won't shut up about? Well, that wannabe—" he jabs a finger in Titania's direction, "definitely hasn't earned it."

"Your hostility toward Tonya is contributing to a lousy climate here at camp," says the country-boy counselor, staring him down across the picnic table.

"But—"

"As they say where I come from, if you find yourself in a hole, you'd best stop digging." Ronnie mumbles under his breath in sulking Spanish—the closest he'll come, I'm guessing, to waving any white flag.

A grateful Titania rewards the counselor with a

flirtatious wave.

"*Thank* you, Dmitri." With her elbow she nudges her toady with the two-toned tresses, who leans in to lap up her every word. "God, Dmitri's so *hot*. How old do you think he is?"

Nissa says nothing but exhales loudly, raising savagely plucked eyebrows into a "trust me, don't go there" expression.

"Do you seriously think 'Hot for Teacher' is the right person to ask?" Frances interrupts, indicating her fellow fangirl. Nissa's brow crinkles at the apparent dig, leaving me wondering how on earth she earned the nickname. "Anyway," Frances lowers her voice, "Dmitri's cute and all, but that twangy accent? Totally unsexy, *y'all*."

"Whatever," says Titania. "I don't need him to talk. Where I'm from, we call that type of guy a 'shut up and
—'"

"Girls!" Ellen exclaims, all squeamish and indignant.

"Oh, come on, Ellen," says Titania. "Tell me you wouldn't like to grab his Texas panhandle."

Ellen gasps and her lower jaw flies open as Mia stifles a laugh. If Mia is the girl next door on staff, Ellen is the sort of uptight chick who, despite being relatively attractive, probably never gets laid. She'll be easy to wind up. Apart from Barb and Nick, all the staffers around here seem young—barely older than the rest of us. Makes sense, though. Staying out in the boonies with a bunch of completely dysfunctional adolescents is the sort of entry-level social-work gig only a recent college grad would be willing to sign up for.

In case you live under a rock, Titania's shoplifting excursions and drunk-driving exploits are sort of legendary. Her face is always plastered across supermarket tabloids with headlines like "Trainwreck Titania" and "Little Girl Lost." I'm a little surprised I didn't recognize her from the get-go, but minus the shellacking of makeup and the glittering "slut"-wear, she's pretty much your garden-variety dumb blonde. Who'd have thought someone like her would end up among the nobodies at this lowbrow brat camp? Isn't she exactly the reason celebrity rehab resorts exist in the first place? She's back to her nonstop talking now, by the way.

"Hey, Peabo, you're into sports and stuff. When's the All-Star game? My agent's booked me to sing the national anthem."

"July fifteenth? Sixteenth, maybe?" As he answers, Peabo, who had been stacking his empty plate in the nearby sink, crosses his arms and leans his spindly frame against the counter in an ineffective attempt to look suave. "Middle of summer, basically." Titania splays her arms out on the table and drops her forehead next to her plate of uneaten food with a melodramatic thud.

"But that's only six weeks away!" She lifts her face up from the table to give Mia and Ellen a desperate glance. "Please say I'll be out of here by then. Will I?"

"That depends on you, not us," answers Ellen. "Well, and Barb, of course."

Right on cue, Barb appears at the doorway, and a hush falls over the room; even Titania ceases her yapping.

"I can see that you all had your fun while Nick and I were away," the camp director says, parading the length of the two picnic tables with the sort of grim-faced scrutiny you'd expect from an Army drill sergeant. "I'm incredibly disappointed in you all. The bunks are barely made; the lavatory is filthy. And who punched a hole in the drywall? Ronnie, was that you?"

"No, ma'am." He and the other kids are practically cowering in her presence. Even the counselors are all glancing down at their plates. She's sucking the energy from the room like an industrial-strength vacuum cleaner.

"Of course not. Because you're all such angels, aren't you? Angels who are going to end up in prisons and halfway houses and welfare lines someday—probably worse, too, unless you figure out a new way to be. Clearly, you guys just aren't getting it, and that's going to change whether you like it or not. We head out tomorrow."

I have no clue what she's talking about, and though everyone is strangely silent, spirits seem officially deflated by her latest newsflash. It's like they've all just given up. Why are they just taking it? I feel that familiar acidic drip starting in my thoughts and winnowing down into my gut. When this feeling kicks in, things never end well.

Once Barb concludes her verbal shakedown, kids and counselors resume talking, only with the volume turned way down low. A few minutes later, Titania launches into a quiet rendition of the national anthem. Eyes closed and nose scrunched, she raises and lowers a hand near her face with every note, like a military salute that can't make up its mind. I seriously wish I could just yank her tongue out. Nissa and Frances—the girls sitting next to her—are enraptured. An engine clicks on in my brain and starts to rev, slowly at first…but building up steam with every whiny high note. Maybe it's irrational of me. I mean, crazy-boy Snout has been imitating a car alarm all through dinner, and *that* I could handle. But it's like a switch has been flipped where this chick is concerned. I can't explain the force compelling me, just as I can't resist the urge to laugh when the hamburger bun I fling hits the unsuspecting diva squarely in the face.

I never quite know what to expect after I go snap-crackle-pop, but I'll let you in on a little secret: I sort of get a contact high from the chaos that usually ensues. Case in point, Titania jumps up from her bench and flings her uneaten plate at me. Sloppy Faux dreck and applesauce pelt my hair and drip down my neck, and now it's on. I fly across the table at her, and we both clatter to the ground in a heap of sharp limbs. The rest of the room is a feverish blur, and things don't come back into focus until Titania has me pinned and is pounding me with her fist.

"Get them apart!" Barb's screaming. She yanks Titania by her hair and pushes her toward Nick, but then *she* takes Titania's place on top of me, urging me to give in as my chin digs into the cold linoleum floor. I'm practically hyperventilating, and Titania is glaring at me like she's possessed as Nick holds her back. "That's it, Robin! This is over!" says Barb, in a tone of finality, easing her grip on me. In one swift motion, I grab a plastic spoon that lies within arm's reach, snap its handle squarely against the hard floor, and swipe it through the air at Barb's face. She may think she writes the rules around here, but she's wrong. It's over when *I* say it's over.

* * *

The water's so cold it hurts. I'm gritting my teeth and

breathing hard, every muscle in my body tensed against the icy shower raining down on me. Though I'm trying to suck it up and act like it doesn't bother me, I'm glad there's a shower curtain dividing me from Ellen and Mia, who are "supervising" on the other side. It's hard to play it tough when you're naked and freezing.

"Warm water would help calm her down," says Mia, appearing to plead my case.

"A hot shower is a reward. You saw the cut on Barb's face. She's lucky it didn't hit an eye." They're speaking low, but I strain to hear every word. Through the dingy PVC curtain, I can just make out their silhouettes. Ellen's considerably taller figure looms above Mia as they lean in, whispering.

"She cooperated during her intake, all things considered. Such a wisp of a kid; I didn't expect this out of her."

"It's a good reminder," says Ellen. "We can't let our guard down around them."

By the time I rinse the shampoo from my hair, they've detoured into "oh-my-god-your-hair-is-so-cute/no-shut-up-*yours*-is" territory.

"He doesn't notice, anyway," Ellen says, clearly unaware that I can actually hear them over the shower. "Not like he used to."

"Oh, honey. I thought you'd gotten past all that."

"Out with the old, in with the new: which is *you*, apparently." She sounds resentful.

"Don't remind me," says Mia. "He's the sort of dude my *dad* would want me to date. You know, the guy who drives a pickup truck and votes Republican."

"Yeah, well, pretend you're me. That's sure to turn him off."

"He'll come around, girl. In the meantime, don't worry. I'm taken." Their discussion veers back into the direction of music and movies, leaving me at a loss to interpret their momentary personal exchange. It's soon clear that I'm not going to harvest any other usable shreds of gossip, which is my cue to wrap up our bathroom trio. With chattering teeth, I peek my head around the shower curtain.

"I got all the food off," I say, reaching for the faucet handle. Mia blocks my hand.

"I'm sorry, Puck," she says. "You've got to stay in here for ten full minutes. Barb's orders."

"What? But why?"

"Good behavior equals comfort. Bad behavior equals discomfort." Something about the way Ellen says this reminds me of a book we read last fall in English class called *Animal Farm.*

"Christ. What *is it* with you people?" I back into the shower again and stare up at the nozzle that's hissing back at me.

"A little water never killed anyone," Ellen says. I close my eyes at these words and brace one hand against the slimy cold tile.

"Shhh!" I hear Mia whisper to her. "You're my best friend, but you can be a real 'B' sometimes."

"Oh, god, I wasn't even thinking," Ellen whispers back. "I forgot, I swear." That's when I'm certain that they know about my past. All of it. Barb must have shared my records with the entire staff. I'll admit I'd been feeling just the tiniest bit of guilt about stabbing her with a plastic utensil, but now…now I'd do it again in a heartbeat—and worse—if I got the chance.

Yeah, a cold shower sucks, but as "consequences" go, they're going to have to try a lot harder than this. And I'll have to work a lot harder at giving them my worst.

All adults have their threshold, the point at which they call it a day and declare me someone else's problem. It'll happen here, too. That moment can't come soon enough. All at once, my face turns hot and my chest shudders. I'm not normally the blubbering type, but today has been…a lot. Anyway, like I said: I'm *really* glad I've got the curtain to hide behind. I stare down at my toes,

34

which have turned purple-ish blue. The water at my feet is swirling down the drain. If only I could, too.

CHAPTER 3

How Long Within This
Wood Intend You Stay?

"Okay, listen up," Barb says, shining a small flashlight on the clipboard she's holding. "Those of you assigned to Group A, head over to Xander and Mia. Group B, over there." She points to Dmitri and Ellen, then holds the flashlight so that it illuminates her face, which has the unintentional effect of making her look ghoulish. Well, more ghoulish than usual. There's a gash just above her right eyebrow held closed by a butterfly bandage—my handiwork from last night—but she has yet to mention anything about the incident this morning. "You know the drill. Nick and I will reconnect with you all this afternoon after our supply run. I expect only good reports from our counselors, or there will be...say it with me, now—"

"*Consequences*," the kids respond in unison, their voices dull.

Adjusting the fifty-pound pack that Nick helped me hoist onto my back a few minutes ago, I join the others, who are staggering like hunchbacked zombies toward the pile of scraggly brush where Freckle Face and Xander are waiting with eager smiles.

Turns out, DreamRoads isn't a typical juvenile detention facility at all; it's a crummy wilderness-survival training program. I'm clearly the last one in on this sick joke, because everyone else seems miserably resigned to our collective fate. Barb's giving us some more instructions (lecturing is her favorite pastime), but my mind has turned her voice into the trombone noise adults make in those animated Charlie Brown specials. *"Bwah-bwah-bwah rattlesnake, bwah-bwah-bwah poison oak, bwah-bwah-bwah black bear attack."* (Yeah, like *that* would ever happen? The chick's just trying to freak us out, but I'm not an idiot. They'd be liable up the wazoo if any one of us got hurt. The only thing we might die of out here is boredom.) Her sermon is also peppered with the same self-help garbage I've heard from adults all my life, though never quite in this context.

"The wilderness will perform its magic on you," she promises in a falsely chipper tone. "It's not going to be easy, and you'll have to work hard, but if you just hang in there, this can be a life-changing experience."

I can't even tell you how many times I've heard speechifying like this from social workers, therapists, ministers, and teachers. In a nutshell, they promise whatever new initiative, grant program, group home, or therapy they're touting is going to work miracles, see? But they're wrong. They never do. *Never.* I'm sure it makes people feel like superheros, swooping in to save me. That's the thing about being a kid like me; all you really are is an opportunity to make other people feel good about themselves, and then when they realize you aren't an easy fix, well, it's like you never existed. In the end I'm basically a living, breathing reminder of their utter failure, and who wants that in their face? (That's a rhetorical question, by the way. The answer is *no one.*)

Forcing me to commune with nature and pee behind bushes is a new one, though, I'll grant you that. I'm not even certain any of this is legal, what they're doing to us. I glance around in the barely breaking dawn, still formulating what my exit strategy will be. Perhaps Barb senses as much, because after her little "rah-rah" motivational speech, her next words seem directed at me.

"I'd like to remind you all that we're hundreds of miles from any civilization," she says, blinding me with her flashlight. "Your only link to survival right now—your food, your water, your basic human needs—is this group.

Abandon the program, and you won't make it far. The coyotes will find you before the cops ever do." Though I'm still pretty sure she's full of it, I grip the shoulder straps of my backpack a little tighter. "That said," she continues, waving her hand as if laughing off her last threat, "we haven't lost a kid out here yet. And we don't intend to. We're about *finding* here. Finding purpose. Finding hope. Finding inner strength. Just remember, the only way home is to finish the course. It's up to each of you to decide how long you want to stay here on the DreamRoad. I need to see a metamorphosis in you before I can make the determination that you're ready to return to the outside world." Butterfly metaphors? What, is she a *poet* now?

Three other kids are with me in Group A, and I'm pretty ticked off to see punk-ass Ronnie among them. He's been staring at me as we've been waiting for Mia and Xander to get this show on the road, and when I make a stealth finger gesture at him in return, his curious expression flips to a leering grin. I'm about to cuss him out when someone else bumps into me and knocks me off-balance. The giant load on my back pulls me over like a capsizing boat, and I land with a thud.

"Don't just stand there, you skinny twerp," I yell at the kid responsible, a boy who's even smaller than I am.

"Help me up!" He reaches a tentative hand down to me, but as I clamor to my feet (no help from his feeble assist), he stumbles backward and falls on *his* butt. His glasses are knocked off-kilter, and his arms and legs flail like the limbs of an upended turtle. If this place didn't suck so bad, I might actually be tempted to laugh at the slapstick. Rocking with great effort to gain some momentum, the kid finally rolls awkwardly onto his side and scrambles back up to standing.

"Sorry about that," he says, nervously. "It was an accident."

His DreamRoads-issued clothing is too big for his small frame, and his eyes are moist pools of agitation magnified by thick lenses. As "juvie offenders" go, this kid doesn't fit the part. I'd peg him for more of a, I don't know, national-spelling-bee champion. In any case, it's vaguely comforting to find someone I can pity more than myself.

"Nevermind," I say, putting him out of his misery. "Just quit being gravity's bitch, man." I whisper this, not wanting anyone to overhear and think I'm going soft on this kid. After last night, people here seem wary of me, and that's just the way I want them. "Has anyone ever told you you look like a Chinese Harry Potter?"

"Only all the time," he sighs. "J.K. Rowling pretty

much ruined my life. I'm not Chinese, though. I'm Filipino."

"Watch out, 'Queer One,'" says Ronnie, butting into our conversation. "Homegirl may carve a lightning bolt between your eyes with one of her plastic cutlery shanks."

"Yeah, well, going under the knife would only help in your case, Ronnie," I reply. "The ugly gene's apparently not recessive in your family." He laughs at my insult before wandering away to hock a big loogie in the dirt.

"My name's Quynh-Wan. Ronnie likes to…get creative with it," scrawny Harry Potter says almost under his breath, "but I go by Quin." Sizing him up more closely, it occurs to me that responding with one of my typical jibes would be a sheer waste of my talents and might reduce this sad sack to tears, for all I can tell.

"I'm Puck."

"I know." He gives me a jittery glance.

"So you saw me go ballistic last night?"

"I was in the bathroom when it happened, but word gets around fast here. Not that anyone ever actually talks to me…Not usually, anyway."

"Okay, listen up, everyone," Xander interrupts, flinging his pack onto his shoulder like it only contains Styrofoam peanuts. "We're hiking until 1300 hours, when we'll meet up with the other group for lunch. Go easy on your water; it needs to last you all morning. We're going single file, and any breaking from ranks will not be tolerated. Mia will lead, and I'll bring up the rear."

"Did he just say 'up the rear'?" I say, more loudly than I'd intended. Frances—one of Titania's ego-strokers from last night—laughs. Ronnie offers me an appreciative fist to bump, but I ignore him.

"Save your breath, Puck," says Xander, unfazed. "Something tells me you're going to need it for the hike."

About fifty yards away, Group B, led by Ellen and Dmitri, is already heading out. Just before he's beyond hearing distance, however, Dmitri turns back to face us, striding backward along the path with a good-ol'-boy grin on his face. His unruly brown hair is brought to heel beneath a straw cowboy hat, and he's sporting aviator sunglasses in the pre-dawn light. Poser.

"Mia!" he shouts. He throws one hand in the air, extending his pinky and index finger—and strangely, his thumb too—to flash her an odd sort of "devil's horns," then swivels to follow Ellen and their deadbeat ducklings onto the trailhead. I hear Xander grumble nearby.

"Relentless," he tells Mia. "I thought you set him straight, but I can see I'm going to have to make it a little clearer that you and I are—" She shoots him a flustered glance before he can complete his thought, giving him a stern shake of her head. *Not in front of the children*, she seems to be implying. While I'm wondering what the deal is, Ronnie steps into place behind me in preparation for the dreaded march.

"Hey," he hisses. I tense, waiting for phase two of the smacktalk he and Peabo initiated yesterday. "Mad props on that beatdown last night. Bitch totally deserved it."

"Oh? I'm glad to know I'm not the only one who isn't buying what Barb's trying to sell around here."

"Huh? I'm talking about that celebrity skank," he continues. "Man, I thought it was bad here before, but then 'Grammy Queen' comes in all whiny and condescending to the rest of us. I've got to admit, watching you bust up on her last night felt damn satisfying. I would have done it myself, but, well, my auntie taught me to never hit a girl."

"Looks like you've more than made up for it with the other half of the population," I say, eyeing his hands, which are scarred and knobby and remind me of a dog's rawhide bone. He slaps the back of one hand against the open palm of the other.

"Somebody comes at me wrong," he says, shrugging, "I might mess him up." His face is incomprehensible. Is the flicker of gloom in his eyes a threat, a regret, or maybe a combination of both? "I've been at camp the longest, though, and know what that gives me? Seniority."

Oh, I get it. Street thug thinks he can boss *me* around? I nod, all meek-like, playing along. Or rather, playing *him*. I need information right now more than I need to school this guy on where we really stand in the pecking order.

"Shake the lead out, people," Xander says, interrupting us. "Let's get a move on."

Keeping step behind Mia and Quin as we set off down a wide dirt road, I toss Ronnie another question over my shoulder.

"How long have you actually been here, anyway?"

"Coming up on six months, I guess." I shoot him another look—*Are you kidding me?*—but he just shrugs, evasively.

I glance back up the trail, feeling a prickling sensation in the shadowy divots behind my earlobes. *Six months out here?* Ahead of me, the horizon has turned from slate grey to a vibrant orange, the color of construction barrels and traffic cones: Proceed with caution. But when have I ever done that?

CHAPTER 4

I Can No Further Crawl, No Further Go

"So then my volcano sort of imploded, but I won an award anyway." Quin is boring me with some of the most lame-ass anecdotes I've ever heard, but I don't tell him to shut it because his stream-of-consciousness rambling is a distraction from both the thoughts in my head and the burning in my legs. And I probably couldn't respond anyway because each gasp of air I take hurts like a mother. The back of my mouth is simultaneously dry and full of mucous (if that's even possible), and my heart feels like someone plunged a knife in it. Not that I ever embraced physical fitness before, but wherever we are must be a bazillion feet higher in altitude than Flagstaff. We've been hiking for at least four hours but have only just begun to ascend from the brush-filled desert into a more wooded area. Suffocating canyon walls rise overhead, and, like a few wayward ants, we're inching our way along a trail that weaves through jagged, rocky terrain. There's a strong floral scent in the air, like being trapped in an elevator with some old lady wearing too much cheap perfume. I push the brim of my floppy safari hat up and steal a quick glance at the sun, which has been slowly rising behind us all morning. Every now and then we walk through a patch of swarming gnats, too many of which zoom up my nostrils. Nature sucks.

"I need to sit down!" I spy a low, gnarled branch on what looks like a poor man's bonsai tree—a perfect bench. Before I can manage to lower myself onto it, Mia's by my side, hoisting me back up by the elbow.

"Nope. Taking a break is going to make it even harder. Just keep walking, and momentum will pull you through. You're stronger than you think you are."

Her "Climb Every Mountain" ploy falls flat. She may be enjoying this little torture trek, but I refuse to be her Sherpa.

"I'm going to collapse, just kick the bucket, right here," I reply in heaving breaths. "And then it'll be on you. You'll have a *dead kid* on your hands." I'm pissed, but too exhausted to put up my normal show of resistance, which frustrates me even more.

"C'mon," she says, nudging me onward up the trail. "Tell me something about yourself."

"There's nothing to tell."

"Okay, then, I'll start. I'm the youngest of five kids, born and raised in Provo. I'm working my way toward an MSW at Utah State, and I've spent the last three summers working here at DreamRoads."

"What's an MSW?"

"A master's degree in social work."

"Oh, you should rethink that plan. I've dealt with *loads* of social workers, and most of 'em seem overworked and miserable. Poor, too."

"Yeah, well, no one gets into it for the money, believe me."

"So why spend your life in such a depressing career?"

"To make a difference. I know that's cliché, but there's no other way to describe it. I guess coming from such a big family, I always kind of felt lost in the shuffle. I want to try to make other people feel like their concerns matter. That, and I really love working with people your age. You're very real, more so than most adults I come across. Anyway, what about you? Where do you live?"

"I don't know where I live. At least, not anymore."

"Well, someone cares about you enough to send you here."

"Yeah, right."

"I'm serious. Do you know how much this place costs? I'll give you a hint—it makes college tuition look like piggy bank change. Somebody clearly thinks you're worth it."

"Yeah, well, nice that my foster mom would rather bankrupt herself than have me in her house one more day; that's comforting." I did wonder to myself how Paula was footing the bill, especially given the upcoming wedding expenses. I still can't believe she's willing to marry the guy, but nevermind—I learned my lesson yesterday about bringing Ted into the conversation. "If this place costs so much," I reflect aloud, "then Barb really *is* a scam artist. She's figured out how to torture children for mere pennies on the dollar."

"That's enough," says Mia. (Notice how she didn't refute me?)

"No, really. She's nuts."

"She's a professional, and it's all a part of her process. Most kids respond well to her firm hand."

"Oh, well *that* doesn't sound sadistic. Are swift kicks involved, too? Whips? Chains?"

"Here's the thing." Mia stops walking and turns to face me. "Barb can either be your best friend out here, or your worst enemy. It's up to you to decide which that will be."

Before I can even question what that means, she gives me a last glance and then, with the spastic energy of a competitive cheerleader, bounds ahead of me to her place at the front of the line, leaving me to wonder what, if anything, she's keeping to herself.

Behind me, the sound of Ronnie's gruff laughter indicates that he is about to weigh in.

"You really think you have Barb's number, don't you?"

"Yeah: six-six-six, to be precise."

"That woman owns your sorry butt, so you had better play the game."

"Believe me, I've got plenty of game. Enough to Houdini my way out of here without having to sell my soul to Dragon Lady."

"I thought that way too, once," he says in resignation. "But even *if* you miraculously outfox Barb, there's no getting around the Stepping Stones."

"What are the Stepping Stones?"

"Figure it out yourself. I'm not your damn DreamRoads manual." Then he, too, charges up the trail ahead of me.

Behind me, Frances is griping to Xander with a nasally voice about a cramp in her side. She sounds like a wuss, and I'm slightly embarrassed to reflect on my own recent woe-is-me attitude. The last thing I want is to be lumped into the same category as *her*, so I resolve to suck it up, even though the blisters on my feet feel like the sting of ten thousand scorpions. In stepping too gingerly while favoring my throbbing heels, I almost roll my ankle on an uneven section of the trail. The four-letter word I let fly earns me another consequence.

"Grab a rock, Puck," says Xander, who's unfortunately within earshot.

"But this makes five now!"

"That's on you. You know the rules."

"Do you even know how liberating it feels to fling cuss words upon the world with wild abandon, Xander? Have you ever tried? I guarantee it offers just as much stress relief as all that meditation garbage you keep swearing by." It's a waste of breath trying to argue the finer points of profanity. I bend down to fetch the smallest rock I can find, but Xander forces me to trade it out for one he's selected that's more the size of a lime. "Geez, why don't you add a few cinder blocks and a truck tire while you're at it?"

"This is a good example of how bad choices become your burden to carry—literally, in this case," he says, unzipping a pocket on the side of my rucksack and tossing the rock in with its four predecessors.

"Puck you," I mumble with the sort of limit-testing defiance I specialize in. Xander seems to consider it for a moment but declines to take the bait. Instead, I'm forced to endure his "Nature Boy" play-by-play of pretty much every wildlife specimen we pass.

". . . and the Pinyon pines you see skirting the trail yield edible nuts. But don't ever ingest anything you find out here in the wilderness. You never know what could be toxic, and it's better to just be safe. Eat only the provisions we give you."

"M'kay," I respond while wondering why he thinks a girl who subsists largely on sour gummy worms and Hot Pockets would suddenly forage for wild berries. I manage to distract him from his treatise on Navajo sandstone long enough to have him explain the "Stepping Stones" Ronnie had earlier referred to.

"Earth, air, fire, and water. They're four symbolic trials you must conquer before your time on the DreamRoad is through," he says. It sounds like New Agey crap to me. Any challenge described as "symbolic" can't be all that intimidating. At least, I hope not.

"Gee, thanks, Your Vagueness. So, 'water trial,' for example. What does that mean, specifically?"

"No need to get ahead of yourself. Just take it one day at a time."

"But just to be clear: if I complete these four tasks, then it's game over? I can leave?"

"Well, that's ultimately up to Barb. She needs to see evidence that you've progressed emotionally, that you've changed your outlook on life and are willing to go forward using the tools you'll learn here to guide you. An attitude adjustment, in other words."

I suspect the victim of last night's picnicware shanking won't be easily moved by any amount of state-of-the-art ass-kissing from yours truly. Barb doesn't have that warm, nougat-y center to target with phony displays of redemption, and frankly, I'd rather be dumped into shark-infested waters than try to bat my lashes and "yes, ma'am" her. Since sucking up to Barb simply isn't an option, I'll just have to take her down, instead. Where there's a will (ill will, in this case), there's got to be a way.

Another forty minutes go by, during which I discover more than I ever needed to know about Frances. She's a one-time handspring champion (is that even a thing?) from Henderson, Nevada, a city she claims is "practically Las Vegas, only *way* classier." She owns two Persian cats named Ramona and Beetlejuice, is allergic to strawberries, and loves throwing the word *ironic* around without appearing to have a clue about what it means. All the yammering aside, she seems strangely reluctant to shed any light on why and how she landed here, yet that doesn't stop her from peppering *me* with questions, fishing for dirt, no doubt. I amuse myself by responding with preposterous fiction.

I convince her that I grew up on the largest pickle-producing farm in upstate Illinois and that I once survived a Midwestern tornado by climbing into the bottom of a Port-A-Potty. It's a good idea to practice my b.s. maneuvers before I'm forced to endure one of the counseling sessions Barb promised we'd be having. (Not that I'm too worried. I've gotten really good at snowing anyone in the business of trying to strip my soul bare.)

We're walking up another steep grade now, this one with a bunch of loose, gravelly rocks and dry clumps of dirt. A cry from the front of our line interrupts the crunching monotony of our feet. I crane my neck to see past Quin and Ronnie. It's Mia.

"Man down," I call back to Frances, who relays the news to Xander. We catch up to Ronnie and Quin, who are both crouched near our pretty leader.

"It doesn't feel broken," Ronnie says. He's feeling around her wrist, his big, meaty hands grasping her dainty, freckled one.

"Get back," Xander orders him. "Don't touch her. Mia, what happened?" He kneels down and puts an arm around her shoulder.

"I think Ronnie's right," Mia says. Her face is flushed, and she's wincing in pain. "It's just a sprain. I lost my footing and landed too hard on this hand. Hurts like a —" She glances at the rest of us and stops herself. "Hurts pretty bad, but I'll be okay."

"It's already swelling. Needs ice, which we're not going to find out here," Xander says, squinting against the sun. "We're only a half hour from the meet-up point for lunch. You can at least soak your hand in the stream when we get there." The way he helps Mia to her feet reminds me of the covers of the cheap paperback romance novels Grandma loved: with hilarious titles like *Savage Destiny*, they featured shirtless men with bad mullets pressed tightly against busty bimbos.

As Ronnie, Quin, and Frances start to plod up the rest of the hill, I spy Xander's hand reach out and rub the back of Mia's neck, just underneath her thick red ponytail. Anyone else might have viewed it as a friendly, consoling gesture, but I'm seeing a more definitive picture. Mia's not just hot for Xander. The feeling is definitely mutual.

* * *

The other group has already arrived at the designated

meet-up point by the time the six of us emerge from the dense brush. In a clearing surrounded by tall trees and scraggy, skeletal pines, the stream that has been running parallel to the trail from a gully far below is now finally within spitting distance. If I didn't hate the water so much, I'd almost be tempted to dive in. I'm hot, I'm sweaty, and I smell completely rank. Despite the pricey cost of admission, they don't provide deodorant here, which is sure to make the rest of this trip a real nostril-burner. I'm fantasizing about chicken nuggets and a McFlurry, though, hell, even Sloppy Fauxs sound pretty good at this point. Mostly, I'm just wiped, so I drop my pack and collapse. The hard ground—sparsely tufted with grass and brown pine needles—digs into my shoulder blades and hip bones, offering a strange relief. It feels sort of amazing to just lay like this, watching sunlight dart in and out among the tree branches. I feel like maybe I could just stay here forever, if all these other degenerates would just go the hell away and leave me alone. I shut my eyes and relax for a minute, my chest still heaving from exertion, but seconds later, a shadow clouds the warm neon pink of my closed lids. I open my eyes and find Barb looming over me, backlit by the afternoon sun. (Regrettably, she has made good on her promise to meet up with us.)

"If you ever expect to graduate from the program,

you need to be able to complete the first Stepping Stone: light a fire without matches," she says. "Ellen's going over the basics." She nods toward a group of kids who are watching attentively as the counselor winds a piece of twine around two sticks. "I suggest you go have a look."

I climb to my feet, not to oblige her but simply to escape her aura of pure evil. After trudging toward the vicinity of Ellen and her firestarters, I collapse again, not much caring what any of them have to say about the finer points of tinder-bundling.

"Why do we even need to know this?" Titania whines, flinging her stick contraption in frustration at the ground. "I mean, isn't this why Benjamin Franklin invented electricity?"

That girl is dumber than a jar of peanut butter. I glance at Ellen, waiting for her to correct the historical facts, but Ellen's not paying any attention, either to Titania or to the fire she's supposed to be trying to ignite. Instead, she's staring directly behind me and looks about ready to spontaneously combust, herself. I follow her gaze to a tree ten feet away. Mia's sitting against it, getting her wrist thoroughly "examined" (i.e. fondled) by Dmitri this time. Geez, the guys in this place are falling all over themselves to be her rescue medic, which is probably what's got Ellen's undies all in a twist.

"Dmitri," Ellen calls over, her tone snappish. "These guys can't figure out how to get any friction going with their hand drills. I need you to come over here and help, if you could possibly tear yourself away from the patient."

"Yes, *ma'am*. Whatever you say, *ma'am*," he responds sarcastically. Not enough friction? That's funny…I'm sensing it in spades.

When Dmitri sidles up to our group, Ellen smiles at him (as if she *hadn't* just made him her bitch) and pats the dirt, indicating that he should sit beside her. He ignores her and squats down next to me.

"Girl's crazy, huh, Cowboy?" I murmur. He's not willing to play along.

"Where's your tinder, Puck?"

"You mean the dating app? Sorry, pal, I'm much too young for you. But pity the fool who stumbles upon Ellen's profile. I mean, yikes, right? And to think we kids are the maladjusted ones."

Dmitri's lips twist into the sort of telltale grimace that proves my cat just got his tongue, but before he can ream me for disrespecting authority, Peabo bounds over to our group, all urgency and exclamation points.

"Barb's got letters, you guys!" Everyone reacts the way you might when a world war ends. I'm not sure why handwritten notes from the very people who banished us to this place merit a celebration, but then again, even dysfunctional child-parent relationships are pretty much beyond my sphere. I'm the lone skeptic in this sudden sea of euphoria.

Barb is full of "drumroll please" suspense as she ceremoniously distributes letters to each camper. They jump up and down and tear into their envelopes like giddy Golden Retriever puppies, each eventually breaking off to read his or her missive in private while choking back tears, soft laughter, or both. I'm standing here like an idiot and feeling as though my "always picked last in gym class" reputation has preceded me here. Of course I hadn't expected anything, but that doesn't explain why my face turns hot once an empty-handed Barb approaches me.

"You just arrived, Puck. I'm sure you understand," she says, and I can hear the condescension dripping off her tongue. It's giving her great pleasure to single me out as the only have-not. "Perhaps there will be a letter for you next time." There's no way to respond without conveying disappointment or sour grapes. Refusing to give her the satisfaction of either, I shrug my shoulders and walk away.

It hurts...*really* hurts, when I take off my shoes and socks and tentatively dip my feet in the stream. I'm sitting alone on a rock near the water's edge, watching the current turn cartwheels over the small stones in its path.

The blisters on the backs of my heels and along both pinky toes feel like fire meeting ice when submerged in the cold water, but within three or four seconds, the stinging melts away. The pain is diluted and delivered downstream—at least some of it. Other things are seeping in, though, the way they tend to do with me. Memories. I used to block the bad thoughts by remembering how good I had it with Paula. But if she was my lifeline, sending me to this place is the equivalent of cutting the rope, and now I'm adrift. The cool water and its gentle movement ferries my mind along, inevitably, to my real mom. I know I shouldn't go there; it's not good for me to remember. Too much hatred and love is knotted all together like this big nasty cobweb in my brain, and whenever I try to unravel it all, it becomes too much, too exhausting. I should have stopped her that day. I shouldn't have let it happen…but forget my boring baggage. As I said, I'd rather not think about it. I glance back at the other kids, all sharing news from loved ones and hopes that they'll be reunited with them soon. The irony is, I've probably had more "parents" in my life than all of 'em combined. Take it from me— quantity doesn't trump quality.

Lifting my feet from the water, I plant them on the warm rock, hugging my knees in my arms for a moment before shaking out my socks and inching them back on my wet feet. I'm tying the laces of my boots when Nick galumphs his way over to me.

"Who wants lunch?" He's brandishing a speckled blue metal camping cup, which he hands to me with a waiter's flourish before taking a seat next to me, uninvited. There's a stick resting in the steaming pile of goop, and I use it to poke at the cup's contents.

"What is this gunk?"

"Ziss, Mademoiselle, is zee chef's special *du jour*," he says in what has got to be the worst French accent I've ever heard. "A *bouillabaisse* of artisanal Asian grains blended in a slow-simmered reduction of zee most exquisite musical fruits, or, as we say at zee Cordon Bleu, 'Le Tooty-Frooty.' Zee more you eat, zee more you toot." My lack of appreciation for his gag prompts him to mirror me with a mime-like frown so extreme it would probably trigger a facial spasm on anyone less buffoonish. The CamelBak hydration pack he's got strapped to his back resembles lederhosen, and, combined with his knee-high white athletic socks, he could pass as a member of the International Yodeling Society. "What? Zee lady does not like zee rice and beans?"

"You want me to eat this with a stick?"

"Yeah, so?" (He's reverted back to an American accent.) "Last time I checked, people still threw down

good money for the privilege at Chinese restaurants."
Though he's clearly proud of his own pointless
observation, the vibe I shoot him—*Dude. Stop.*— sobers
him up. "Cutlery is something you have to earn here," he
continues, "and, well, Barb's not too keen on the idea of
you wielding any more utensils just yet. *Capiche?*"

"I'm not hungry," I lie, shoving the cup back at him.
He takes it and sets it gently beside me.

"Okay." Staring off at the stream, he casually picks at
some weeds growing up from in between the rocks. Oh,
brother. Ten-to-one odds, he's practicing a non-
confrontational tactic learned at some touchy-feely
psychology seminar. "Well, maybe just try to eat a few
bites before we set out again. We'll be hiking till
sundown."

"You mean limping? My feet are in shreds."

"Common entry-level complaint. They'll toughen up
after a few days in the trenches. Just try to block it from
your mind until then." He pulls with two fingers at the
laces on my right shoe, as if testing it. "This is no good,
for starters. These should be a lot tighter so your feet
aren't slipping around in there. You may as well be
walking with banana peels tied to your soles—which I
have, in fact, tried and *do not* recommend." He shifts to
his knees and begins retying my boot, yanking the laces

loose down toward my toes and starting over from the bottom. I feel like I'm four years old again, but I decide to use this opportunity to gain some emotional leverage with the guy.

"Thank you," I say, attempting to block any sarcasm in my voice. (Never an easy feat.) I grab the cup of rice and beans again and shovel a spoonful of the flavorless mixture into my mouth.

"For what?" He stops in his task to offer me a puzzled expression.

"For just being cool about things," I answer between chews. I see his eyes brighten with self-conscious pride. The sucker is taking the bait, so I pile it on. "For not freaking out on us every other second. As far as old people go, you're all right, I guess."

"'Old people?' Zounds!" He falls back on his heels and pretends to pull a dagger from his chest.

"You know what I mean," I say, pretending to laugh. "You're not like Barb, who seems more like a dominatrix than a therapist." (I'm pressing my luck, I know, but what can I say? I live dangerously.)

"She just takes some getting used to is all," he says, returning his focus to my bootlaces. "Heck, I'm married to her, and she's *still* a riddle to me at times, but she always —"

"Wait, what? She's your *wife*?"

"Yep. Married fourteen years this September. She'd just graduated from college back then, but I'll tell you this: she's every bit the looker now as the day she first inscribed her name on my heart. Me, on the other hand?" He pats his midriff. "Well, let's just say I'm showing my mileage."

"Married," I say, genuinely floored. "But, I don't get it. I mean, the way she bosses you around . . ." He chuckles softly and shrugs his shoulders, almost sheepishly.

"You must not have much experience with married couples. As for orders, I'm happy to take them. She's the one with all the fancy degrees and letters after her name. I can't tell you how many kids I've seen make a one-hundred-and-eighty-degree turn in their lives, thanks to her."

"Well, maybe you don't have formal training with cast-offs like me," I reply, "but at least you seem to understand. I can't say the same thing about your old lady. She's not exactly a people person." Nick doesn't dispute this but instead seems thoughtful, as if reflecting on dark sentiments he'd rather not voice. I'm touching a nerve, and I decide to take it one step further.

"No offense, but it sort of seems to me that she treats

you like some beast of burden." He gives a dismissive wave.

"I'm happy to take a supporting role. Barb's got her own way around here, and maybe it's for the best," he says. "I have a habit of getting too attached to you kids."

"Oh, right. God forbid somebody actually cares about us for more than two seconds. Doesn't it occur to anybody that's what we might need most? Somebody who will just accept us for what we are? Not having that is probably the reason most of the kids here are acting out in the first place."

"Acting! *Now* you're speaking my language!" he proclaims, his eyes lighting up as if he'd been waiting this whole time for me to stumble upon some magic password. (Or maybe he's simply anxious to steer the conversation away from the topic of his iron-fisted spouse.) Reaching into his back pocket, he pulls out a bulging leather wallet, from which he produces a small frayed card with a circular insignia on it. "See, there." He hands the card to me, pointing emphatically at the official lettering above his name.

"*The Dramatists Guild of America*," I recite from the card.

"Not to brag or anything. It's my other passion: the theatrical arts." (I decide not to mention that the membership's expiration date is more than ten years passed.)

"What, you do plays and stuff?"

"Writing, producing, 'treading the boards,'" he says, needlessly using finger quotes. "Barb may be the 'director' of DreamRoads," (Finger quotes again. Jesus.) "but when it comes to the show we put on for Parents' Weekend, I'm Cecil B. DeMille."

"A variety show? Sounds...*great.*" I don't know what's worse: the prospect of being forced against my will to sport jazz hands, or getting paraded around in some stupid 'Look at all the progress we're making!' b.s. aimed at parents. I doubt Paula would even come, anyway—not that she counts as a parent or anything—especially not now. "I'm afraid my only talent is ticking people off."

"No, no, this is not your garden-variety ventriloquist acts and boring interpretive dance," he assures me. "You'll be *immersing* yourself in a character. We're talking Broadway-caliber. Well, maybe off-off-*off* Broadway. I've been tossing around some ideas for the next show: a little something I've written myself, which I'd describe as 'David Mamet meets Andrew Lloyd Webber.' I'm still trying to get Barb on board with the idea, though. She thinks it's too 'experimental' and 'derivative.'"

I have no idea what he's talking about, but I

recognize in his face the fleeting wince of a man who knows his wife sits atop the food chain while he's a mere bottom-feeder.

"Sounds like it could be cool," I say, putting my ego-stroke offensive back on track. "Plus, you'll have a legit Hollywood celebrity to star in it."

"Tonya, you mean?" he asks. I nod. "We'll see how that goes. Between you and me, I'm not sure our amateur production will be worthy of her *prodigious* talents. She's already digging in her heels pretty hard, saying she won't participate."

"Titania shunning the spotlight? Go figure."

"Yeah. We'll have to work on her, huh?" He hoists himself to his knees, then his feet. "I'm glad we got a chance to chat, Puck. I know you made a rough debut here, yesterday, but I think you're going to do just fine out here in the wilds."

I nod my head in fake agreement. Knowing I'm going to turn on Homer Simpson here the minute he lets his guard down, I almost feel guilty, for half a second, but if this dude chose Barb for a wife, he's clearly got *sucker* stamped on his forehead. Dumb people don't get a free pass, in my book.

I'm still considering this when all kinds of chaos erupts a few yards away. I jump to my feet and Nick and I both race over (him out of concern, me out of morbid curiosity).

Joining the others, I see that Titania is having another one of her hissy fits, and Snout is crouched down on all fours barking like a rescue mutt or something. Their respective freak-outs don't seem to be related in any way, but it sure adds up to one supersized order of pandemonium.

"What on earth is going on over here?!" Barb asks, directing her question at the pop star. Strangely, everyone seems to be ignoring the canine-boy in our midst.

"Someone stole something that belongs to me," Titania screams. "I want it back. *Now*."

"What is it?" asks Barb.

"I'm not going to specify." Tears are streaming down her face. "I hate this place so bad! You all suck!"

"There's no equipment missing from her pack," Ellen reports to her boss. "We can't figure out what she's even referring to."

"*Someone* knows, all right," Titania seethes, staring directly at Ronnie. "And he's going to pay."

"Why don't you ask Nissa, your number one fan? She's the klepto of the group, after all."

"How dare you bring that up, Ronnie!" Nissa shouts. Her tone is shrill.

"I still don't get why someone with a thirty-two-year-old sugar daddy has to steal anything in the first place." This second comment of Ronnie's amps Nissa up to gasket-blowing range right alongside Titania. Ellen and Mia step forward to calm her.

"Not cool, dude," Xander says, glancing at Ronnie with reproach. "How many times have we told you? Campfire confessions stay at the campfire."

"Are you for real?" Ronnie says in disbelief. "Nissa's been bragging about hooking up with her teacher from the minute she got to camp. It certainly hasn't been a *secret*."

"Ronnie, we'll deal with you in a minute," says Barb. "Tonya . . ."

"Whatever you're going to say to me, I don't even care. All I want is to get out of this place," says the singer, clearly happy that the drama has swung back in her direction. "I have rights, you know. I can't believe my parents signed off on this." She reaches in her pocket and produces the letter—from them, presumably—tearing it into pieces before tossing it over her head like confetti. "I *knew* I should have sued for emancipation! They don't *deserve* me!" Snout, meanwhile, is lying on the ground doing snow angels in the pine needles and screaming, "NEE-ner-NEE-ner," over and over like he's some sort of emergency siren.

"What is wrong with that dude?" I wonder aloud.

"He's *insane!*" Titania answers in an angry shriek. "That's what *INSANENESS* looks like. And no wonder; this place is demented. That's why I'm getting out of here."

"You're not going anywhere," Barb answers calmly. "I'm guessing that whatever you claim was stolen is contraband." She stares at the group. "If any of you know about this, you should come clean right now, because I *will* find out the truth. Snout," she adds, directing her attention to our own resident nutjob, "nice try, buddy, but no one's falling for it. Get ready to hike again, everyone. We've still got a long afternoon ahead of us."

Five minutes later, Xander finishes wrapping up Mia's wrist in an Ace bandage, while Ronnie, Frances, and I wait for our marching orders.

"Where's Quin?" Mia asks, glancing around. "Did he already leave with the other group?" About twenty yards away, I see him, sitting on a fallen log and staring off into the forest. With his pack on, he's clearly ready to go, but he looks lost and so small among the trees. I trudge over and offer him a hand.

"Time to roll," I say, leaning backward as a counterbalance to successfully help him to his feet. "Hey, look at us, finally nailing this whole 'standing upright' business, you and I. Why are you hanging out way over here? We almost took off without you."

"There could be worse things." His baby face registers resignation. "Especially here," he adds. "You'll see."

"If you're trying to freak me out, you're going to have to up your game, bro. Worse is a word that doesn't scare me, because *I am THE* worst, according to ten out of twelve foster parents and principals." I snatch his canvas hat from his hand and settle it securely atop his head. "I know I'm small and don't look like much, but that's the one claim to fame I've got going for me. The worst?" I point to myself, definitively. "You're looking at it."

"Ten out of twelve," he says skeptically as we walk back toward the others. "That's only, like, an 83 percent disapproval rating."

"Whatever, mathlete. Are there going to be any pop quizzes out here? If so, I'm copying your answers."

"I still can't believe I'm even here," he says, and I can't contain a scornful laugh.

"Yeah, join the club."

"That's the problem. I didn't fit in out there…" he gestures to the woods, but I understand that he's talking about the real world. "And I *definitely* don't fit in here, either."

"Do you really want to?" I side-mouth this comment, eyeing him like he's nuts.

"I guess not. Maybe. I don't know."

"Way to be decisive." He only stares at me, unblinking, so I set aside my signature sarcasm for the time being. "Look, I'm not winning any popularity contests here, either. So why don't you and I help each other out? I can't make them like you, but I won't let any of 'em mess with you."

"Why are you being so nice to me?" he says, suspiciously.

"I don't know. I guess you kind of remind me of some kid I knew, once. Come on, let's go. You can bore me with more science-fair stories on the way."

CHAPTER 5

I'll Make Her Render Up Her Page to Me

Primitive man managed to start a fire with basically a snap of the fingers. My fingers may as well be coated with fire retardant for all the good they're doing. Though the sun set only a few minutes ago, I can already feel the cold through my parka. Who knew Utah's climate could be so schizo?

"Time to let the pro take over?" Peabo asks, eyeing Nick hopefully.

"We all know how good you are at lighting fires," Nick replies. "Unfortunately, that's a contributing factor in your being admitted here, son."

"*Ar*-son," Ronnie fake coughs from the peanut gallery.

"It's why you're exempt from the fire-building challenge," Nick continues. "Puck, on the other hand, needs to conquer that Stepping Stone in order to graduate, just like everyone else."

"But look at her!" Peabo gestures at me. I'm hunched over my little pile of dead leaves and pine needles, rolling a stick furiously between the palms of my hands so that it bores into a flat piece of bark on the ground. "She's like an OCD chipmunk doing the hand-jive." I stop just long enough to scowl at him and then proceed to work even harder, desperately hoping I can show them up. "If we have to wait for *her*, we'll either freeze to death," he says, "or be forced to spoon each other for warmth. And my girl back home would *not* be down with that, let me tell you."

"Considering your girlfriend's name is *Chastity*, I'm guessing she's not down with much. *If* she actually exists, that is," Ronnie says.

"Not only is Chastity real, she's also a complete fox. She can light anyone's fire." Peabo checks my progress. "Puck, not so much."

"Here, let me give it a try," Ronnie says with a sigh, kneeling next to me. The whole twig contraption goes flying out of my hands as it has done every ten seconds for the last fifteen minutes. I sit back on my heels and wipe my brow, wondering what the hell his sudden agenda is.

"Ronnie, you're offering to help?" Nick clutches his chest and stumbles backward, pretending he's in a state of

73

complete shock. "By Jove, Barb!" he yells over his shoulder to his wife, who's currently nowhere in the vicinity. "Our camp fixture is starting to understand the value of teamwork! Maybe he's actually learning to get along with others."

"Okay, whatever." Ronnie shrugs in embarrassment, gathering up my fire-starting tools of failure, which are strewn across the dirt. "Just go away and give us some space so we can concentrate."

Hands in his pockets, Nick walks away with feigned nonchalance, whistling like one of the Seven Dwarfs. (Dopey, obviously).

"This is the blind leading the blind if I ever saw it," says Peabo. "Dude, you've been stuck in this limbo land for six months because you couldn't complete the Fire Challenge, and now you fancy yourself an instant flamethrower? I could die laughing if I weren't so frigging cold. Hell, *Titania* even figured out how to light a fire before you!"

"We can't all be pyromaniacs like you." Smoothing his barely-there 'stache with his thumb, Peabo seems to take Ronnie's dig as a compliment.

"What can I say, man? When you've got it, you've got it."

"Shut up."

"Gladly. Now excuse me while I go freeze my balls off somewhere else," Peabo says, turning away from us. As soon as he and Nick are both out of sight, Ronnie turns to me.

"Out of my way," he orders.

"I'll go when I'm good and ready," I say. "So let me get this straight: you've been here for six whole months because you can't light a fire?"

"What of it?" He shoots me a look that almost (*almost*) makes me flinch.

"Well…it can't be *that* hard, can it?"

"Not anymore, it's not," he says, lifting up his parka and reaching into his waistband toward his…oh *good god,* no.

"What are you doing? Don't even think about whipping that thing out in front of—"

"Relax," he says, giving me a devious smile. Withdrawing his hand from his crotch, he covertly opens his fist to give me a glimpse at what's within.

"A lighter? Where the hell did you get that?" His devilish grin offers up no clues. "I could totally narc on you."

"True. But you won't."

"Oh? And why is that?"

"Because you hate Barb way more than you hate me." After checking to ensure that no one's watching, he grabs a leaf and holds it up to the lighter, then flings the caught flame onto the pile of tinder. I'm already one step ahead of him, however. Leaping to my feet, I scream like a winning game show contestant. (You snooze, you lose.)

"I did it! Oh my god, I actually did it!" I squeal, jumping up and down. "I started the fire!" Stepping Stone Number One: Light a Fire. *Check.* (Light, steal... whatever.) Only three more Stepping Stones to accomplish, and given how I operate, it's going to be a cakewalk. Before Ronnie has a chance to react, I grab the lighter from his hand and cram it into my parka.

"You selfish bitch," he says, stuffing his hands in his pockets and walking away. The player is angry that he just got played, but so what? The way I see it, that's not selfish. That's survival. I'm quick, and I'm crafty, and anyone who doesn't like it can suck it.

Campers and counselors alike all come running with woo-hoos and enthusiastic high-five hands at the ready. Everyone's stunned and amazed that I lit a fire on my second day at camp, and Barb—who's been helping Titania and Nissa set up their tent—eyeballs me with a curious and confused expression. She didn't think I could do it, the shrew, and, well, okay, so maybe I *didn't* do it.

But who is she to underestimate me? The thought of defying her low expectations brings me tremendous satisfaction, something I didn't expect to experience out here in this wasteland. I'm a rock star right now.

Only there's a problem. The *real* rock star is having none of it. Titania glares at me from across the campsite. She knows I didn't do shit, and it immediately dawns on me where Ronnie got that lighter. I can see by the look on Titania's face that she'd love to destroy me, but saying anything would only incriminate herself. I'm spared, for now, but between this and our throw-down last night, I can already tell that this chick is going to be a major burr in my butt.

* * *

Dusk has passed its baton to darkness, now, and I'm sitting cross-legged, with a mug of tepid herbal tea, waiting for the quackery to come. Directly across from me, her face flickering in the campfire flames like some sort of demon, is Barb. I can tell she's trying to catch my eye, but I pretend not to see her and stretch my legs out again. Considering how I stole Ronnie's fire, I feel the defiant bliss of a shoplifter who's made it past store security. The warmth creeping through the soles of my boots is soothing. For a moment, I can almost block out Titania's yammering in the background. Almost.

". . . but the real problem is," she says, projecting her voice in that way people do when they think everyone else is enthralled by what they have to say, "they were just jealous of me. Know what I mean?" Predictably by her side, Nissa and Frances wag their heads, backup singers performing a well-rehearsed routine. Everyone else is dead silent. Group therapy by campfire is exactly like group therapy anywhere else. Not that I expect it to be anything different. Whether it's in a church basement, an RTC (that's a Residential Treatment Center), or any number of other places, there are a few things you can count on: uncomfortable chairs, cheap snacks, and (I've saved the worst for last) always, *always* the one person who, like the recipient of mouth-to-mouth resuscitation, sucks up all the air. You'd think that under this seemingly infinite black canopy of sparkling lights, it would be impossible to feel suffocated. And yet, somehow, Titania is managing to make me feel just that. Silver lining? The more *she* talks, the less the rest of us will have to. Speaking of the rest of us, most of the other kids have (probably deliberate) blank looks on their faces. Snout's mouth is hanging open, and, I swear, there's a spot of drool on his chin.

"Tonya," Barb finally interrupts her. "I'd like us to go back to something you touched on earlier." Titania is only too thrilled to oblige her. "The party for your first single: where were your parents?"

"My mom was there," she answers in a softer voice, and for the briefest moment her expression flickers from vapid to sad.

"What did she say when you told her what happened with that guy…the record exec?" Titania is silent. "Did you tell her about the drugs?"

"No."

"Why not?"

"I didn't have to. She already knew."

"You mean she was with you in the bathroom?"

"No, but she saw us go in."

"She didn't do anything to stop you?"

"No." Titania is almost whispering at this point. "She was high, too. Frankly, I don't think she cared."

"Your *mom* actually parties with you? That's kind of awesome." Frances is incredulous. "God, you're so lucky."

"Don't be such an *idiot*," I say, under my breath. I glare at Frances, who's so busy worshipping at the altar of Titania that she doesn't even notice. Quin, who's sitting to my right, flinches. This kid is high anxiety, and for the

79

umpteenth time I wonder what he did to end up with this group.

"Can we talk about something else?" Titania asks in a simpering tone that I'm guessing is at least partly for effect.

"Okay. Let's give someone else a chance to talk," Barb says. I'm hoping I'll get to hear the juicy dirt on Nissa and her thirty-two-year-old lovaaaah, but Barb apparently has other ideas. "Frances, why don't you tell us about your mom?"

"What's to tell?" Frances says with a shrug. "She's a prison warden in yoga pants. Her only job in life—besides watching her weight and getting her highlights done—is jumping all over my case. I'm grounded 90 percent of the time, and it's her fault I'm here, missing what could have been the greatest summer of my life. Maybe if she actually *trusted* me and treated me like an adult—"

"My mom says since I make more than anyone in our family *ever*, I've earned the right to be treated like an adult," Titania chimes in, obviously jonesing for any opportunity to worm her way back into the center of the conversation.

"Tonya, remember, we don't interrupt," Barb says, using the first person plural favored by counselors and hospital attendants everywhere. "That's your second infraction tonight. Frances—what makes you think your mom doesn't trust you?"

"Well for starters, she snoops at my texts, and I *know* she searches my room when I'm not at home. I'm beginning to understand why my dad took off. I mean, my little brother has more privacy than I do, and he's only five!"

"What do you think your mom's motivation might be?"

"To make me miserable?"

"Don't you think she might be doing it because she cares about you and wants to protect you?"

"Oh my god," says Frances, rolling her eyes. "This conversation is beyond pointless." Barb ignores this comment.

"Let's go back to why you're here. You say it's your mom's fault. You don't feel you bear any of the responsibility?"

"I never said I was perfect. But I don't get why people say that I'm two-faced. They see me as someone who's pretty and popular and then label me a 'mean girl,' and, well, maybe I am—*sometimes*. But there are things about my life that none of those people could even fathom."

"Okay," says Barb, "so why don't you tell us about that?"

"I'd rather not." Frances folds her arms across her chest and lowers her eyes. "It's not a big deal."

"I disagree. It's a very big deal. It seems like your mom has a pretty good reason to be concerned about you, don't you think?"

"Please." Frances's once-stony face is twitching. She's fighting the onslaught of tears. "I don't want to talk about that in front of everyone."

"I'm sorry, Frances; I've been patient, but there's a reason it's called 'group' counseling."

As vain and ditzy as she can be, even I am feeling sorry for 'pretty, popular' Frances. I glance around the campfire and notice that everyone else is staring either at the dirt or vaguely into the flames. We're collectively holding our breaths because we know sooner or later each of us will have our turn wriggling under Barb's microscope.

"You just told us that 'trust' is important to you, right?" Barb says, insistent.

"Yes." Frances's voice is so low that I have to strain to hear her.

"Well, being honest about ourselves is how we establish trust within the group context. Do you understand?"

"Yes."

"So, where were we? Oh, yes. The reason you're here. You wound up in the hospital getting your stomach pumped. Do you want to talk about that?" Frances is silent. "You almost died that night. Isn't that correct?" Still no answer. "You must know that this is what terrifies your mom, far more than all of your acting out and infractions at school, right?" Frances's lower lip trembles, and she glances skyward before shutting her eyes tight. "Frances?"

"This is sadistic," I murmur. And that's when Barb turns her attention to me.

"Puck," she says. "Is there something you want to share with us?" I shake my head and train my eyes on my feet. "As you know, interruptions count as a strike. I'll give you a pass, since it's your first session, but only on one condition: that you make a positive contribution to this conversation." I say nothing. "Opening up with the group for the first time is difficult," she continues. "It gets easier, I promise. It's like ripping off a Band-Aid—best to just get it over with. Maybe you'd like to tell us something about *your* mother."

"I-don't-have-a-mom." I say this quickly, before my voice has a chance to quaver on me.

"That's not exactly true, now, is it?" Barb says, persistent. "Why don't you tell us one thing about your mom. Could be anything."

My mom. I lift my chin and look upward, wishing I could fly off into the air like fucking Peter Pan. I can feel the tears in my eyes attempting to jump ship. I will myself to hold them back.

"Didn't you hear me? I haven't seen my mom in years. I don't even remember her," I lie. My fists are scrunched into a ball, and I force myself to address Barb directly. Her face is eerily calm, and the gleam in her eye tells me that she's taunting me.

"I think you remember quite a bit more than you claim," she says. I stare defiantly at the now-unbandaged mark on her face where my fork grazed her forehead.

"Well, um, will you look at the time," Nick says in a muffled tone, almost as though he's clearing his throat rather than speaking. He taps at an imaginary wristwatch. "Whose turn is it to help me clean up? Puck, right?" Barb glares at him, but he looks away like a sheepish dog that senses it's about to get kicked. I look back and forth between them, uncertain but hopeful that Nick's obvious ploy is successful.

"Yes, it's getting late," Barb finally says, to my relief. "Tomorrow night we'll continue where we left off." She stands up and dusts off the back of her pants. "In the meantime, I'd like you all to think about something. *Trust* is a two-way street. Each of you is here because you've betrayed the trust of the people who care about you the most. The sooner you can face that fact, the sooner your real healing can begin."

My cheeks are still hot—both from the fire and my anger—as I trudge over to our camp's makeshift cleanup station. Nick hands me a ladle that's crusted over with a dried paste of rice and beans, and I plunge it into one of the cast-iron cooking pots that's now filled with soapy water.

"Hey, know much about astronomy?" he says, tapping me on the shoulder and pointing up to the sky. I sigh in annoyance but shift my gaze up to the chaotic array of stars. (He *did* save me from Barb's interrogation, after all.) "Yeah, me neither," he continues when I fail to answer his yes-or-no question. "It's like the ancient version of Where's Waldo?, only I can't pick out a thing. I *do* like the stories, though."

I say nothing, returning my focus to the sticky brown goop I'm trying to scrape off the ladle with the edge of my fingernail. "Take the princess Andromeda, for example,"

Nick continues. "Her mom, Cassiopeia, was a real piece of work. She sacrificed Andromeda—her own kid, mind you! —to a terrible sea monster. The poor girl got chained to a rock overlooking the sea and left for dead. She made it out okay, though."

"She survived?" I ask in as casual a voice as I can muster, tossing him the ladle to dry.

"Yep. The great hero Perseus came to Andromeda's rescue. Or, if you want to get technical, I suppose Medusa really saved her."

"Medusa. Wait. You mean that monster lady with snakes for hair?"

"Right. Now remember, Medusa was a Gorgon. Anything that looked in her eyes turned to stone. So Perseus, see, he had managed to cut off Medusa's head, and he had it with him in a bag."

"Eww. Gross."

"Right? 'Hello, sir—paper or plastic?' So anyway, when the sea monster comes along to gobble up Andromeda, Perseus just reaches in the bag, grabs Medusa's head, and points it like a weapon. Badda-bing, badda-bang, the sea creature gets turned to stone."

"What happened to the horrible mom?" I ask a few minutes later, interrupting the silence that had settled back over us like a soft flannel blanket. Nick tosses his drying towel over his shoulder and places both hands on his hips for a moment.

"Come to think of it, I don't know," he says. "Although…I'm not even sure it matters. It was never her story to begin with."

"Yeah." I plunge my hands back into the lukewarm soapy sludge water that's now got nasty remnants of rice and beans floating on the surface. "All I know is, she must have been really messed up, to have done that to her own kid." It's clear now that neither of us is talking about constellations anymore, and somehow that's okay with me. I chalk it up to the darkness, our mundane task, and the weird combination of exhaustion and relief I've been feeling ever since we left the campfire.

"I'm guessing so," Nick says quietly. "That's usually the way those things work. In fact—"

"That'll be enough, Nick," Barb interrupts, stepping forward. I get the sense that she must have been listening in on a good portion of our conversation, and her next comment only proves it. "I don't think Puck needs any more astronomy lessons. And if she *wants* another astronomy lesson, I think *I'm* the authority on that topic—don't you?"

"No disputing that," Nick says, following his response with an uncomfortable chuckle. He glances at me tentatively, as if to apologize for this abrupt end to our conversation, and I feel a familiar electric current begin to zap its way through my system as Barb walks away.

"You're just jealous," I yell to her before my brain has the chance to tackle my tongue into submission. She slowly reels around to stare at me. She's holding against her chest a thick three-ring binder loaded with paperwork —her closely guarded psych workup of all us nutjob kids. Shadows of light from the campfire skitter across her face.

"Excuse me?"

"You know that Nick has a better connection with the kids here than you ever will," I continue. "And you hate that!" She stifles a soft laugh and places her thumb and forefinger against the bridge of her nose as if digesting the theory I've just presented.

"What I'm *concerned* about, Robin, is your ability to manipulate people, to prey on people's kindness, and I suspect Nick might be an easy target. Don't you get it?" she says, turning back to her husband. "Don't be such a fool. This is what she *does*. It's why she's here. She did it with her foster mom, and she'll do it with you. It's nothing but a game for her, and if you can't recognize that, then —"

"But, Barb...," he interrupts.

"No, Nick, don't bother," I say. "She's already made up her mind about me. I'm just some clinical case. Some category in her stupid therapist's manual. I guess you'll find me under 'L' for 'Lost Cause.'"

"See what she's doing, Nick? She's invoking the pity party. But what she's *really* trying to do is play us against one another."

"You think you get me?" I yell, my voice shaking. "Well, I get you, too. You're a modern-day Medusa. You're cold and heartless, and you turn things to stone. Maybe even your own marriage, too, once Captain Intellect here has the sense to figure out what you really are."

"Don't go there, Puck." Nick is standing off to the side, staring at me like I'm a stranger.

My face flushes even hotter than before. The words are spilling out of me before I can sort out what it is that I even mean to say or who I even mean to hurt. Something inside is screaming, *Just stop?* But I can't stop. That's always been my problem, and I can't help but wonder if it's something in my DNA—something dark and crazy.

"How much money are you getting for me to be here, Barb?" I ask. "You're not going to get rich off of me, because, mark my words, *I* will make *you* pay. I will be more plague to you than a mosquito spreading malaria or a tick that gives you Lyme disease. I will be the ugly, indelible stain on your pristine, white existence. I am the giant pothole on your stupid DreamRoad, and I lead down to the very depths of hell. Someday, if I can get so lucky, you'll be rid of me, but know this: every scrape and bruise you suffer, every parking ticket and pile of dog crap you step in, will be a reminder of me. Because I wish those on you. I wish every ill of the universe on you, and then some."

I'm about to cry, and I know it, but I would rather drink dirty dishwater than bawl in front of Barb. Instead, I force back my tears, reach forward, and rip the binder out of her arms, flinging it into the watery dregs of the filthy cast-iron pot. With a shriek, she reaches to retrieve it from the soapy stew, but I push her away. Nick approaches Barb and grabs her shoulders, either protecting her from my violent outburst or allowing me the chance to fully vent—it's impossible to tell which. I lift the heavy pot, give her one more parting glare, and stride angrily to the campfire, where I hurl the entire contents, binder included, onto the flames.

It feels like minutes later, but it's probably only milliseconds before Xander and Dmitri have me by the elbows. The other kids all hover in my periphery, slack-jawed, as the black binder—evidence of all our faults and failings—melts into a wet, ashy mess. My eyes follow the dancing trail of embers that spiral upward into blackness.

* * *

"Burpees," Barb says, managing to make the funny word sound ominous. I'm standing in line with my fellow campers, firing-squad style, while she and the counselors shine their flashlights at our feet. Ronnie grunts his disapproval, and Snout kicks the toe of his hiking boot angrily into the dirt. "You heard me. Now drop and give me forty."

"But *we* didn't do anything!" Frances protests. "Just because Puck pissed you off—"

"Not another *word*, from *any* of you," Barb says. "Wrong behavior hurts *everyone*. You'll be doing fifty of them, now. So go ahead. Start."

I have no idea what a burpee is, but as I join my cohorts on the ground at the top of a push-up and follow their motions, I'm clued in to what's happening. Collective punishment. I knew my latest act of defiance— obliterating her paperwork—would go hand in hand with a pretty gnarly consequence, but I never suspected she'd make everyone else suffer for it, too.

The exercise is just four basic moves: start in plank position, hop both feet forward to your hands, jump off the ground with arms raised, then crouch and return to plank position. Again. And again. And again. It sounds simple enough, but after the first five, I am struggling. My body is beyond wrung out. To eke out forty-five more seems an almost-impossible feat.

Barb keeps time, slowly calling out the number we've completed with a whip-cracking brutality in her voice. If someone's feet fail to leave the ground on the jump, she doesn't count it. If someone fudges his or her push-up position, she doesn't count it.

"*TWENTY-FOUR!...TWENTY-FIVE!* . . ." I'm positioned close enough to my torturer to overhear a subtle call for mercy, from Nick, of all people.

"They did hike all day, Barb. Maybe they can pick up the second half tomorrow morning."

"Please be quiet, Nick. You're making me lose track of the count," Barb says. I haven't heard her speak in such a severe tone with him before. Man, is she ticked. "So where was I?" she continues. "*SEVENTEEN!* . . ." We huff and puff our way through the exercise—a bunch of big, bad wolves brought to our knees.

"Excuse me? Ma'am? I think you're mistaken," Dmitri says. "They'd just done twenty-five." I pause in my crouched position on the ground and glance up, silently blessing his little ol' heart, as Grandma would've said. Next to him, Xander's and Ellen's eyes both widen in alarm.

"Thank you, Dmitri, but your interruption has me quite confused again. Perhaps we should just start over from the top. ONE!"

Next to me, Quin lets out a whimper. I promised to have his back, and instead, I'm putting him through more misery. Forcing everyone else to pay for my misdeed, Barb clearly intends to bring me to heel by pitting them against me. The other kids' resentment goes unspoken, but it hangs in the air. I can feel it, as surely as I can feel the burn in every muscle of my bone-weary body. Knowing they all despise me bothers me more than I ever thought it could. The tears are like shards of glass pressing against my eyelids, and I focus my thoughts on holding them back. *Seven, eight, nine . . .*

* * *

Much later, I'm in my sleeping bag, yet the last thing I'm able to do is sleep. My hostility toward Barb is still smoldering like an abandoned cigarette butt. The people I've encountered in life all seem to fall into one of three categories: bad people who do bad things, good people who are bad at doing good things, and bad people who masquerade as good people. Barb falls into that last category, and it's her type I hate the most. She and Paula's fiancé, Ted the Interloper, go together like guns and ammo. They both have their acts down, all composed and concerned, so enlightened with their tight, fake smiles, but it's all just a ploy to manipulate you. Therapist? What a laugh. Barb's a *sadist*. The scowls and shade everyone threw me when we finally retreated to our tents said it all. If I wasn't before, I'm now officially a pariah around here as a result of our forced late-night calisthenics, and on top of that, my abdomen feels like it's been gutted with an ice cream scooper. For the first time since bedding down, I roll gingerly onto my left side to peek at my tent mate. Frances's quiet, hiccupy sobs have finally given way to the monotonous sounds of sleep-breathing. Barb took twisted delight in broadcasting her personal baggage tonight, although I'm not sure why the girl from privileged suburbia would have it so bad she'd almost drink herself to death. Whatever; I'm not in the business of judging other people's emotional garbage. Not this, at least.

I try to wriggle into a more-comfortable position, but I've got that "Princess and the Pea" feeling—only in my case the pea feels more like a tennis ball lodged where my heart ought to be. As much as I fight it, my mind keeps looping back to the single topic I spend pretty much every moment of every day trying not to think about. During tonight's counseling session, Barb practically came at me with the conversational equivalent of a crowbar, which means I'll be spending every night hereafter evading her attempts to lure me into a fireside chat about Mom. At least Paula knows better than to try to talk about all that with me. At least Paula…*No. Screw Paula*, I angrily remind myself, remembering that she's the reason I'm here. With one arm, I reach up and partially unzip the front flap of my tent, then scooch over to where I can see through the opening. Overwhelmed by the stars, I finally spot the Big Dipper—at least I think it's the Big Dipper. I hadn't been putting Nick on earlier: I've never been one for stargazing. Then again, where I come from, the stars never shone so brightly, either.

I can still remember Grandma in the hospital, her gasping to me with that plastic tubing shoved up her nose. *"I'll be a star when I'm gone, darlin'. I'll be up there in the sky taking care of him soon. Just look up, and you'll find us."* Great for them, I guess, but what about me, the one who got left behind? What good are a couple of celestial pinpricks for salvaging the shitty life I was left with? The stars here in Utah are too numerous to count, and they have a strangely hypnotic power over me. Sleep steadily reels me in like a hooked fish, but then a rustling in the woods behind the tent snaps me back from dreamland. I tense up, imagining that a menagerie of all those ferocious animals we'd been warned about are out there in the darkness, just waiting to pounce. Instead I hear a burst of giggling and shushing.

"Ouch, you stepped on my foot!" I can't be sure, but it sounds like Ellen.

"Shhh…," replies a male voice that isn't much quieter. "You'll wake up Barb."

"Hang on a sec. My shoelace is coming untied." (Yep, that's definitely Ellen.)

"Hey, I thought you said Mia was coming, too." Recognizing the drawl as belonging to Dmitri, I briefly consider letting them know I'm awake. But where's the fun in that?

"She's with Xander, and I think they want to be alone. We should give them their space."

"Like hell! As if Mr. Namaste has any actual moves beyond Downward Dog. I'm sorry, but what a joke. That dude's got nothing on me."

"You're preaching to the choir, babe."

"Um…do me a favor and don't call me babe, okay? It's just *weird*."

"You never used to mind."

"I know." Silence. "It's just, you're like a sister or something."

"Oh." In that one tiny syllable, I can hear the air deflate from Ellen's soul. "So, um...do you feel like hanging out? I've got a few airplane-sized vodkas hidden at the bottom of my pack I could go get."

"Wow. I didn't have you pegged as the smuggling sort."

"Yeah, well, sue me, but after days like this one, I need a freakin' drink."

"No kidding. Barb was on a rampage tonight."

"So what do you say? Care to join me?"

I have half a mind to jump out of my tent and slap the desperate out of her, but I'm dying to know how this soap opera moment will conclude. (And note to self: uptight Ellen has booze!)

"No, thanks. I'm going to go find Mia," Dmitri answers.

I hear the sound of footsteps retreating from my tent, and then Ellen whispers a bit more urgently.

"Wait for me! I know where they went! I'll take you."

As they scurry off into the brush, I think about what the counselors' midnight mingling means and, more importantly, how and when I can use it to either blackmail or bribe my way to freedom. Ratting them out is one option, but I'm no snitch. Besides, the only upside of selling them downriver is to win points with Barb, and god knows I've dug too deep a hole for myself after tonight to make up for it by turning informant.

It's all coming together in my head now: Xander loves Mia, Mia loves Xander, Ellen loves Dmitri, but Dmitri loves…Mia. I may suck at algebra, but even *I* know that's not a balanced equation. And it dawns on me now: the wonky devil's horns gesture Dmitri had flashed Mia on his way out of camp this morning was also sign language for "I love you." Xander had realized that—no wonder he pitched an insta-fit. Grandma would be lapping up this sort of lovers' drama, by the way. I, on the other hand, take only a strategic interest in this romantic equivalent of musical chairs. After tonight's run-in with Barb, I'm more determined than ever to ditch the DreamRoad by any means possible. Could Cupid's four victims somehow lead to my out? As God is my witness, I'll never do burpees again.

CHAPTER 6

Such Tricks Hath Strong Imagination

"Can someone please explain why I feel like roadkill?" I ask, poking with a stick-spoon at my tin mug full of unflavored oatmeal. I've been aimlessly roaming the wilds of Utah with this merry band of misfits for more than six days and feel no closer to appreciating any facet of the so-called Great Outdoors.

"Could be withdrawal. Your body's still feeling the effects of a world without cigarettes, booze, and all that other nasty stuff," says Ellen with a note of authority. I'm propped against a fallen log beside the breakfast fire at an hour I would classify as criminal. Everyone's got laughable bedhead, and we are all struggling to hoist our eyelids up—Ellen included. I'd bet money she and the other counselors stole away last night for another late game of mixed doubles.

"Or maybe it's just my body's revolt at being woken every morning at the buttcrack of dawn," I reply.

"Waking up to your potential means waking up early," says Barb, who's just ambled up, looking as refreshed as a vampire. "The strenuous hiking we've been doing this week is helping detox your system," she says. "And speaking of 'systems,' everyone should see to their bathroom business in the next five minutes."

"Aw, *man*," Peabo gripes. "You act like we can just do that on command. I need some time—and a copy of *Sports Illustrated* or something."

"While we're on the subject," Barb continues, "someone failed to bury his or her number two last night in the latrine area. If it happens again, we'll be chaperoning everyone's bathroom breaks, and frankly, I don't think any of us want that. Get your mess kits washed and your beds rolled in ten minutes."

"Are we hiking again today?" I ask.

"As a matter of fact, no, Puck," answers Barb. "Today is a 'stay' day."

No hiking? I'm momentarily stoked, but the harmony of groans coming from my fellow campers harshes that buzz. I even spot a grimace flash across the face of the otherwise-accommodating Quin. Uh-oh.

"What's a 'stay' day?" I ask once Barb saunters off.

"The slow and agonizing death of our dignity," Ronnie answers. He stands, tosses his uneaten oatmeal into the fire, and storms back to his tent.

"Put a rattlesnake, a rabid wolverine, and a hungry bear in a cage, and ask 'em to hug it out. Barb thinks we all should be singing 'Kumbaya' or something by the end of it." Nissa's explanation is cryptic, so I glance over at Peabo, hoping he'll clarify.

"You missed the first one," he says, sensing my confusion. "It's like this weird, touchy-feely Olympics: emotional exercises, socialization activities…basically all the stuff that gets therapists turned on, with a bit of hard-core boot camp mixed in."

"Oh, god," I say, piecing together the enormity of this bad news. "Please tell me you don't mean 'trust falls' and that kind of garbage."

"Afraid so," says Frances, joining in on the conversation. "Only I think they've eighty-sixed any more trust falls. Ronnie almost wound up brain-dead after the last one."

"Quin and Titania were paired up to catch him," Peabo recalls, laughing. "Like dropping an anvil onto some saltine crackers."

"He was *heavy*!" Quin says, putting forth a half-hearted defense and glancing around to make sure

Ronnie's not within earshot. Poor Quin. Making a kid this scrawny do teambuilding courses is no less cruel than taping a "kick me" sign to his back. "Ellen, where are the other counselors?" he asks, changing the subject.

"In the woods, getting everything set up for today," replies Ellen, with less than zero enthusiasm. I imagine Mia flitting about the forest with her two starry-eyed suitors, and here sits Ellen like one of those despondent early rejects on the pathetic television dating shows Grandma used to cackle over. Coming in second place is really just being the first loser, as they say, and Ellen is living proof. She's about to walk away when it occurs to me that this is an opportunity to do a bit of strategic sucking up.

"Hey, Ellen, can you show me again how to roll my tarp and sleeping bag? It's like wrestling a giant jellyfish every time I try."

I'm alone in the tent with her when I test the waters. If I'm ever going to get the hell out of this place, I need the counselors squarely in my corner.

"God, I wish I were as tall as you are," I say. "You could be a supermodel or something." She pauses in aligning my bag and gives me a skeptical glance. I may be laying it on too thick, but then again I don't have much time for subtleties. "I'm serious. And I'm not the only one who thinks so. The way Dmitri checks you out? Not that it's any of my business or anything," I hastily add.

"He doesn't think of me that way. You're imagining things," she says, but the tone in her voice seems to be saying, *Tell* me more! I cast my net a little wider.

"Promise me it gets easier. You know, with boys and all that." I concentrate on wrapping my sleeping bag as snail-shell tight as I can, hoping my face won't betray what utter b.s. I'm dishing out.

"That is something I most definitely *can't* promise. What makes you bring this up?"

"Well…there's a guy I sort of like back home."

"Yeah?" she asks, helping me secure the rope around my bag.

"Yeah," I reply glumly. "Only he's madly in love with my best friend. I mean, she's pretty, I get it. But what am I, Purina Dog Chow?"

"Oh, honey." Ellen grabs me gently by the shoulders, every adult's prelude to attempting an inspirational lecture. "I've been there. *Believe me*, I've been there. And it hurts, I know. Love can feel like a game of tag. The more you care about someone, the more they seem to run away."

"I wish it were that simple, but you don't get it," I continue, worming my way further into her confidence.

"We're all at school together, and I have to see these people *every single* day. Do you understand what a roach that is?"

The look in her eyes tells me I'm homing in directly on the target.

"Yes, Puck, I do. Sometimes it can feel like everyone else is happy except you, and that sort of thinking will throw you into a complete shame spiral." (The psychobabble in this place is never-ending.) "The bottom line is, love doesn't always work the way we might want it to. I wish I had the magic solution, but all I can say is, don't give up hope. Things have a way of sorting themselves out. Do you understand?"

"Sort of." I force a fake sniffle.

"I'm sorry." Ellen sits back on her heels and clasps her hands behind her neck. "I'm the worst person on the planet to be talking to you about this, especially with the way . . ." Stopping mid-sentence, her wistful eyes drift in the direction (at least, I imagine) of where Dmitri is out there in the wilderness trying to out-Romeo Xander in some Mia tug-of-war. As if thinking the same thing, Ellen's eyes narrow into slits. "This so-called best friend of yours. What does *she* have to say about all this attention she's getting?"

"Oh, you know how pretty girls can be," I say, batting my eyelashes dramatically and affecting a phony Southern drawl. "'Who *me?* But I never did a thing to lead him on!' And the whole time, I just feel like a colossal jerk, because the truth is, she is just a maddeningly good person. Of *course* the whole world would love her. It's just . . ."

"Hard," Ellen answers. "I know. I'm glad you had enough trust in me to confide all this, but maybe you ought to tell Barb how you're feeling." And with that, the spell I've just cast on her is suddenly broken. "She's got some great insights."

"Sure. I guess." (Translation: Not in a million years.)

* * *

I'm stuck to the pop superstar like a conjoined twin, and neither one of us is very happy about it. We're standing back-to-back, a wide Velcro band tightly affixed like a girdle around our waists.

"Stop elbowing me!" Titania says, stomping squarely on my instep.

"Ow! *You* stop, skank!"

"You're pulling my hair every time you fidget!"

"Well then quit whipping it in my face like a dirty old rope mop."

"FYI, a celebrity stylist does my hair at $400 a pop... I'm assuming a paper shredder is responsible for your *interesting* look."

We're standing in a small clearing surrounded by the three other protesting groups of two. Barb, Nick, and the four counselors are nearby, sideline coaches to the spectacle that's about to begin.

"Our first game of the day is Octopus Opposites," Barb announces with a smile on her face, as if we're preschoolers at recess. "You've each been strategically paired with the person we feel can most challenge you and help you to grow as a person."

"Grow? More like a *growth*. He's diseased. I'm going to need a rabies shot after this," whines Nissa, making a face at the thought of the monkey on her back. (In the most literal sense of the expression; she's Velcro-wrapped to Snout, who is currently pounding on his chest and yelping like a howler monkey.)

I feel like howling, too, when Barb spells out the rules of her absurd little game. The gist: Stumble through this wilderness wasteland with your "opposite" while using a compass and map to locate a hidden treasure chest containing a pictogram. Decipher the pictogram's coded message in order to finally "be liberated" (at least, from each other).

Each team of two has been assigned a counselor to referee and keep us from cheating—god forbid we so much as breathe without a babysitter.

"The winners get to share *this*," Nick says, revealing a bag of Flamin' Hot Cheetos he's been hiding behind his back. It might as well be a suitcase full of stolen cash the way everyone's eyes light up.

"Come to mama," Titania purrs.

"*Must. Have. MSG*," says Ronnie, reaching his hands toward the prize like a salivating Frankenstein. "Hey, nerdgasm—don't screw this up for me." He glances over his shoulder at Quin, whose ashen face makes me wonder if *pre*-traumatic stress disorder might be a real thing. Lashed to Peabo, meanwhile, Frances resembles someone about to be burnt at the stake.

"Set aside your differences, people, and work together as a *team*," Barb instructs us. "Cooperation and mutual respect will carry you farther than your own ego ever will. Is everyone ready?"

I roll my eyes and glance at our chaperone, Xander.

"Is this one of those stupid Stepping Stones?" I ask. "Do I need to do this to get out of here?"

"No, not exactly," he says.

"That's what I thought." Barb has just blown the whistle, signaling the start of the race, but I bend my knees and sink my butt to the ground, bringing an unsuspecting Titania down with me.

"Hey! What the?!" she sputters.

"Wake me when it's over, 'cause I ain't playin,'" I say. "I don't need to race around like a lab rat for some grub-shaped hunk of bright-orange cornmeal."

"The hell you don't!" Titania shrieks. "Do you know how long I've gone without junk food? Get your butt off the ground."

"Make me."

"*Bite me.*"

"Ladies," Xander says in a reprimanding tone. "Not off to a great start, now, are we?"

"Consider this an 'Octopus Opt-out,'" I say, digging in my heels on the ground. "If this game doesn't help get me out of here, then what's the freaking point? Are you people filming us for a reality series? That would explain the celebutante, at least." Barb has ambled over to us and is sizing me up with her arms crossed in front of her. I scowl and spout off the one thing I remember from school last year. "It's called civil disobedience," I huff. "You can't make me do anything I don't want to do."

"Yes, that's true," she says. "Making your own choices also means living with the ramifications of those decisions. In this case, that amounts to spending the rest of the day shoulder-to-shoulder with Tonya, which, come to think of it, would probably do you both no end of good. Of course, if you change your mind, you can always go ahead and jump in the game. Xander, if they're not going to play, why don't you catch up with the others? Nick can stay back with these two." With that, she strides off to let us stew—me quietly, and Titania at several decibels above tolerable.

"You understand that they're just manipulating us, right?" I say. "Don't fall for it. They're trying to bribe us into conforming like some sort of obedience school for aggressive dogs."

"That explains why you're being such a bitch. Plus, you owe this to me and you know it," she says, elbowing me hard in my right tricep. We sit in angry silence for approximately two minutes before she starts humming. Shit.

"All right, fine," I finally yell, interrupting before she gives way to any more of her screeching. "We'll go get the stupid Cheetos. The faster we finish, the faster I ditch you."

We sidestep and hobble our way through low-lying scrub brush, each taking turns biting the dust and bringing the both of us careening down to the dirt with a thud. (Full disclosure: I may have hit the deck a few times on purpose just to piss her off.) Hoofing it this way for at least twenty minutes occasionally brings us into contact with the other teams, who look just as bent as we are.

"Anything?" I ask Ronnie when he and Quin pass us.

"Like I'd tell either of you," he mutters, wiping sweat from his brow. I glance at Quin. He shrugs and shakes his head; they've got nothing.

As we walk off in another direction, I think back to stealing the lighter from Ronnie. Wait a minute! Why should I have to play fair when this whole situation is anything but?

"Keep going," says Titania. "We haven't checked over behind that clump of trees, yet."

"Screw it. We're going to do this another way. Just follow my lead. Hey, Nick," I call out, glancing at our chaperone, who's trailing us. We wait to let him catch up. "Titania and I were just talking about your show for the parents and how cool it sounds!"

"We *were?*" Titania says, confused.

"Don't play coy," I tease, smacking her hard on the thigh with my fist.

"Oh. Yeah, right. We were. *Apparently*," she corrects herself.

"Titania is wondering if you might be willing to cast her as the lead, when the time comes."

Once again, she stomps her heavy hiking boot on the instep of mine, and I wince, but Nick's too stoked by the news to even notice.

"Really? That's great! Because, I mean, if you're willing, then I'd probably stick with our 'musical' format. *Cats*, maybe? You'd be just purrrrr-fect as Grizabella." Titania remains speechless. "Wow, cat's got your tongue, I see. Okay, well, if you're thinking something more dramatic, there's always *Streetcar*. Tennessee Williams in teen speak; now *there's* an idea." He claps his hands and points them skyward before frowning momentarily. "Of course, Barb will want to keep it G-rated, which could be a problem. *Streetcar Named Maguire*? Well, we can work out the details later."

"Whoa, whoa, whoa, back it up." Titania attempts to climb out of the hole I've dug for her. "I don't just perform on command. There are, like, contract minimums and guarantees that need to be met. My lawyer and manager need to sign off, and—"

"What she's *trying* to say," I interrupt, shooting her a dirty look she can't even see, "is that she knows you can't actually pay her to appear in the show—I mean, how *ludicrous* would that be? But maybe, you know…maybe you could just help us out from time to time here at DreamRoads. Make her dreams come true, if you get our drift?"

Nick eyes us askance, as if we were asking a prison guard for a cell phone.

"The Cheetos, man," I sigh, amazed at how dense he can actually be. "She wants the Cheetos. Help us get 'em, and the starlet's ready to hit the stage."

"Puck, can we talk privately for a moment?" Titania yanks me about fifteen feet away. "What the hell are you doing?" she asks.

"What? You want the Cheetos; I'm getting them for you."

"By starring in his ridiculous little camp show? If the tabloids ever caught wind of something like that, my career would be in the toilet. Forget it. I have my dignity, and it's not worth the price of a bag of Cheetos." I can't see her face, but I can tell, just by the tone in her voice, how riled up I've got her. Miss Famous thinks she's too good for Nick's stupid little amateur production, and her snotty tone pisses me off. She thinks she's such a great actress? I'll show *her* great acting.

"You really don't know, do you? I figured you were already clued in, with being in show business and all that."

"Know what?"

"Wow. Okay," I say, lowering my voice even further. "I'm going to tell you this, but you've got to keep it on the down-low."

"Fine, what?" She's irritated. I glance covertly at Nick.

"He's related to Martin Ford Scorpio."

"As in the director? Oh, what a load of—"

"I'm not shitting you. You know how it is with big Italian families. That family tree has a lot of branches, and he happens to be one of the, well, low-hanging ones. The bushy hair. The prominent ears. The portly physique. Can't you see the resemblance?"

"Well, now that you mention it…not really. Wait, are you serious?" She wants to believe it. This is going to be so much easier than I thought.

"Like once-removed or something, but basically, yes. Why do you think he's so into staging shows here?" I can't see the look on Titania's face since we're standing back-to-back, but her silence tells me she might actually believe my whopper. God, I love messing with people. "It's a win-win for you," I hastily add, in case she's still wavering. "Agree to do his stupid show and you could end

113

up with more than just a bag of Cheetos. He calls his peeps, and this could be your ticket to an Oscar, for all we know."

"I could wear Alexander McQueen on the red carpet," she muses, dreamily.

"Become Nick's leading lady, and it'll get you out of here faster, for sure—probably in time to sing at the All-Star game, if you're lucky. So, c'mon." I yank her back toward Nick. "Just don't let on that you know about his 'connections.'" We stumble and hop the few strides back to where Nick is standing.

"So, Nick, do we have a deal? Where's the treasure chest?"

"Sorry, ladies, but helping you win the game is against everything we stand for here." Nick has that disappointed expression on his face again, as though my attempt at coercion is just another act of personal betrayal, and maybe he's right. "I'd love for you to headline the show, Tonya, but, well, I simply can't pay you in ill-gotten Cheetos."

"Oh, that's no problem," she quickly replies, in as congenial and polite a tone of voice as I've ever heard escape her lips. "I understand, and just know that it would be a thrill and an *honor* to participate in your production in any capacity. *Sir.*"

* * *

"Quin, Ronnie—I'm not impressed by much, but I'll hand it to the two of you. Those were some serious skills out there in the field." Dmitri whips off his bandanna and runs his fingers through his unruly mop. "Nice work, y'all."

"Once we figured out how to get around quicker, it didn't take us long to find the box," says Ronnie. "I could hoist Potter on my back like Luke did with Yoda and just take off running. He probably weighs less than my rucksack, so we locked elbows and motored."

"I just lifted my legs off the ground and held on for the ride," Quin adds. He's stone-faced and soft-spoken, as always, but I can tell he's kind of exhilarated.

"Your abs are going to be paying for it tomorrow, bro," Ronnie assures Quin before turning to the rest of us. "Sensei Wu, here, went all 'boy genius' on the pictogram," Ronnie continues. "The little dude brought it and then some." He raises his meaty arm into the air above Quin, who flinches for a second before realizing he's being offered a high five, not a certain pummeling.

"Congratulations, gentlemen," says Barb with all the satisfaction of a woman who's transformed pit bulls into puppy dogs. Nick steps forward and kneels before the boys like a knight before royalty, presenting them with the nine-ounce bag of Cheetos. "And to the victors go the spoils."

The rest of us hover like a pack of starving hyenas. Despite my earlier protests, even I feel tempted to execute a snatch-and-grab on the coveted cheese puffs. Ronnie proudly accepts the prize but then looks toward Quin, and, after hesitating for a moment, they nod in agreement.

"So, Quin and I talked about this, and we've agreed we're going to split these among everyone. I mean, if that's okay with you, Barb?" Ronnie couldn't lay it on thicker if he were using a cement trowel, but hell; if I get a handful of salty, hydrogenated junk food, what do I care if he's become a total sellout?

He and Quin painstakingly distribute their take like mental-ward nurses handing out nightly meds, and we're all, at least temporarily, happy campers. The adults disperse, leaving us to enjoy our feast in private. I scarf down my take in about three seconds flat, but the others are taking their time. Nissa slowly nibbles the end of a Cheeto. Snout is sniffing his as though it's a fine Cuban cigar, while Peabo sucks the end of one that hangs limply from his mouth.

"Leave it to the new kid to blow through her stash already," he says, nodding at me.

"For someone who wanted to boycott, you sure didn't waste any time inhaling those, girl." As she says this, Titania stares methodically at the eight Cheetos lined up neatly (by order of size) in her palm. "You should have savored them. Who knows when we're going to get something like this again?"

I shrug to mask my faint sensation of binger's remorse.

"Get while the getting's good," I say. "You never know when it's all going to be yanked away from you, right?" No one responds, and though it doesn't necessarily seem like a slight, I have to wonder if they're all still pissed with me about the burpee incident. Only Quin glances at me curiously.

"You can have the rest of mine, actually, Puck," says Nissa. "I don't like them anyway." Her offer prompts everyone else to pitch a major fit—"Why should *she* get them?" "She hasn't been out here as long as the rest of us!"—until a tournament of rock-paper-scissors is set in motion. Frances starts a shitstorm by throwing down a pinky finger in the semifinal round.

"'Dynamite?'" Ronnie asks. "I call foul."

"Yeah, that's completely bogus," Titania says in agreement. "You made that up."

"It's a real thing," Frances argues. "Dynamite beats rock by exploding it, and it beats paper by burning it. But scissors can beat dynamite by cutting the wick."

"But, from a physics standpoint, paper *could* beat dynamite by smothering or snuffing out the wick," Quin says, almost enthusiastically. "I'm with Ronnie on this. Adding in dynamite just throws off the mathematical odds of the whole thing." Nodding emphatically, Ronnie offers him a bro fist. Quin's face turns pink, but he smiles as he sheepishly bumps him one back.

"For christ's sake, people," says Nissa, exasperated. "It's just a *game*. Who *cares* who gets four extra Cheetos, anyway? What I really want is something that will get me buzzed." I see Snout smile in appreciation. "Hey, Physics Boy," Nissa continues, elbowing Quin, "put on your chemistry hat and figure out how to make us some moonshine. What?" she asks, when we all eye her skeptically. "Gin comes from juniper berries, right? You can't spit out here without hitting one of those bushes."

"Sure," scoffs Peabo. "Quin will get right on that with the *miniature distillery* he'll MacGyver out of twigs."

"Forget fancy cocktails. I'd just settle for a spliff," Ronnie says. "There's grass freaking everywhere. Sadly, the wrong kind."

"Irony," Frances says.

"Yeah, tell me about it," adds Quin, rolling his last Cheeto between his fingers like he's about to take a toke. The gesture launches Ronnie into a full-on laughing fit.

"Look at geek-ass homeboy trying to pretend he's one of us! Like you've ever actually burned one."

"I've done drugs," Quin insists, but not convincingly enough for the rest of us.

"Oh my gosh, that's adorable," says Titania. Even crazy Snout (who never seems to be following a conversation) cracks another grin.

"Why are you even here, Quin?" Frances says, asking the question that's on all our minds. "Let me guess: you *studied* someone to death."

"Lay off him," I say, my mood turning spiky.

"No wait, wait—he got an *answer wrong* on the SATs." Peabo drops his voice to an ominous whisper. "The *horror*."

All the Cheeto-victory joy vanishes from Quin's face. He averts his eyes and crosses his spindly arms across his chest. I'm teed off now, because bagging on Quin is too easy. The poor kid was just trying to fit into the group; did they really have to tag-team him like that? I'm as curious about Quin as the rest of them because, no joke, he's a serious outlier at this place, but judging by the anguish on his face, I guess even he has some hidden box of hell locked deep inside. Just as I'm wishing that I could carefully roll him up in bubble wrap and ship him somewhere much safer, another manifestation of hell walks up to the group and casts her cloud of doom over our conversation.

"Okay, everyone," barks Barb. "Break time's over."

CHAPTER 7

So Quick Bright Things
Come to Confusion

"I was going to wait until tomorrow night to distribute these," Barb announces mysteriously, just before dinner. She's gripping a tote embossed with the words *'Your Freudian Slip Is Showing*.' (Therapist joke; I don't get it either.) "However, since you all displayed some real progress during today's challenges, I've decided to hand them out tonight as your reward for good behavior."

She holds the tote aloft with one hand and makes an encouraging motion with the other, inviting us to circle up. My fellow campers scurry to her side while I hang back, warily eyeing the canvas bag as though it might contain a "rhumba of rattlesnakes." (Shout-out to Xander for teaching me the term.)

I've been wholly unimpressed with Barb's so-called reward system. The scant bite of warm Cheeto I'd hoovered up earlier today was tasty, sure, but it certainly wasn't a come-to-Jesus moment. "Stay Day," contrary to being the easy, nonstop siesta-ville I'd hoped for, has been nothing short of torture. The humiliating physical challenges were bad enough, but coupled with all the positive-affirmation overkill sprinkled in between, let's just say I happily welcome the return of our grueling death marches.

So forgive me if I'm skeptical that the contents of Barb's tote will have any redeeming value. Sure enough, she reaches into her canvas bag and pulls out something far worse than a severed Gorgon head. It's more letters from home. As my fellow campers jostle one another, jockeying for prime position in their greedy quest for news from the outside world, I back away toward the fringes. My own shadow looms long on the ground in front of me, and the horizon is tagged with sprays of neon pink and purple. There's probably only about a half hour of light remaining before the day calls it quits. These stages of the sunset have taken on a comforting familiarity, and, almost without realizing it, I've begun to sense what time it is by the sun's position in the sky.

"Puck!" Barb's shrill voice reaches out and lassos me, checking my attempt at a silent retreat. "There's one here for you, too."

Sheer relief damn near cracks the granite expression I've been struggling to maintain, but I manage to keep it together, forcing a scowl for good measure.

Nissa, who's standing just behind Barb, gives me a congratulatory thumbs up, as if we're all receiving acceptance letters to the colleges of our dreams. I ignore her, taking the envelope from Barb's hand and turning it over to see my name written across the front in Paula's perfect handwriting.

When we'd driven away in the van, I'd made up my mind that I'd never speak to her again. Ever since, I frequently envision her pleading with me, tears streaming down her face. I fantasize about what would happen if I actually bite the dust out here, and Paula, wracked with guilt for sending me to an early death, has to come to claim my body. But who am I kidding? She's probably so happy to be rid of me, relieved to be free of the pet project that went toes up. Paying for my camp incarceration is, I'm sure, just her way of feeling as though she's done her duty, whatever it takes to wash her hands of me. We left on such horrible terms—the incident with Ted still makes me sick—that I didn't expect to hear from her again. Maybe this is a "goodbye, so long, don't-let-the door-hit-you-on-your-way-out" letter. Or maybe she wrote it to alleviate her guilt. Either way, there's no point in reading it.

But what else do I have to do between now and dinner? Everyone else is engrossed in theirs. At least I might have the satisfaction of an apology, even if it's one I'd never (*ever!*) accept. I tear open the envelope and pull out the enclosed sheet of paper. For not giving a crap about what she has to say, I feel strangely sick with anticipation.

> *Dear Puck,*
>
> *I'm writing this letter without much hope that you'll even read it. I know that anger isn't something you let go of easily. After everything you've been through, who could blame you? But I know what hides behind that anger. I could read it all on your face the morning you left: the hurt, the disappointment, the fear. "Not again," you were thinking. "Not her."*
>
> *You're probably wondering how I could send you away, and the truth is, I wonder myself, sometimes. Please, try and understand that I feel I had no choice. Letting Barb take you away was the most difficult thing I've ever done. What I*

hope is that maybe, just maybe, it's also the best thing I've ever done, too.

Fourteen months ago you entered my life. You were feisty, funny, smart, and tough as that old pair of Dr. Martens you insisted on wearing every day. You were also scared, and here's something you might not know: I was scared, too. I wasn't sure if you'd ever be able to trust me, though over time, you began to. I'll admit we've hit more than a few speed bumps, but we've also shared some incredible memories I wouldn't trade for anything. I've watched you dart in and out among shadows since then, and I know you have good reason for all that cynicism. But I also know that you are one of the smartest, strongest people I've ever met, and I'm absolutely certain that deep down, underneath all the anger, the Puck I know and love is still there. Yes, kiddo, you are loved. And that's what I want you to know. No matter what happens—no matter what has *happened, happiness is still attainable. I want you to come home. But in order for this to work, I need you to do one thing: graduate from DreamRoads. Puck, I know you've got it in you to do this. Don't let your anger get the best of you. Take all that grit and*

stubbornness and use it to come back to me. Your
room is waiting for you, exactly as you left it. And
so am I.

    Love,
    Paula

After reading the words (and noting that there's no mention of Ted in them), I stare down at the page for what feels like a long time, letting the letters blur in and out of focus. You know when you combine too many colors of paint and it all turns a muddy brown? That's the best way I can explain what's happening inside me. It's impossible to pick out one emotion from the next, because they're all flooding together—guilt, anger, confusion, indignation, skepticism, relief—filling me like a thick liquid, from my toes right up to my head, where it seems like I have only an inch or two left to breathe. I'm suffocating, and all I want to do is get rid of this letter and get out of this place. I glance up and see Barb standing practically forehead-to-forehead with Quin, who looks stricken—by either her general oppressiveness or the contents of his letter, I'm not sure which. They're bathed in an eerie spotlight from the sun's descent. Nick and the four counselors are undoing the giant "spiderweb" we'd made earlier in the day out of rainbow-colored yarn (don't ask), and I realize, this is it: my chance to disappear.

I make a run for it (well, okay, more like a fast walk), crossing paths only with Peabo, who wonders where I'm off to.

"I've got to take a piss," I mutter, stomping away and ducking under the branch of a nearby pine tree. In front of me is a thick clump of bushes. If I get to the other side, it'll give me a window of time to be completely out of sight. It'll be dark soon—they'll never be able to track me. Beyond that…never mind, I can't think that far ahead. Once again, my body overrides my brain, shoving all rational thoughts aside. All I know for sure is that I'm done here. I inch my way through this natural barrier, struggling to part unyielding branches as I navigate my small frame through whatever openings will permit me. With enough foliage now screening me from behind, I hold up Paula's letter and reach into one of the pockets of my army fatigue pants. First things first. Flicking the lighter to give up its flame, I'm about to set one corner of the paper to it when I hear some sort of whimpering. Christ. I squat low to the ground, trying not to move a muscle, peering through my leafy-green scrim to get a glimpse of who's there. About twenty feet away, I finally make him out, sitting on the ground. His face is buried in his arms, which rest on bent knees. Ronnie is the last person I'd ever expect to see blubbering out here.

"Hey, man…are you okay?" I ask, approaching with caution. He stiffens up at the sound of my voice, and even in the dim light I can tell that he's been crying.

"Leave me alone," he answers, hiding his face again.

"Your letter sucked, too? Well I say screw 'em." He looks up at me, his face registering confusion.

"Speak for yourself," he answers. I see now, between his legs and his chest, that he's guarding a few pages of lined paper, the ends ragged, as if ripped from a spiral notebook. He glances down at them. "He's all I got."

"Who's he?"

"My baby brother, Eduardo."

"How old?"

"Eleven. My auntie works two jobs, so he's by himself most nights. I'm supposed to be there. I'm supposed to be helping look out for him."

"I guess that explains your stealing Titania's lighter. You'd do anything to get home to him, huh?"

"I won't ever see Eddie again."

"What do you mean?" I feel a familiar dread rise up in me. "Oh, god, did something happen to him? Is that what the letter is about?"

"He's okay. But I can't go back there."

"When you graduate from here, though. Right? It shouldn't be much longer."

He shakes his head. "I won't go home. I'll join the military, maybe; run away, if I have to. It's better for everyone that way."

"But if you got a letter, then that must mean—"

"He deserves better," he interrupts, his meaty fist brushing away more tears that are pooling under his eyes. "I've done bad things."

"Join the club."

"I hurt someone."

"I piss off people all the time, too, man. It's not—"

"You don't understand, Puck. The person I hurt…he isn't pissed off," Ronnie says quietly. "He's in a coma." I take a single step back. My mind races frantically, searching for something to say, but no words form. "I didn't even know the guy. It was just some stranger on a crowded bus. He was minding his own business, staring at his phone, but he brushed past me on the way to finding a seat, and it felt like such massive disrespect. I called him out, he turned around and told me to chill, and that was it. I lunged for the guy and just started pounding on him. Even after the driver pulled over to the curb, I didn't let up. I was so filled with rage; it's like my brain blacked out and my fists just took over. It seems like I've been angry like this for as long as I've been alive."

I know the feeling, I think to myself.

"I'm only here because I'm lucky. The judge must've been in a good mood on the day of my hearing," he continues. "He went easy on me. Said this place could probably help me more than the alternative."

I want to ask Ronnie why his little brother is living with the aunt—where are their parents?—but I know better than to snoop.

"Don't you see?" I ask, instead. "Even a judge thought you deserved one more chance."

"I guess, yeah. But my auntie and Eduardo, all I bring them is problems. They deserve to be free of all that. Sometimes I wonder if there's ever any going back. From some places, maybe you just can't." We remain frozen in silence. Two scrub jays bicker loudly in the dark branches overhead. "You got any brothers or sisters?" Ronnie eventually asks.

Just as I shake my head no, my hand loses its grip on the letter I forgot I was holding. It's carried away by a faint breeze, which jerks it, teasingly, in midair until it finally lands on the dirt a few feet closer to Ronnie. I stoop down to retrieve the single piece of stationery and fold it along its original lines, which I crease hard with my fingernail. "Actually, yes. A younger brother." Ronnie offers me a small smile.

"How old?" he asks. I shake my head again—*no*—averting my gaze.

"Oh, Puck. Damn. That's…I don't know what to say."

"Don't say anything. Just . . ." I inhale deeply to keep my voice from cracking as I hold out the lighter, which I'm still clutching in my right fist. "Here. Take it. Use it to go home to yours." He hesitates for a moment but then accepts my offering, holding my gaze just long enough to establish that we understand each other. "Come on, we'd better get back," I say, "before Barb 'consequences' the shit out of us."

* * *

I thought Quin was a total square when it comes to recreational pharmaceuticals, but, apparently, he's got the rest of us beat.

It's his turn under the blinding scrutiny of Barb's campfire interrogation, and once she puts the screws to him, he almost seems relieved to fess up.

"I forged the prescriptions," he says, digging at the dirt near his feet with a long stick that, in a better world, could be used to toast marshmallows. "After it worked the first time, I just…kept doing it."

"You had to have known, Quin, how risky it was to play around with those kind of medications," Barb says, her expression solemn. "They're addictive—and so dangerous."

"But not taking them," Quin answers back, "that would have been worse. Believe me."

"Can you explain what you mean by that?"

"The pills got me through the day on four hours of sleep. They helped me focus. I was juggling four AP courses, cramming for the Academic Decathlon, trying to get out my college applications—"

"Oh my gosh," Nissa interrupts. "He really *did* study someone to death. Himself, practically."

"Basically true," Quin replies, unfazed, "and if I didn't keep a perfect GPA, then . . ." He stops mid-sentence.

"Then what?" Barb prods.

"Then nothing. That's not even an option in my family."

"But, Quin, no one's perfect."

"That's not true. In my family, we are. No excuses, no exceptions. If you're not a concert-piano-playing rocket scientist by the age of nineteen, you're *nothing*."

"So what you're saying is your parents have high expectations of you." The rest of us die laughing at the understated ridiculousness of Barb's comment. Only Quin keeps a straight face.

"My mom and dad weren't born in this country. They worked hard to get here. They suffered and sacrificed everything to get ahead, and they did it for us. Perfection is the only acceptable return on their investment, and to let them down...there's no greater shame in my culture."

"But that's insane, dude," interrupts Peabo.

"Seriously," says Titania. "You're, like, every parent's idea of the perfect kid."

"Guys, guys," Barb cautions, trying to keep control of the dialogue, but Quin is already speaking again.

"Not to mine, I'm not," he says. "I just totally cracked. I was walking around like a zombie those last few weeks, and I knew if I didn't nail my SATs then I wouldn't get into Stanford *or* Caltech, and—"

"Are you kidding me with this?" Ronnie wonders aloud. "I call b.s. on your drama. I *wish* I had parents who rode my butt. If I had, then maybe—"

"Okay, okay," Barb interrupts, slapping her palms on her knees. "Since everyone here seems so intent on throwing in their two cents, we're going to try something a little different. I'm going to let the rest of you conduct

133

the session. You guys talk things through amongst yourselves." There's nothing but silence in response to her suggestion, so, of course, she does what she does best: prods us. "So, then. Who wants to talk to Quin a bit more about what he's been dealing with? Anyone?" After a few more beats of silence, I can't take it anymore.

"I, for one, would be incredibly interested to hear what Snout's take is on all this," I say. The other kids instantly lose it, and Snout—our resident Looney Tunes— drums his fingers mischievously across his mouth. Even the counselors exchange smirks at my (apparently successful) attempt to break the ice. Quin's cracked a smile, too, but the only one who's not amused is Barb.

"I think we'd all be keen to witness that, Puck, but in the meantime, do you have any perspective for Quin? Any questions for him, maybe?"

There's no way she's going to get me on board with grilling the guy, so wrongly doomed to this backwoods equivalent of juvie hall.

"You don't belong here, Quin," I tell him. "The last thing you are is a delinquent."

Quin's chin drops to his chest, and then he mumbles, "I am, though. I got arrested. Breaking and entering."

"Whoa." Peabo voices what the rest of us are thinking. "Seriously, man?"

"Bad. Ass," Ronnie says. "You're full of surprises, eh, Potter?"

"That's enough, Ronnie," Barb says. "Frances, why don't you give it a try? Ask Quin a follow-up question."

"I'm not sure what to ask. Could I have a hint or something?"

"This isn't exactly Twenty Questions," Titania says.

"I'd start with the obvious," Barb says, not even attempting to hide her sarcasm. Frances's expression, at first dull with confusion, brightens in comprehension.

"Okay, right." She turns to face Quin. "You want to walk us through what happened?" He is silent.

"It's okay, man," Peabo says. "You can tell us. You've heard our stories, right?"

"How bad can it be?" Titania says.

"If he doesn't want to tell us, he shouldn't have to," I say in his defense.

"No, it's okay," Quin says. "I might as well get it over with." The rest of us wait patiently for him to continue. He's quiet, too, but eventually, staring into the fire, he begins.

"The SATs were only a week away. All semester, I'd been so careful. I'd taken the bus to a different pharmacy every time. I obviously used a fake name, but I was in a hurry that day. My parents had asked me to walk my little sister home from her cello lesson. I decided to take a chance and go to the drugstore in our neighborhood so I wouldn't be late to pick her up. I guess maybe I'd gotten a bit overconfident, too."

"You got cocky." Ronnie nods in brotherly solidarity. Quin leans into the fire, warming his hands. The flames flicker in the reflection of his glasses. The rest of us remain silent, giving him time to collect his thoughts. I sneak a glance at Barb, who, for once, doesn't look menacing, only thoughtful, as she rests a hand under her chin.

"I pulled a Dodgers cap out of my backpack and put it on before I went in," Quin finally continues. "I didn't recognize the woman behind the counter, which was a relief. She told me I'd need to wait a few minutes for the prescription to be filled. This was totally copacetic—"

"Copa-what?" Peabo asks.

"Co-pa-cet-ic," Barb pronounces slowly. "It means *fine*; normal. Go ahead, Quin."

"And so I headed over as nonchalantly as I could to the magazine aisle. That's when things got weird." He pauses again, comfortable enough now to make eye contact with the rest of us.

"Weird how?" I urge him, hanging on to his every word.

"I felt paranoid, like someone was watching me. I glanced over my shoulder, and the woman was whispering to another man behind the pharmacy counter. They were both looking at me."

"Damn," Ronnie says. "Dude's about to get *made*."

"That's exactly what I thought. Even though I was panicking, I put down the magazine as casually as possible and headed toward the exit. Once I was outside, I ran as fast as I could down the street. That night, I kept waiting for the phone to ring, or for the cops to knock on the door, but it never happened."

"So you didn't get busted?" Titania asks.

"Not for that," Quin answers. "If I had stopped there, none of this would've happened. I should've learned my lesson, but I didn't. It was like a warning, and I completely ignored it."

"Why?" Peabo asks the question we were all thinking.

"The SATs. I still had to take them, and I was convinced I needed the Ritalin to do it. My mom was friends with a woman across the street, and she'd mentioned her son was on Ritalin. They'd gone out of town for the weekend."

"Uh-oh," Nissa says. Then, registering Quin's obvious misery, she claps her hand over her mouth and mumbles, "Sorry. Go ahead."

"That's okay. Anyway, I waited until my family was asleep, and then I snuck out. I'd never done that before. I felt so guilty. Like, what if the house burned down while I was out, and my dad tried to save me and I wasn't even there?"

"You *never* snuck out?" Nissa asks. Quin shakes his head.

"I used a hammer to break a window in the back of their house, and then I shimmied through. I was in the bathroom rifling through their medicine cabinet when the police arrived." He shudders and puts his head in his hands. Nissa, who's sitting next to him, timidly places a hand on his shoulder.

"The next-door neighbor had heard the glass shatter and called them." Quin stares helplessly into the palms of his hands, as if searching for answers there. "Want to know the funny thing? There was no Ritalin in the house, anyway. It never occurred to me—and I'm supposed to be so smart, right?—that the family would've taken it with them." His laugh sounds bitter. "The worst part? When they led me out of the house in handcuffs, my parents and my sister were standing on our lawn. The looks on their faces…I'll never be able to unsee that. My mom was crying." He puts his hands underneath his glasses and rubs his eyes, because now he's crying, too.

"It's okay, man," Ronnie says, lobbing kindness toward him like a ball Quin can't quite catch.

"We've all been there," Peabo adds. "You don't even *want* to know how many times I've disappointed my family, and yet they still ponied up the dollars to send me here. Not like I deserve it. Your parents did the same."

"No, they didn't."

"What do you mean?" Titania asks.

"My uncle pays for this place," he answers, and then he looks around at all of us. "My letter today? It was from my father telling me that he and my mother will never be able to forgive me for humiliating them. I'm basically being disowned."

As everyone else expresses sympathy and support, I stare intently at the ashy white logs crumbling in the base of the fire, a ghostly blue glowing from their center. Most of the kids sitting around me are the duds, the misprints, the flawed products. DreamRoads is like one of those robot arms in a manufacturing plant, deftly plucking us from the conveyor belt of life and tossing us in the scrap bin. We deserve to be thrown out, because we don't meet a certain standard. And I guess that's what's got me all bent out of shape about Quin. He's a good egg—not rotten like the rest of us. This kid with so much potential, just cast aside. If he doesn't make the cut, the rest of us never even stood a chance. Quin has me beat by miles in the brains department, but there's one thing I *do* know that maybe he doesn't. He's still crying, sitting there across the fire from me, and I just can't take it. I stand up and storm over to him.

"Get up." He glances up at me, almost frightened by my blistering tone. I offer him my hand, and when he grabs it, still confused, I yank his small frame to his feet. We're standing just about eye-to-eye, and the words spill out of me, the mantra I've learned to live by from a very young age. "If they don't want you, eff them. You kick their dust off your shoes, and you go it alone. No matter what kind of 'failure' they say you are, tune them out. Who cares about being perfect? Who cares about what *anyone* thinks? It's your life, not theirs. There are a million people in this world who will try to drag you down, including the people who are supposed to love you most. Whatever happens, you'll be okay."

"Yeah, man," says Ronnie, chiming in, "you're going to be some super-rich genius-type, like that Bill Gates guy, and we'll all be able to say we knew you back when you were a high school twerp."

"Right on," Titania says. "You'll be so famous that the tabloids will rat out all kinds of dirt on *you*, and they'll finally leave me in peace."

Quin exhales a chuckle and stretches up his shirt collar to dry the tears on his cheeks and wipe the fog that's accumulated on the underside of his glasses.

"Even if you end up as one of those guys who swing cardboard arrows at street corners, we'll still think you're an ace," says Peabo. "Not only do you have awesome nerd cred, I'm just stoked that I finally have somebody to call whenever I've got computer trouble."

"You'd actually stay in touch with me?" Quin asks, his wet eyes widening.

"You're my Double-O, man—Octopus Opposite," Ronnie says. "That means we've got each other's backs. Always."

"I'd add you to my contacts right now if Barb would give us back our cell phones." Peabo clasps his hands in front of his chest and glances all "pretty please" at Barb.

"Not a chance," she replies. Her face is stony, but her eyes are dancing, the way they always do when one of us is having a campfire crisis. I swear, the woman gets off on taking us to the brink of anguish. As Quin contemplates the campfire, I can tell he is somewhere far away, thinking about his parents. Like a pocket-sized drill sergeant, I slap both of my hands squarely upon his shoulders.

"You don't need them, Quin," I say. "You don't need anyone. In fact, flying solo through life has its privileges. Take it from me. When I finally age out of the foster-care system, it will be like the sweet taste of freedom." This seems to bring him back around, and he does something kind of out of character for him: he looks me straight in the eyes.

"How do you do it?" he says. "How are you not terrified to soldier through life...alone?" I blink hard. He hasn't said it to be cruel, but like the razor-sharp edge of a blade of grass, his simple question cuts, and I brace myself, half expecting the starry sky to collapse onto me like a defective circus tent. When it doesn't, I have no choice but to pull out the same emotional sleight-of-hand tricks I've been practicing for years. Not for my own benefit, mind you—but for Quin.

"I guess it's like that old saying: 'Wherever you go, there you are.'" I shrug, trying to force a smile. "Right now, I'm here, and call me crazy, but I don't feel very alone." I glance around at the rest of the circle, meeting the stares of all these broken-winged birds. "What do you think, guys? Am I alone?"

Nissa's the first one on her feet, striding over to wrap both of us up in a hug.

"No way, girl," she grins. "And neither are you, Potter." Within seconds, the other five are swarming us, and we're a jumble. Though jostled against Quin's bony frame, my nose is practically shoved up into Snout's toxic armpit, and from behind, Frances hugs me to her like she's about to administer the Heimlich. From the outer edge of the huddle, Titania tussles Quin's hair, which prompts Peabo to yank playfully on her ponytail.

"Looks like you're stuck with us," I say, nudging Quin in the ribs with my stomach. He laughs. In the gap under Snout's arm, I see the fire, and beyond that, Barb. Her face is expressionless as she watches us, and I wonder how she could be so mercenary as to accept a kid like Quin into this program, a kid who hardly deserves to be here at all—everyone knows it. It's no matter to her, though; it's all about the almighty dollar. Barb shifts her gaze, and maybe I'm wrong, but it seems like she's staring straight at me—even buried in all these bodies. The corners of her mouth turn up in a barely perceptible smile like some Disney villainess, wickedly smug. I shut my eyes and burrow tighter into my comrades, the only true source of light in this otherwise dark forest.

CHAPTER 8

From Heaven to Earth,
From Earth to Heaven

Day seventeen (I think?). I'm standing in the middle of a ditch I've been digging since daybreak. My palms are like raw flank steaks flung on a searing-hot frying pan. My neck, back, and biceps are screaming murder, and the sun is cutting no slack. Though the other kids are scattered within shouting distance, we're all too zonked to talk. We're not allowed to stop digging until we're each into it up to our shoulders. The counselors, along with Barb and Nick, are making their rounds, from hole to hole, checking our progress. I've barely reached waist level, but it's getting increasingly harder for me to hoist out spadefuls of dirt.

I'm about four gallons of sweat into the Earth Challenge. It *might* be more tolerable if we were actually doing something productive, like preparing for trench warfare, but I'm pretty sure there's no endgame to this little exercise beyond turning everything we do into an emotional metaphor.

"Today is about digging deep," Barb says as she parades above us, Queen of the Mole People. "Who you are on the surface is *not* necessarily who you are underneath. Consider this an archaeological dig of the soul."

Shrinks sure do love to force the symbolism. When I was eleven, some complete whack-a-doo thought I'd benefit from carrying two suitcases full of clothes around a gymnasium for forty-five minutes to demonstrate how much "baggage" I needed to let go of. Ass-backward, of course. *This*, on the other hand, is ass-backward *plus* needlessly heat-stroke-inducing. The part that's getting me though is the sound of all our shovels scooping and dumping: *Skrisssh, thwap. Skrisssh, thwap.* I feel strangely chilled and almost faint as a long-buried memory rises to the surface, floating at the edge of my thoughts.

A seven-year-old doesn't understand (can't, really) the concept of putting someone she loves in a box and putting that box in the ground. Everyone thought I should be at the funeral to say goodbye, as if witnessing such a ritual wouldn't scar me for life. Thinking back, it's sad how few people were actually there. Just me and Grandma

145

and a handful of her friends, many of whom dangled rosaries from bony, spotted hands with raised purple veins. Grandma's lilac-colored polyester dress smelled like mothballs. I wore patent leather Mary Janes, borrowed, and a size too big. I didn't know I wouldn't be able to keep them, and the only time I actually cried that day was when I had to take off those damn shoes. Looking back, what I remember most is the smell of the earth, freshly dug after a rain. That, and the strange expressions of the mourners as they reached down to shake my hand or pat me on the back. Now I can see it for what it was: pity, and probably a little disgust. No one likes to be that close to tragedy, as if it's something you can catch, like the measles.

Dredging up that awful crap while I slowly entomb myself is turning me into my own ridiculous cliché. It's probably what evil Miss Metaphor was hoping would happen.

A few hours later, when we've all dug holes more or less to her satisfaction, Barb calls off the charade and tells us to climb on out.

"When you're in too deep, sometimes you need help," she explains when none of us have the upper-body strength to hoist ourselves up. She then signals the four counselors to haul us out, one by one, to illustrate her point. "Unless you're capable of sprouting wings, you'd be a fool not to take that help when it's offered to you." Dmitri and Xander grab me by my sweaty forearms and pluck me from my pit.

"I guess I'm supposed to thank you," I tell them in between panting breaths, "but, c'mon, it's not like I ended up down there of my own doing. It was kind of forced on me."

"Was it, Puck?" Barb says, having overheard. "Because I disagree. Different choices on your end might have prevented you from standing in the bottom of that hole, or being here at all, in fact. Refusing to take any ownership for where you are in life seems to be a throughline with you."

Presuming she knows all the details of my past, her words are not just malicious; they're downright inhuman. I want to scream at her that I've been taking ownership for what happened for the last eight years of my life, that I've wanted nothing more than to duct tape shut the mouths of every well-meaner who has patted my shoulder and said, "It wasn't your fault." They may have believed it, but I never will. If taking ownership is the ticket to salvation, then, hell, I should be the most enlightened person on the planet. But there's no point in explaining any of that, so instead of answering Barb, I clam up. To engage her at all is to trigger more verbal spewage from her mouth, so no, thank you.

"Thank god that's over," says Nissa, who is sitting a few feet away from me, letting handfuls of sandy dirt run through her fingers.

"That sucked," agrees Peabo, who is sprawled on his back, "but at least it earned us another Stepping Stone." Nearby, Ronnie is leaning against a tree gulping water from his canteen, which he lowers to let out a laugh.

"Newbies, newbies. So naive."

"Meaning what?" I say. Before he can answer, Barb's back, handing out short, eraserless pencils, loose-leaf paper, and squares of flimsy cardboard to provide flat writing surfaces.

"Is this a pop quiz?" Frances whines.

"Not exactly. This is Part Two of the Earth Challenge," Barb answers. "Don't worry; it's nothing taxing. You only have to write. It could be a letter to yourself, or to someone you love—someone you've hurt, perhaps. It could be a letter to the Tooth Fairy or your own rap song for all I care. The most important thing you need to know is that no one else is ever going to read what you write, and that is my solemn promise. This is a one-way missive, so get it out. Get it out of your head; get it out of your heart—whether it's a fear or a secret, a confession, a promise, or an apology. Only you know what you need to write, and only you will ever read it. All I ask is that you write honestly." Frances raises her hand.

"How do we *know* no one's ever going to read it?" she says.

"Why don't you ask Ronnie?" Barb answers. "He's got a few of these under his belt already." As DreamRoads's not-so-distinguished veteran, Ronnie shrugs an embarrassed assent.

Twenty minutes go by, and the others are dutifully hunched over their assignments. Perched on a small boulder, Snout is scribbling like some Neanderthal academic; whether it's actual words or gibberish, I can't be sure. It's "Sniffles Central" over where Titania and Nissa are sitting, whereas Frances seems more thoughtful than teary. Quin's pencil is balanced lengthwise between his lips, but he's staring hard at his paper, reading what he's already jotted down. Standing at the perimeter are the adults, looking as hawkeyed as teachers on testing days.

"Puck, I haven't seen you write anything," Barb says.

"Huh?" I respond, snapping to.

"If I don't see your pencil moving soon, I can't allow you to pass this Stepping Stone," she continues. "You're running out of time. Five more minutes, everybody!"

Flicking my pencil against my makeshift writing tablet, I pretend to concentrate, but my gaze wanders back to Barb. Her eyes are boring into me. I think back to what she said to me when I'd gotten out of the hole, about being responsible for the shitty cards I've been dealt. Blackness seeps into all the little tiny gaps, flooding my insides. *Write honestly.* Like the first three people in a mob to break through the police line, the words suddenly appear on the paper:

> *I*
> *hate*
> *her.*
> *I hate her.*
> *I hate her. I hate her.*
> *I hate her. I hate her. I hate her. I hate her. I hate her.*
> *I hate her. I hate her. I hate her. I hate her. I hate her.*
> *I hate her. I hate her. I hate her. I hate her. I hate her.*
> *I hate her. I hate her. I hate her. I hate her. I hate her.*
> *I hate her. I hate her. I hate her. I hate her. I hate her.*

I hate her. I hate her. I hate her. I hate her. I hate her.

The repetition puts me in a trance. I don't care if Barb reads it. I don't care if anyone reads it. It's the truth. She has made my life a living hell, and I'm sick of feeling like there's something wrong with me for not being able to square what's expected of me with what I actually feel.

"Okay, people, let's wrap it up," says Barb. "Fold your paper and go stand by the edge of whichever hole you've dug." While the other kids slowly mobilize, I glance down at my graphite chicken scratch, feeling cheated, somehow. Those three words, written to Jupiter and back, would never be enough. Barb's barking more orders, but her words vanish in the air before they reach my ears or brain. Almost as an afterthought, I squeeze one last line in tiny print at the bottom of the page:

If I could kill her, I would.

I drop the piece of paper into the hole I've dug, and I begin to backfill, tipping the spade so that dirt cascades over the small, folded square. We're supposed to feel resolution, says Barb. But I feel nothing. It's just dirt. Paper. Words. She wants us to purge, to get it out of our systems so that we can get closure. To leave it here in this spot, forever, so that we can walk away. It doesn't work like that, though. What's buried isn't forgotten.

CHAPTER 9

Fetch Me That Flower

Being high removes you from the rest of the world. You can let your mind just zone out. It's an escape, a dizzying sensory overload. Dangerous? Maybe, if you end up doing something stupid, I guess, but I tend to find it therapeutic. It's the next best thing to flying.

It's why I'm feeling pretty at ease backing out over the ledge of a hundred-foot cliff. The only things gnawing at me are the harness cutting into my upper thighs and Barb's totally pointless pep talk.

"You can do this, Puck. The first step is the hardest, and after that, gravity takes over."

Of course I can *do this*. Why else does she think I volunteered to go second? Barb wants to believe that Stepping Stone Number Three (the Air Challenge, which I'm mere minutes from acing, thankyouverymuch) has me pants-pissing scared, but she's wrong, as usual. She should be focused on talking everyone else down off the ledge (literally) because the last things I see as I descend into the void are my fellow campers' gaping mouths and horrified expressions.

"Atta girl, you're doing fine!" says Nick, cheering me on. "See what she's doing, kids? Your instinct is going to be to pull forward, but you have to fight that urge and lean back. Trust your harness, and sit into it."

I only paid attention to about ten of the forty-minute "Rappelling for Dummies" seminar Nick and Barb gave us in preparation. I've got to assume they're not in the business of allowing children to plummet to their deaths. Besides, how hard can sliding down a rope actually be?

Okay, so I'm admittedly a bit choppy at first, tentatively feeding the rope through the figure-eight-shaped ring that's clipped, by a carabiner, to the front of my waist. My right hand is gripping the rope that dangles down past my right side to the ground, where Ronnie and Mia watch with craning necks. Xander's down there too, harnessed to the other end of the rope, ready to halt my descent if things go badly.

I'm about a quarter of the way down when I stop by wrenching the rope in my right hand behind my back, hard, and gripping the taut rope above me with my left.

My heart is slamming itself against my ribcage with every beat like it's a club kid on a crowded dance floor.

"Puck? What's wrong?" yells Barb from the ledge above me. "You're doing great; keep going."

But I don't want to keep going. I've been so focused on the technical part of descending this sheer drop that I haven't had the chance to appreciate the journey. When the hell am I ever going to get another chance to hang off the side of a freakin' mountain?

Glancing over my right shoulder, I see the canyon spread out before me like some fake scenic backdrop. I can't remember ever seeing landscape so devoid of civilization—no buzzing freeway or ugly radio towers. Thin, jagged clouds stretch like giant claw marks across an expansive blue sky, while the sun casts shadows behind trees that, from far away, appear miniature.

Above and below me, the shouting continues. They all think I'm having some massive freakout, but I just ignore them. It feels too peaceful, hovering in this halfway place like a puppet on a string. Glancing at the rock face in front of me, I lose all sense of depth perception, and my thoughts turn to my first (and only) Ferris wheel ride.

I don't remember where we were—some church festival or county fair, I guess—but I do remember the three of us gripping the wide metal bar that locked into

155

place in front of us, the way we screamed with terror and joy each time the wheel peaked and made its swift, stomach-lurching drop. I'm surprised they even let Shane on the ride—he couldn't have been older than three at the time. (Not that my mom was ever a stickler for child safety.) But, anyway, I can still see his soft cheeks formed into perfect, pink spheres when he grinned, and that cute gap between his front baby teeth. "More!" he kept shouting. He never wanted it to end. None of us did.

"Puck, listen to me!" Barb is yelling down, and for once, I'm happy to have her bust in on my thoughts. I glance up to see Barb's and Nick's heads peering over the ledge like stickpins. "I know you're scared," she shouts, "but you have complete control over this. All you have to do is take it one inch at a time. Breathe…and *go*."

More encouragement rains down from my unseen fellow campers behind her, garbled words hinting at phrases like *You can do it!* and *Quit being such a wuss!* I check the ground, where Ronnie and Mia wait. For once, I feel liberated from this place and all these jerk-offs. You might even say it's the best I've felt since arriving at camp. I'd happily hang out in this limbo forever. Wherever he is, I hope Shane feels this free.

I position my feet against the rock face and take a deep breath, leaning back as far as I can. I notice Xander's left a lot of slack on the line.

"There you go," yells Nick. "Just lean into it, like I said."

"I've got you, Puck!" Xander shouts up. "You're not going to fall!"

Oh yeah? I believe you. Here goes nothing, I think to myself before letting go. Xander's not expecting me to drop without any warning, and before he can adjust the safety clip to stop me, I've dropped twenty glorious feet. The whir of the rope through the metal ring at my waist buzzes like an insect until I stop in midair. What an incredible rush. Halfway down the cliff now, I dangle horizontally by my waist. My arms are outstretched, and my head's tossed back in delight as I laugh at the echo of screams that ricochet through the canyon. I scared them good. I'm spinning clockwise, like a yo-yo that's punked-out to gravity. Xander slowly lets his end of the rope feed up, up, up through his hands, and I slowly drop down, down, down. Xander finally drops me with a thud onto the ground. Ouch.

"What the hell was that?" he asks sharply.

"Ah-ah-ah…*language,*" I remind him. He throws the end of the rope at me. Mia stoops down to unfasten my carabiners.

"That was incredibly stupid, Puck," she says. Only Ronnie offers me a hand and hoists me up. He's still wearing his harness, having descended just before me, and we walk over to a nearby boulder to get out of earshot of Xander and Mia.

"That was *sick*," he says in a tone I take as a compliment. "Your real name is Robin? It ought to be *Danger Bird.*"

"Whatever," I say, almost embarrassed by how much I'm enjoying his kudos.

"Was it worth it?"

"What do you mean?"

"Forfeiting the Stepping Stone. They only bring us to this cliff once a month or so. You're going to have to wait for a batch of new recruits for an opportunity to do it again."

"But…I mean, technically, I *got down*," I say, furrowing my brow. It's sinking in that I may have just screwed myself. Again.

"You think Barb's going to see it that way?"

"Whatever." I unbuckle my chin strap and toss the helmet next to his on the ground, where we both drop to our butts. "Anyway, you sure did shred it." He shrugs.

"My fourth time down," he says. "I've had some practice in six months. But we may be here a while now that you've scared the shit out of everyone else up there." He glances to the top of the cliff, where Barb, Nick, and Dmitri are attempting to coax a very reluctant Titania to make a go of it. Even from way down here, I can hear her shrill crying.

"I'm not buying her claim that she zip-lined from the rafters onto center stage at Madison Square Garden," I say.

"Yeah, not likely. Man, speaking of, did you hear her and Nick talking about the show on the hike up here this morning?"

"No, but I'm all ears," I say, brightening to think of my pet project underway. He shakes his head in disbelief.

"She used to only hate on that doofus, but now it's like she's his deranged disciple." I don't tell him that it's all my doing, but I'll admit, it's hard not to claim credit.

"Are they still going with Nick's original idea?"

"Yeah. Nick's promised her an epic death scene," he says. "Too bad it's only pretend."

"What's the point of the show, anyway? He told me it was part of some parents' weekend?"

"It's basically graduation, at least for some. We look 'adorable,'—they want to take our sorry butts back home, I guess." *Not likely*, I think to myself. "If your parents aren't in the audience, that's a sure sign you're staying put —maybe even a 'lifer,' like me."

"Not anymore, you're not. Not after that impressive fire you 'started' this morning." I see the corners of his mouth twitch upward.

"I tossed the Bic afterward," he says. "It was almost out of juice, anyway. The last thing I need is Barb catching it on me."

"Speaking of the Stepping Stones, the only one left now is the Water Challenge."

"Yeah."

"So what's involved with that? Please tell me it's not some cultish baptismal crap." *Or swimming. Please not swimming.*

"No. River rafting."

"Like, raging rapids?"

"I wish. It's pretty tame-slash-lame. Barb's got this whole 'go with the flow' analogy she always does once we're in the boats. You know how she is."

I nod, letting a certain familiar tension in my body go slack. Boats I can handle. We stare up at Titania, who is descending at a sloth's pace, all while screaming at Xander every ten seconds to slow her down. If God has any sense of humor whatsoever, maybe the rock star will crap herself somewhere between here and terra firma. (There's an album cover for you.)

"You know, I'm curious," I say, keeping my gaze trained at Titania. "Who's the craziest kid you've come across since you've been in this program?" Ronnie's eyes narrow as he considers the question. He pushes his sleeves up to his elbows, exposing on his left forearm a tattoo of a mermaid riding on a dolphin's back.

"Snout's a rare breed," he says.

"Yeah, but he's just a head case. C'mon, you must have heard some pretty wild stories from the other kids who've come and gone over the last six months."

"What happens at the campfire stays at the campfire," Ronnie says, delivering a fairly clutch impression of a DreamRoads staffer. "The DreamRoad will work *magic* on you, praise Jesus!" He tosses his head back and throws his hands in the air like he's at some gospel revival.

"The wilderness will scoop you up in a big ol' headlock and deliver you from evil," I chime in, laughing.

161

"Exactly! Who needs an *actual* mother when there's Mother Nature to watch over you?" His last sentence instantly sobers us both up, and he fumbles to change the subject before a grey cloud settles over us. "Come to think of it, there *is* something I heard out here, and I don't even know if it's true…it's probably complete b.s., actually."

"Go on."

"So this one guy who came through, he was a first-class junkie. Dabbled in just about everything—stuff I never even heard of, which is saying something."

"So. What of it?"

"Well…you've seen those big white flowers that grow on bushes out here?"

"Of course," I say. "They're everywhere."

"Angel's Trumpets. This kid told me they can take you on a pretty epic trip."

I give Ronnie a skeptical glance. He merely shrugs.

"Wait a second," I say. "Xander has pointed those flowers out to me before. He calls them moonflowers, but he never said anything about them being hallucinogenic."

"You think he'd tell *us* that?" says Ronnie. "According to this kid, if you brew them into a tea and drink it, you'll get the most crazy high of your life. 'At one with the universe' kind of stuff. Peace, love, and harmony. Pink elephants on parade."

"He tried it?"

"Nah. He was way too spooked by the stories he heard from other people who *had*. Apparently if you take too much, it's really, *really* 'no bueno.' Know what I'm saying?"

"From a glorified daffodil? Oh come on, I'm not buying any of this," I say. "You can't seriously think Barb would be marching a bunch of losers and users through the Utah equivalent of an opium crop, do you?" Ronnie shrugs, his arms folded against his chest.

"Who knows? Maybe there's some truth to her claims that the wilderness can 'set us free.'"

Ignoring him, I spring to my feet and wave my arms over my head.

"Come on, Titania! You can do this!" I shout. "I believe in you!" I glance behind my shoulder at Ronnie, who's staring at me like I'm some kind of traitor. "Don't hate," I tell him. "You're the one who said I need to 'play the game' to get out of here."

* * *

By the time everyone has finally joined us at the bottom of the canyon, I've all but sprouted pom-poms at the end of my hands, which are numb from clapping. Hopefully, cheering on my fellow campers and radiating shiny, happy positivity will be enough to squeak under the radar. Truth be told, it's not *entirely* an act. I'm kind of caught up in the excitement everyone else seems to be feeling at having conquered the mountain. I join in on high fives and back-slapping hugs. Barb's self-satisfied smile as she watches us convinces me that I'm going to get a free pass for my forbidden freefall.

"Congratulations, guys!" she says, wiping her brow and taking a swig from her canteen. "I know that was a first for most of you, and we're so proud of the way you tackled this challenge, even in the face of fears and doubts. You channeled those emotions, you focused on the task at hand, and you should feel so good about having passed this Stepping Stone."

We all let loose with a few more victory whoops. Frances, Nissa, and I start to get our groove on, but then Barb stops me mid-shimmy, grabbing me firmly by the shoulder.

"*Not you,* young lady."

"What?" I say, my voice cracking. She doesn't respond; she only shakes her head, sternly. "But I...I made it down, too!" My face burns, and for some reason I feel completely humiliated.

"What you did up there was reckless," Barb says. "You didn't pass this Stepping Stone, and I'm sorry to tell you I don't even know when or *if* I can trust you enough to let you attempt it again. If this is some kind of game to you, then I've got news for you: you lost today, big time."

She turns on her heel to walk away, and I know that if I let this conversation end here, I might become a "DreamRoads Lifer."

"Wait!" I shout, grabbing her by the elbow. (Not a good idea, as it turns out—Nick, Dmitri, and Xander nearly pounce on me before I quickly let go of Barb and raise both arms in surrender.) "I didn't drop like that on purpose! I don't know what happened to me, I just…felt upset and confused, and—"

"You didn't look upset. In fact, you looked positively gleeful."

"No! No, that's not what I was feeling at all! I got halfway down the cliff, and maybe you couldn't tell from where you were standing, but I was terrified. I was *traumatized.*"

"You were…*traumatized*," Barb repeats, her hands on her hips, her expression dubious.

"Yeah," I continue, trying to think of anything to convince her. "Please don't penalize me, Barb! You've got to understand that I…I started to think about bad stuff

165

that's happened to me, and well, I just kind of lost it, that's all."

Her eyes pierce me with all the focus of a sniper's lens.

"Go on. I'm listening," she says.

"Well, um…it's something that's painful for me to talk about." She nods, taking a step toward me as if I'm a skittish colt she's attempting to throw a bridle on. "I don't think I'll ever forget what he tried to pull with me, that sicko," I continued. "He was my foster mom's fiancé, and I trusted him. But Ted stole my trust. And he tried to steal…my innocence, too."

"Riiiiight," Barb says in a voice that, unless I'm reading her wrong, is marked by doubt and annoyance.

"I just got confused up there," I plead. "I was so excited about this challenge, but halfway down, it's like something just snapped. It was out of my control."

To Barb's right, Nick has a sympathetic look on his face.

"She *did* volunteer to go right after Ronnie, and she started off so well," he says. "I can see where maybe she might have gotten her bearings all mixed up, especially if she…er, lost her focus, like she said."

"Okay," Barb finally agrees, crossing her arms decisively across her chest. "I'll go ahead and give you the

166

benefit of the doubt this time. In return, I believe it's time for us to sort some of your confusion out."

"I'm not sure I follow," I say, blinking hard.

"*Tonight.* At the campfire. It's *your* turn."

"Da-da-da, dum-de-DA, dum-de-DA," Snout chants. This homage to Darth Vader's theme is the closest thing to human speech he's managed yet.

It's an easy walk back to camp, and everyone's in a dorktastic mood. Frances sings some lame Girl Scout song about people with stank-ass feet, which is cracking everyone up. Everyone but me, that is.

It's *my turn* at the campfire, Barb had said. As in, my turn to be raked over the coals, skewered, and grilled like a piece of meat. I knew it would be coming, eventually, and I guess it's a miracle I avoided it for this long. Over the past few weeks, I've managed to dodge the inquisition, dancing around her pointed, "So, tell me, Puck" questions with the verbal agility I've used all my life to get out of jams. But in hinting at my personal baggage just now, I made a rookie mistake. She's going in for the kill tonight. The thought makes my head throb, and I feel like I'm overheating. If I'm lucky, I'm coming down with some horrible flu, and they'll end up having to medivac me out of here in the next five hours. Huh…not a bad escape route, actually. Only how to make it convincing?

"Yo, Dangerbird!" Ronnie calls back to me, glancing over his shoulder from the front of the line. "Head's up, three o'clock. Just sayin'!"

I glance to his right, and there, low to the ground, is a patch of dark green foliage brimming with trumpet-shaped white flowers. Ellen and Dmitri are behind me, but it's clear they're in the midst of some intense conversation. *Act first, think later.* I drop to the ground and pretend to re-tie my hiking boot.

"C'mon, Puck," says Ellen, trudging past me. "Keep up."

"Be right there!" I answer. From my stooped position, I reach an arm out and yank a white blossom off the bush, stuffing it down the collar of my T-shirt before jumping to my feet and skipping to catch up with Ellen. Dmitri, now hauling ass further up the trail toward Mia and Xander, has left poor Ellen eating dust.

CHAPTER 10

But, Being Over-Full of Self-Affairs, My Mind Did Lose It

I used to find plenty of fun after dark. Back in Flagstaff, I'd sneak out the window of my bedroom at Paula's condo to go prowling for trouble, which often led me no farther than the jungle gym in the schoolyard of Athens Elementary two blocks away. It's where a few other misfits from school and I would "loiter" when all other ideas went bust. We were broke and bored, but we ruled the night, backlit by the glimmer of streetlights, cell phone screens, distant car headlights, and the glowing tips of our cancer sticks. Out here, though, it's *scary* dark.

It may be the reason we're all nervously cracking jokes while Barb and Nick finish up their nightly staff meeting with the counselors. The early July sky turns a deeper shade of purple, silhouetting the ridgeline looming in the distance. Our conversation turns to the stupidity that is Nick's show.

"I'm sorry, but this version of his is completely *mental*."

"It's called 'artistic license.' Why don't you freaking evolve, already, Nissa?" Titania is defending our director's wacked-out retelling of *The Wizard of Oz*. "It's metaphorical; don't you get it? Or maybe just meta. At least, I *think* it is? Nick has his reasons, so don't question genius."

"Am I the only one who finds it a little…confusing?" asks Peabo, referring to the bizarre plot twists Nick had spelled out during our afternoon rehearsal.

"My agent says acting is the natural next step in my career," Titania says with a shrug. "This is a dream role."

"Look out; the ego has landed," Ronnie says.

"It's ridiculous," Frances scoffs. "Nick cast me as 'Glinda-slash-Flying Monkey.' That is some messed-up shit."

"Well, I'm 'Yellow Brick Road,'" Quin counters. "I'm basically scenery with dialogue."

"I'd trade you in a second," I say. My cheeks are toasty from the flames, but I feel a slow chill spreading across my back. "I don't get why I have to be Dorothy. Shouldn't that be your role, Titania?"

"Too safe," she responds with a shake of her head. "Yeah, sure, I'm probably the obvious choice for the quote-unquote heroine, but playing Dorothy would stifle my intensity. I need a character that's powerful enough to show my range."

We all stare at Titania, mystified.

"You hear that?" says Ronnie, cupping his ear. "That's the sound of nobody caring."

"I don't care if none of you get it. Nick understands," says Titania. "He knows what my process is. God, he's such a generous director…and a master of allegory."

"If he only had a brain," I say, shaking my head. Everyone except Titania laughs, but I feel pretty awful when I glance over and see that Nick, Barb, and the counselors are within earshot.

Nick steps into the circle and places a kettle of water into the fire to heat. Mia and Xander hand out the blue speckled mugs for our nightly cups of herbal tea, a.k.a. "sewer water."

"I have a little surprise for you guys," says Barb. "Instead of tea tonight, you'll each be getting a packet of instant cocoa—*with* mini marshmallows."

The other kids are instantly stoked, but I sit quietly, knowing there's a catch. There's *always* a catch with Barb.

"First things first, though," she says, settling onto one of the rocks that serves as seating in these parts. "Nissa, let's begin with you tonight."

I'm instantly thrown off by whatever game Barb is playing. I thought for sure she'd start in on me straightaway—I even had my opening remarks all planned out like some newly appointed member of the Deadbeat Debate Team. Then again, being spared the interrogation a few minutes longer isn't exactly a *bad* thing. I'm focusing hard on trying to keep my own story straight when, after a few minutes, I can't help but be drawn into Nissa's.

"Deep down, I knew it was wrong," she says. "But it felt like something I couldn't undo. I was the one who hit on him in the first place. It was my fault."

"Nissa," Barb says, "he was the adult. He was in a position of authority, and the responsibility lay with him, not you."

"But I love him."

"I believe that *you* believe that. But—"

"He's only thirty-two years old," Nissa interrupts, her face registering defiance. "If I were a few years older, no one would even blink an eye."

"He was your teacher. He crossed major ethical boundaries, not to mention the fact that he was married."

"So they send me here until the shitstorm dies down. Sorry, I don't mean to cuss, but it's true. The school board, my parents…everyone just wants me to disappear so they can get rid of the problem."

"Let's not forget the shoplifting incidents, the drinking, the self-destructive behavior. Your involvement with this man led you down a bad path; don't you see that?" Nissa only shrugs. "Okay, so four months into this affair, how did he respond when the two of you were found out?"

"He told the police that, well…he said I seduced him."

"He blamed you. He *blamed you*."

"But it's the truth." Her voice is getting shaky now. "I'm not going to pretend that I didn't flirt with him, because I did. I wanted it, I asked for it, I got it. God, I'm either a skank or a victim in everyone's eyes, and I don't want to be either!"

"Let's back up a moment," says Barb. "You said earlier that you knew it was wrong. That you wished you could have undone it."

"It's not like he molested me or something!" Nissa says, tears brimming up in her eyes. "I knew *exactly* what I was doing. I did this to myself!" Barb shakes her head sadly and glances down at the ground as if deeply disturbed by Nissa's last remark. "Yeah, *of course* I feel used, but I can't act like I have no blame in this, when there are other people who . . ." Nissa hesitates, glancing at me, snot trickling out of her nose. "Puck, I'm so sorry. I know how insulting it must be for you to listen to this after what happened to you…with your stepdad, and all. This doesn't even compare. God, I feel like such a loser."

No, no, no, no, no . . .

Every eye is trained on me, and I feel the way I imagine you must when a gun is pointed to your head. I chew anxiously on my thumbnail, preparing to utter some of my pre-rehearsed saga, but after listening to Nissa— hearing the sincerity in her voice—I'm not sure I can go through with any of this.

"Well, Ted is…not my stepdad," I clarify. "He's my foster mom's fiancé. And…what happened to me, it's, uh, totally different. Anyway . . ." I lock eyes with Barb. "I don't want to distract from the emotions Nissa is feeling right now. That wouldn't be fair to her."

"No, honestly, Puck, hearing your story—if you have the strength to talk about it, I mean—maybe it could actually help both of us." Nissa's voice sounds fragile.

"Go ahead, Puck," adds Barb. "We're all listening."

Christ. I've never wanted to escape from this place more than I do at this moment. I wish I could just implode and leave a smoldering black hole on this lumpy rock I'm sitting on. I want to keel over dead; hell, I don't care. Anything but this.

"Well, to the outside world, I suppose Ted seems nice and all," I continue, "your typical goober, always asking you how your day was, quoting *The Simpsons* and stuff like that."

"It's always the ones you least expect," murmurs Frances, who, along with everyone else, is hanging on my every word. I mentally reflect on Ted the Turd in his dorky high-waisted jeans, the guy who will someday be loafing around on Paula's couch in his boxer shorts spouting lame knock-knock jokes and leaving the toilet seat up every time he takes a piss. I remember the tears in Paula's eyes —tears of stupid joy—when they'd sat me down on Christmas Eve to tell me about their engagement. Then more tears, a few months later, when I told her what he'd done to me. My eyes water, even now, thinking about how horrible it all is. On the bright side, a few tears may help me pull off what I'm about to do. But…oh, crap. I thought I could do this. I really did. But I can't.

"I can't," I whisper. I'm not quite sure how, but Barb seems to know exactly what's stopping me, and I can tell that she's not going to pluck me from this terrible tide that's about to take me down.

"Are you ready to tell the truth, Puck?" Barb says. "Doesn't Nissa deserve that? Doesn't everyone here who has shared their difficult stories deserve that much?"

Seated next to me, Titania places her hand on my shoulder in a gesture of support. Her touch is gentle, light as the wings of a butterfly, but I buckle under its weight. I feel my soul plummeting, and the sensation is terrifying— nothing like my joyful freefall earlier today.

"I guess I kind of, sort of…*made it up*?" The words tumble out like marbles dropped on an ice rink, scattering everywhere. Titania slowly lifts her hand off my shoulder like I'm toxic. And let's face it: I am. I steal a sheepish glance and see only shock, disgust, and outrage directed back at me. I am an abomination. "You've got to understand," I stammer, feeling my face grow hot, "he wasn't good for us. Paula and me, I mean. I tried a million things to get him to just…go away, but the guy stuck around like a malignant tumor. We were doing just *fine* before him." Across the fire, Ronnie is looking at me like I just crushed a kitten's skull under my heel.

"You Judas'd a brother because you were *jealous*?" he says. "That's low. That's *beyond* low." Next to him, Quin eyes me warily.

"You're nothing but a fraud," Titania adds. "A fake. A phony. And another f-word I'd love to say, but I won't."

176

It's clearly not the best time to get all snarky and point out that *phony* doesn't start with f, so I remain silent. Nissa, springing to her feet, screams at me, her face all pinched and pink.

"Have you been conning us all this whole time? Who would even *want* a pathetic liar like you to be their kid? Your foster mom dodged a bullet, if you ask me. It makes me *sick* to look at you!" Ellen jumps up and throws an arm around Nissa, who collapses against her, heaving sobs.

"You're right," I say quietly. "I'm sorry."

"All right, everyone, let's take a moment," says Barb. "Maybe this is a good time for that cocoa break."

The angry villagers drop their pitchforks at the thought of having their sweet tooths satisfied, but there's still an unsettling silence as they swarm Barb for their packets of powder. I throw my empty cup to the ground and walk over to my tent, which I silently slip inside.

A few minutes later, a rustling shadow approaches, and I see the inside zipper of the tent creep slowly upward. I'll be damned if things aren't about to take a bad teen-horror-movie twist. Barb pokes her face in. (Close enough). God, what now?

"You're missing out on hot chocolate," she says, noting the obvious.

"'*Consequences*,' geez, I get it already. Can't you just leave me alone? Or are you here to order up a new batch of burpees?" I say, undoing my bedroll.

"What do you mean?" she asks with that classic note of false concern.

"You got what you want. Everyone hates me now. Isn't that punishment enough?"

"No one's punishing you," she says as she climbs into the tent without asking first. The nearby campfire throws just enough ambient light to make her vaguely visible in the darkness. In her right hand, she's holding out a white paper envelope; in her left, my speckled tin mug, steam rising from the top. "Careful, it's hot."

"Wow. This place really *is* some sort of perverse, head-wrecking experiment, isn't it? You've been punishing me for weeks for so much as breathing wrong, but when I admit to something unforgivable, something heinous to the core, you're all, 'Congratulations! Swiss Miss!'" She cautiously sets the cup on the ground, and it's only through complete willpower that I keep myself from snatching the mug and tossing the scalding water into her condescending face.

"It's just cocoa, not a conspiracy theory. Although I have to say, the fact that you're so upset about what just happened out there is…encouraging." Ahh, so *that's* what this visit is all about. She's here to gloat.

"What's it like performing the equivalent of a root canal on someone's psyche? You take perverse pleasure in it, don't you?"

"It can hurt a lot, but it's necessary, to piggyback on your analogy. And it will save you a whole lot of pain in the long run."

"Well, congratulations, you pried the truth out of me using Nissa as your pawn. And now she's collateral damage. Did you see the look on her face? She hates me. They all *hate* me, now."

"They feel betrayed, with good reason," says Barb. "Isn't it funny? You never used to care what any of them thought of you."

"I know what I did was awful," I say, my voice trembling with anger. "But here's what gets me: they *all* took Ted's side. Paula, social workers—even the cops. One minute they were buying it, and then, poof, the charges were dropped, and no one even seemed to give a damn about what I had to say."

"Because they knew you were lying."

"It was my word against his, and my word counted for nothing. I mean, Paula's actually still planning on marrying the guy, for crying out loud—not plagued by even a shred of doubt that her foster kid might be right. No wonder victims never report this kind of stuff."

"Again, because she *knew* you were lying, Puck."

"No one knew I was lying!"

"How about that Internet chat room?"

"What?" I say, feeling my face start to burn.

"Everyone leaves a digital footprint, Puck. The police seized Paula's home computer."

"Right, to see if Ted had child porn or whatever."

"Exactly. Didn't you know they could trace your activity, too? You basically confessed to all of cyberspace about what you were going to do to get Ted out of the house."

"Anonymously," I say, sulking.

"Yeah, see…anonymity doesn't really exist online. Especially not where law enforcement is concerned."

"I don't understand," I say, blinking back tears. "Why didn't the cops ream me? Why didn't Paula say anything? She didn't even mention it in her letter to me here. God, I feel so stupid."

"What would calling you out have accomplished? You needed to come clean about this on your own, and that's part of the reason you're here. What you did was beyond serious. Extremely troubling, in fact. But it's within your power to fix." I know she's trying to edge her way into shrink-mode now, and though I hate to give her the satisfaction, I'm curious.

"How?"

"By being honest." *Oh, here we go again.*

"What do you think I just did out there?!"

"Being honest with yourself, I mean. Tonight was only the beginning. Thoughts can be deceptive, you know. Memories, too. You give them safe harbor for long enough in here—" she points to her chest, "and they start to harden into the truth. You can take away their power; you just have to want to." I don't like what she's hinting at. Lying back onto my pillow, I ball up into a fetal position, my face turned away from her.

"The only thing I want is to go to sleep."

"Suit yourself, but you'll be missing all the fun. Nick's going to be sharing his infamous ghost story about 'Old Nellie Bones.' If past tellings are any indication, I'm pretty sure you won't be able to fall asleep through the laughter."

"I'll survive."

"Surviving is one thing, Puck," she says, before backing out of the tent. "Living is something else entirely."

CHAPTER 11

It Is Not Enough to Speak,
but to Speak True

Okay, okay, I get it. My credibility is completely shot to hell. I'm the kid who cried wolf. (Or, well, "molester," in this case, and you don't have to tell me how effed-up that is.) I'm not going to sit here and try to claim that I've been racked with guilt over the whopper I told. In the beginning, it felt damn satisfying to manipulate a situation that wasn't working for me. Conjure one little lie, and chaos becomes control. Power. I drove the train, and it never, ever occurred to me that I might derail the whole thing. My plan had been to make sure no *real* harm was done by simply claiming I was too emotionally fragile to press charges against Ted if it even came down to all that. I didn't want the guy to get into any actual legal trouble. I'd just wanted Paula to send him packing.

But as upset as she was, Paula never bought my story, which is, I guess, how I ended up here. This place is my punishment, and there's a part of me that knows I deserve it. But here's what you have to understand: I basically had no choice. Imagine finally having everything you ever dreamed about: security, the promise of a home, a life where I was *wanted*—not just some ward of the state. I had it all in front of me, gleaming like some beacon of light, the expectation of a future that I didn't have to shield my eyes from or dread. That was all Paula. She never tried to fix me; she just accepted me, to the point where I'd finally figured out how to stop holding my breath and expecting only the worst. Things weren't perfect, but they were good.

Then Ted entered the picture. Paula was happier than I'd ever seen her, but, let's face it, love does stupid things to people. She got totally caught up in the fantasy—she let him call her "Polly," for Christ's sake—but I wasn't falling for it. It was only a matter of time before Ted would have convinced her to toss me back into the system, and once that happened, it would be too late to save Paula from her own heart. I couldn't just sit there and wait for any of that to happen, so I took matters into my own hands. It wasn't pretty, but I'll go so far as to suggest that I actually did Paula a huge favor. Too bad it cost me everything.

So now you know the worst. Yes, I lied about Ted, and no, I'm not proud of it. If I dwell on it for too long, I could make myself crazy: What if I got it all wrong? What if Ted's "nice guy" act was never an act? What if, at the end of the day, I ruined three people's chances at happiness for no good reason at all? That's the scariest part about being such a good liar. Spin enough yarns, and you can start to get confused. Eventually, you can't even tell when you're lying to yourself.

That's why I'm calling it quits. No more half-truths, no more tall tales. And no more manipulations. I'm ready to play it straight once I get back to civilian life. I guess you could say I'm having some sort of giant life epiphany, only it feels a bit like finding a winning lottery ticket in the street seconds before a semi truck turns you into a pancake on the pavement. In this case, the eighteen-wheeler is Barb. Our conversation just now has sent my self-protective radar into overdrive. I know, I know; she seems all supportive with her offerings of cocoa and "I'm proud of you" pats on the back. And I'm fully aware that my word is pretty much crap, at this point. If I'm Judas, then she shakes out as Jesus in the court of public opinion, right? So believe what you want, but I swear on the soul of my little brother—that woman has it in for me. I can't explain how I know; you'll just have to trust me, despite everything. She's after the *whole* truth, and if I give her what she wants, it will destroy me.

* * *

Trying to sleep on a sopping-wet pillow is the pits. My breath keeps catching in my chest, my head is throbbing, and I'm in a constant panic that my tent mate, Frances, is going to come in and discover the blubbering idiot I've become—or worse—go aggro on me about my emotional forgeries. I will myself to fall asleep, but it's not happening; I can't help thinking about how pissed the other kids are with me because of my campfire confession, and the conversation I had with Barb still has me on edge. Then there's the atmosphere outside the tent, which has morphed into "open-mic night" starring Nick as the most hilarious man on the planet. I can only hear snippets of whatever story he's telling, but the high-pitched screams and staccato snickering of his highly amused audience need no real explanation. The dude is clearly killing it.

"*. . . only I didn't realize the Pepto Bismol had turned my beard purple!*" His voice peals through the night like a bullhorn, followed by more group hysterics. What, are they all drunk or something? Their laughs echo through the canyon like reverb through the cold halls of some institutional looney bin. God, I want out of this place.

I sit up and reach for my canteen. Empty. I'd neglected to refill it tonight before I stormed off in disgrace. In the moonlight that's filtering through the netting of my tent, I spy the tin cup Barb had brought me ten minutes ago. I take a sip, but it's still too hot to actually quench my thirst, so I carefully pour it into my canteen for later.

As bad as DreamRoads had been up to this point, at least I'd had the other kids who were in it with me. Now, my tribe has ditched me, all because of a momentary lapse in my fiction-telling skills. Whatever jerkface first claimed "The truth will set you free" has some serious explaining to do.

". . . suddenly, I heard my cue, and I tried to get up, but 'someone' had crazy-glued the toilet seat. Talk about improv!" Nick's line is followed by another bout of shrill screams from his fans. There's a strange fluttering sensation in my armpit, as if a wounded butterfly has gone there to die. I root my hand through the neck of my shirt, frantically fishing around for what I hope to dear god isn't some giant flesh-eating spider. When I pull out what resembles a soft, shredded wad of Kleenex, I realize it's

actually the trumpet flower I'd plucked on our hike earlier today. I'd forgotten all about it. It's wilted and practically disintegrating, but I can't help but wonder…could there be any truth to Ronnie's claim that this is Nature's "feel-good" flower? If so, I can't think of a more perfect time to test out its mythic powers, even if all it does is help me to feel a little less raw. He'd said you just brew it, like a tea. And here I am, with a canteen of hot water. If this isn't fate screaming, "*Duh!!!*" then I don't know what is.

Xander's been all "broken record" about not eating anything we find in the woods. But it's not like I'd be *eating* it. Besides, that whole story about being able to get high from it is totally bogus, I'm sure. I study the wilted flower in my hand like Alice down the rabbit hole with a bottle that reads, "Drink me." What do I have to lose? No doubt, the same kids who were so easily won over by Barb's cocoa ploy will give me a hero's reception when I reveal my homebrewed hooch. I crumble the perfume-y flower between my fingers and feed it carefully through the opening of a canteen, my sad little attempt at a peace offering. To be safe, I'll insist that everyone sticks with just one sip. Worst-case scenario, we can make ourselves throw it up. Best-case scenario, I get my friends back and maybe even shake a few of the demons off my own damn tail, at least for a little while.

I exit the tent and return to my place by the fire, setting the canteen on the ground by my feet and zipping my parka to my chin in defense against the chill (both literal and figurative). My reappearance has thrown cold water on the laugh riot that had been in full effect seconds earlier.

"What's so funny?" I say, leaning toward Peabo for the CliffsNotes version. Refusing to make eye contact, he snaps the twig he's holding and tosses it into the fire.

"Nothing," he mumbles. "You kind of had to be here."

"Welcome back, Puck," Nick says, attempting to usher me back into the fold. "Your fellow campers were just obliging my long-winded ghost story about the misadventures of Old Nellie Bones and the Hempen Homespuns."

The mere mention sends giggle-fits rippling through the group, but they flitter away into more stony silence. I glance from left to right, feeling like the buzzkill who's just flipped on all the harsh, cold gym lights during a high school dance.

"I guess I missed it."

"Maybe next time, Puck," says Barb with a pat smile, and I know what she's implying: I'll get to hear an encore performance in who-knows-how-many months, because

I'm stuck here indefinitely now. "All right, everybody," she continues, rising to her feet, "finish your hot chocolate, if you haven't, and let's rinse out those cups and get ready to turn in. We've got another big day in front of us tomorrow."

"Oh, Barb, speaking of," says Ellen, "the other counselors and I still have a few details to discuss for tomorrow's activities. Is it okay if we grab a lantern so we can go over the essentials before we bed down?"

"Yes, of course," says Barb. "Take the one that's sitting in front of my tent."

"Thanks," says Ellen. "Mia, I'll meet you over at the guys' tent."

"C'mon, Xander. I guess that means we should go straighten up the 'frat house,'" says Dmitri, hoisting him to his feet. "Ellen, don't forget the clipboard."

"Oh, trust me. I wouldn't *dream* of forgetting the clipboard." Clipboard? I'm not exactly sure what they're talking about, but I can tell you what they *ain't* talking about: clipboards. Barb, though, seems none the wiser.

While the other kids are rinsing out their cups over by our kitchen station (a.k.a. two buckets filled with water and a drying rag hung over a tree branch), it occurs to me that I would actually *kill* for Barb's stupid cocoa. I mosey back to my tent and retrieve the single-serve packet I'd

189

left there, ripping off the top and tossing back my head to shake the envelope's contents into my mouth. The gritty mixture has the consistency of brownie batter, and with the crunch of dehydrated mini marshmallows, I can feel a shit-ton of endorphins race through my system. If a little sugar can make me feel this good, imagine how incredible an Angel's Trumpet chaser will feel. I hurry back to the fire and retrieve my canteen, but a few more minutes pass before I finally manage to corner Ronnie away from the others to offer him a sample of my liquid stash.

"Fancy a spot o' tea?" I ask him in a poor attempt at a Cockney accent, pointing to my canteen. I blush as soon as I say it, realizing it sounds ridiculously Nick-like. "The Angel's Trumpet," I add, practically tripping over my tongue. "I cooked some, man." (Oh brother, now I'm coming across like a meth peddler.) "Want to test-drive it?"

"Are you serious?" His eyes widen. Bingo. He's obviously awestruck by my skills. We'll be comrades once more. "It's bad enough that you're a liar, but now you have a deathwish?"

Oh.

"But I thought . . ."

"What the hell is wrong with you, anyway?"

"Nothing! I mean, a week ago, everyone was talking about how much we were all jonesing for a joint. What's the harm?"

"What's the harm . . ." he echoes my words with a sad shake of his head, and then he leans into me, lowering his voice. "I told you that stuff will *mess you up.* I don't fly that way anymore; don't you get it? Keep your trippy-ass tea away from me, Puck."

"But you're the one who pointed out the flower to me! I thought that meant—"

"Yeah, well, you're obviously confused, so let me put you straight: you don't know me. You don't know *shit.* I bet everything about you is a con. Did you even have a brother?"

"That's not fair."

"Yeah, well, welcome to human existence, sister." His nostrils flare, and he takes a step back, shoving his fists into the pockets of his parka. "Better get comfy with those camping skills. Your 'DreamRoad' isn't going to lead you anywhere. It's a treadmill. A hamster wheel. There's no way Barb's gonna let you loose."

"Not so fast, *Papi.* We both know you didn't *really* light that fire. If you graduate, it's only through the grace of my locked lips."

"Is that a threat?"

It's happening again. One of those conversations that's escalating into something awful and angry when that was never my aim in the first place. How is it that things always seem to turn inside out without my even trying?

"Easy, man," I say, attempting to downshift this confrontation. "Blowing your cover would mean blowing mine, too. I want us *all* to get out of here, believe me."

"Then you should do yourself a favor and forget about whatever's in that canteen," he says, pointing to the metal flask at my hip. I turn, and in my attempt to storm off, I nearly sideswipe Nissa.

"Excuse me," I mumble, keeping my head down.

"There's no excuse for you," she says, her voice cold.

"I know. Look, I realize this explanation isn't worth much, but I just want you to know that I came clean tonight because of you. I'd rather have you hate me than keep on deceiving you."

"Like I should be flattered?! I always thought you and I had this connection over what we'd each been through. But you were just mocking me."

"No! I understood! You were just trying to be happy…to be loved. I *do know* what that feels like."

"But you were lying."

"I know. Ted never touched me. You have every right to hate me."

"*Something* happened, though."

"What?" I lock eyes with her for a moment, taken off guard.

"Something you're not saying. You only act the way you do because something happened to you. Something messed up."

Before I can respond, Titania's nasally whine pierces the night like a screech owl.

"Pleeeeease," she says, following Nick back to the campfire like a stalker fan. "But you're hilarious! Do it for meeeee . . ."

"What's going on now?" Barb says, leaving off from her nightly tasks to address the commotion.

"Tonya is lobbying for one more of my legendary yarns," says Nick. He shrugs his shoulders as if put upon, but it's obvious that he's basking in the glow of Titania's admiration.

"Come on, Barb, will you let him?" Titania begs. "I haven't laughed so hard in weeks."

"Even Quin lost it during that last one," says Ronnie, for once in agreement with the pop star. "He needed it. We *all* need it."

Nick's trying to play it cool, but I can tell he's desperately hoping Barb will cede the campfire circle to him for a few more minutes.

"One more! Just one more!" says Peabo, sidling up to the group with Quin.

"Oh, all right, but only until the last of the fire's burnt down," says Barb with a grudging smile.

"Yaaay!" squeals Titania. Swivelling on her feet, her natty platinum ponytail splays outward like a whirligig. "Nissa, Frances, get your butts over here! The 'Nick Chronicles' are back, by popular demand! Get ready, Puck," she says, and I'm a little startled when she laces her elbow in mine and leads me to a seat next to her by the fire, "you're not going to believe what a trip this is."

She's right. A few minutes later, we're all listening to the most ridiculous, embarrassing, tears-streaming-down-our-faces funny bedtime story I think I've ever heard (Peabo's right; you have to be here). What seemed absolutely fubar for me forty minutes ago now seems… well, not *better* exactly, but somehow okay. Nick, god love him, has no problem making a complete jackass of himself for our amusement, and as counterintuitive as it may sound, I respect that. Our laughter launches into the night like bottle rockets, ricocheting against towering pines and imposing granite walls before disappearing into that protective, dark sky. I've never bought into my grandma's idea of god or heaven, and anyone who claims prayers get answered is pulling a way bigger con than I ever could.

But I will grant you this: sitting out in the middle of nothing (or everything, depending on how you choose to look at it), there's a strange force that settles over me, like two gentle hands pressing down on my shoulders. *Stay a while*, it seems to whisper, and I think of Grandma and Shane and wonder if they're together, if they're anywhere, that is.

My fellow campers surround me, their faces illuminated by the last flickers from the dwindling campfire. With the added light of the full moon, I can see each one of them so clearly. It's in this moment that I realize—and it's a stunning revelation—this motley crew of ne'er-do-wells and misunderstoods *is* family, in a sense, with all the messy, mystifying, occasionally difficult awesomeness that the word implies. Yeah, they're probably still royally pissed at me, but here we are, huddled side by side, laughing. Life goes on. (Maybe that's *not* just some dumb platitude.) I'm suddenly certain I'd rather be in the here-and-now with these guys, even on my worst day, than trying to duck out on reality with some "hallucinogenic" tea. My gaze lifts to meet the moon, which is shining brightly, and I'm grateful for its defiance against the scope of so much darkness. Somehow I just know with absolute certainty that things are going to be okay.

CHAPTER 12

Lord, What Fools These Mortals Be!

The birds again. Their gentle chirps and perky whistles are preferable to the obnoxious alarm clock better known as Barb, so it's nice that I've been lately waking up on my own, five or ten minutes before her official "up and at 'em" blitzkrieg. Staring at the ceiling—or rather, the top of a khaki-colored nylon tent—I fill my lungs with morning's crisp air and nestle a little deeper into my sleeping bag. Though last night's confession was all kinds of awful, this morning I feel strangely content. It would be an almost-perfect moment if it weren't for the small, nagging dread I feel about the stupid Water Challenge. Could it really be as straightforward as Ronnie made it out to be? I push the thought out of my mind and try to focus, instead, on identifying the different bird songs Xander's been teaching me on our hikes. The low, raspy call outside the tent this morning is one I definitely can't identify.

Whatever kind of animal that is, the noise it's making sounds curiously like someone…puking? I quietly unzip a portion of the tent's window flap and peek through the black netting.

Eww. It's not a bird; it's Ellen, on her hands and knees just outside of the tent she shares with Mia. She's only wearing a sports bra and a pair of navy blue track pants, and she's spewing the contents of her stomach like that chick in *The Exorcist.* My mind does a quick rewind to her "clipboard" conversation with the other counselors. Someone clearly went on a serious bender last night. My own gag reflex is *this close* to being triggered by the sight of her ralphing, but before I can turn away in disgust, I see another sickly face—the last one I'd expect—emerge from her tent.

"*Ellen?*" Xander moans her name with eyes at half mast, his cheeks splotchy and his expression puzzled. "Oh, god, I think I need to be sick, too."

Wiping a string of bright yellow spit from her mouth, Ellen glances at him wearily.

"Did we…?" As gossip goes, it doesn't get much juicier than this. I strain to hear their hushed voices.

"I don't *think* so?" He pauses for an episode of dry-heaving, then glances at her. "Sorry, it's not you, it's just . . ." He practically hisses his next remark. "What the hell happened to us?"

"I don't know. I thought it tasted weird, but I didn't expect it to get us so…wait, where's Mia?"

Before Xander can answer, a piercing scream comes from the direction of his tent—the one he evidently hadn't slept in last night. Xander comes to life and half-scrambles, half-stumbles to his tent, proceeding to hurl himself through the unzipped canvas flaps. Two seconds later, he's hauling Dmitri out into the first light of dawn. Mia climbs out behind them in a daze, her unkempt hair strewn with grass and dead leaves like some stoner Coachella chick. She's wearing an oversized Dallas Cowboys hoodie that just barely covers hot pink undies. (PhD not required to figure out who the sweatshirt belongs to.)

"What the hell…?" she says, hopping up and down on one foot while trying to cram the other into one of her hiking boots. "No, no, no, no, no. This is *not* happening right now. Please let me still be hallucinating!"

Dmitri and Xander are already going full-sumo on each other in the dirt, and the commotion is waking the others. A groggy Frances has scootched next to me in her sleeping bag to get a glimpse out the window, too.

"What's going on?" she asks in a gravelly tone, squinting through eyelashes dusted with eye crust. I press my forefinger to my lips, hoping to witness more of the counselors' morning-after mortification. Barb must have heard it, too. She's skulking out of her tent in a black thermal shirt and long johns that make her look like a cat burglar. Nick follows in maroon velour lounge pants and a dingy T-shirt that reads, "Hittin' the Hay."

"Is everyone okay?" Barb asks, approaching her young team. Though her attitude is one of concern, it quickly turns to disgust once she susses the situation.

"Barb, this isn't what it looks like," Xander says from astride Dmitri's chest. "I don't know what this is, per se, but I *do* know it's, er…just, *not* what it looks like. If we can all take a moment to breathe, I'm sure—" He's interrupted by Mia, who holds her head in both hands as if attempting to prevent it from splitting in two.

"Xander, babe, I swear, I passed out before Dmitri and I . . ." She blushes, and her brow furrows. "It's all such a haze, but I'm sure that he and I never…*wait a minute*." Mia's eyes slowly travel from Xander to Ellen, who is still bent over clutching her abdomen. "Were you with *her* last night*?!*"

Xander's about to protest, but faster than you can say *prissy girlfight*, Mia runs and vaults onto her friend's back like a rabid spider monkey. She's got Ellen's neck in a choke hold with one arm, and she grabs a fistful of her hair with the other, giving her that much more leverage when Ellen springs upright and careens first right, then left, before eventually whipping round in a circle.

"Let go of me," Ellen howls, trying to escape her tiny assailant.

"Never, you man-thief!" Mia shouts. Ellen succeeds in prying her friend off her back and spins to face her with the stance of a ninja ready to strike.

"Oh, that's rich, coming from you. Isn't Xander enough for you, Mia? Did you have to bag Dmitri, too?"

"I don't know how I ended up with Dmitri, but whatever you're implying is just…eww!"

"Hey, now!" Dmitri protests. He's still pinned to the ground by Xander, who gives his rival's ear a sharp flick with his fingers. (Who knew Yoga Boy would end up besting Texas Two-Step in a battle of brawn, by the way?)

"God, you're such a little slut," Ellen says.

"Who are you calling *little*, you hideous giraffe? I'm not too short to claw your eyes out! You did this just to spite me! You're jealous, so, what, you poison us all just to even the score or something?"

"*Me?!* Do you honestly think I would…oh, wait a minute. I see what this is. This is some twisted joke the

three of you conjured up, isn't it? 'Poor, single Ellen...
let's roofie her and have a big laugh at her expense!'" Her
face crumples, and tears take over where her words leave
off. I almost pity her. It's strange to see our counselors,
typically so zen and pulled together, cracked open and
exposed like this. "I thought we were friends, and that's
what hurts the most," she adds, pausing to wipe her eyes.

"Ladies, ladies," Xander says, playing pacifist even
while his knee is jammed into Dmitri's rib cage. "We're
all more than a little confused right now, but if we could
just try to find a moment of equanimity, I'm sure that we
could—"

"Shut up!" both Mia and Ellen scream at him.

Barb brings all this fun to an end just when it's
getting good, of course. Grabbing Xander by the elbow,
she throws him off Dmitri, who rolls onto his stomach and
groans.

"In my office, all four of you," she yells, pointing to
her tent. "*NOW!!!*"

Both sobbing, Mia and Ellen join their respective
bedfellows in Barb's tent. For a few seconds, the only
sounds I can hear are the oblivious birds, still chirping
away. Then, like one of those comically vocal moviegoers
who can't resist talking back at the screen, Ronnie's voice
slices through the tension.

"Dayyyyum!"

In our tent, Frances and I glance at each other and giggle, and a titter of laughter ripples like a chain reaction from the rest of the tents situated in the clearing, making it pretty obvious that all of the other kids here have enjoyed this morning's reality-show antics as much as the two of us have.

* * *

With the counselors having their moment of reckoning, the rest of us are left to fend for ourselves. We huddle over cups of oatmeal, whispering about the twenty-somethings' crazy exploits and speculating about their potential fate.

"What on earth do you think's going on?" Nissa asks.

"They got plastered or something," Frances responds.

"If that's true, they're my new idols," Peabo says. "But come on, how likely is that? Where would they get booze all the way out here?" Frances shrugs.

"So what are you thinking?" Quin asks. "Weed? It'd be small enough to stash in their backpacks."

"A few blunts never got anybody *that* messed up," Ronnie says. "And none of them strike me as the sort who would do anything harder. Especially that straightedge,

Ellen. Though, come to think of it, she *did* say something about roofies."

I'm about to interrupt and explain that the so-called straightedge actually smuggled a mini wet bar in her backpack when Nick approaches and cuts our gossip session short.

"Okay, folks, while we're waiting, I'd say now's as good a time as any to rehearse the show," he says. "Places, please. Let's start with Dorothy's first encounter with the witch." We all migrate to our regular rehearsal spot near an oversized juniper shrub and take a moment to find our marks, mumbling half-hearted protests through it all. I'm standing opposite Titania, with Snout (a.k.a. Toto) on all fours by my side. The rest of the kids are kneeling in a line behind us, pretending to be munchkins. Nick has them positioned in order from smallest to tallest, with Ronnie closest to me and Snout.

"Vocal calisthenics!" Nick says. "Repeat after me: Rocks, shocks, locks."

"Rocks, shocks, locks," we all mumble in unison.

"Don't forget to enunciate, people! Now to stretch our soft palettes: Car, far, mar."

"*Car, far, mar.*"

"And now we'll release tension in our jaws with a *Nee-Yah! Nee-Yah!*" (This embarrassing exercise continues for the next five minutes as we trill our tongues, vibrate our lips like motorboats, and contort our mouths to resemble gaping fish. The only one among us who appears even remotely at ease is Snout, though Titania seems to be drinking the Kool-Aid as well.)

"So, to remind you of my critique from yesterday, I'm not seeing quite enough in the way of emotion at this point," says our director once we're vocally limber enough to proceed. "We need to play to the nosebleed seats, know what I mean? Puck, imagine stumbling upon a frightful witch."

I think: *I have: your wife.* Snout, meanwhile, isn't paying one lick of attention, seeing as how he's too preoccupied with sniffing the ground and panting. ("*Method acting,*" or so claims Nick.) I take a swig from the canteen that hangs by a strap across my body.

"Put yourself in Dorothy's headspace, Puck," Nick continues. "Try to consider how strongly she might react to a situation that's so alarming."

Spitooie! Right on cue, a spray of clear liquid shoots from my mouth in a dramatic *sploosh*. In my exhaustion last night, I'd totally blanked on dumping out my canteen full of moonflower punch. Using the crook of my elbow to swipe at the acrid liquid that's dribbled down my chin, I attempt to hide my distress. My scene partner, Titania, jumps back and screams in revulsion.

"Are you kidding me?! There is *no way* I'm getting drenched in backwash for this show!"

Nick seems lost in his own world. He tilts his head thoughtfully and runs his large, hammy hand through his curly hair.

"You know…I never even considered playing the scene for laughs. A spit take…what a bold choice, Puck! And Tonya," he adds, almost as an afterthought, "the shriek was absolutely spot-on."

"*Really?*" Titania asks, a hesitant smile eclipsing her anger. "Does the scream need more vibrato, in your professional opinion? How might I make it more nuanced?"

I'm not listening to the obsessed thespians talk shop, because I'm grappling with one hell of a question: why does the liquid in my canteen taste exactly like…raspberry vodka?

A stealth glance at the underside of my canteen confirms the worst. In black Sharpie, bold block letters spell out E-L-L-E-N where my name ought to be. *Oh shit.* While Nick and Titania are convening, I step over Snout and sidle up to Ronnie, who's kneeling at the end of the row of campers.

I squat down and nudge him with my canteen, flipping it over to reveal Ellen's name. He gives it his furtive appraisal, his eyes widening as he connects the dots.

"Ellen must've accidentally picked up my canteen. It explains everything. What are we going to do?" I ask.

"What's with the 'we'? This ain't no 'we,'" he says, crossing his arms.

"What should I do?" I whisper. I'm fully freaking at this point, but he just shrugs and scratches his jaw.

"You'd better fix it, before they figure it out," he says through gritted teeth. "If they haven't already."

My fear propels me like a slingshot to Nick.

"May I be excused, please? I have to use the facilities. I mean, really, *really*." He frowns for a moment, and I jump up and down on my toes to emphasize my distress.

"Okay, but be quick," he says. "We need you for this."

"Sure thing. Be right back."

The designated "latrine" (if that's what we're calling shrubbery these days) is located clear on the other side of our circle of tents. I speed off in that direction, my feet barely skimming the surface of the earth. On my way, I unscrew the canteen cap and empty its contents onto the ground. Pausing at the campsite, I take one quick glance over my shoulder to make sure no one's paying attention. The only one with his eyes trained on me is Ronnie, so I dart inside Ellen and Mia's empty tent. There, I spy the strap of my canteen, tangled in a balled-up heap of sleeping bags. I grab the container, shaking it to test how much is left. Mere drops, from what I can tell. I can't remember letting it out of my sight last night, but I must have set it down near the fire when I'd gone to polish off that hot cocoa mix in my tent. Ellen probably picked up mine by mistake. An honest switcheroo, but I'm bound to get seriously busted if I don't undo this screwup, pronto. Flinging Ellen's canteen onto the pile, I'm ready to skedaddle when I hear voices approaching. I freeze like a terrified squirrel, only instead of a nut, I clutch my canteen to my chest. This is the beginning of the end for me. I helplessly watch the tent flap inching up from the outside. As I race through possible (but mostly pathetic) defenses in my head, the flap falls back in place. That's when I remember to breathe. I'm safe. For the moment, anyway.

"Go away. I don't want to talk about it anymore." It's Ellen, and her voice sounds like dead soldiers strewn upon a battlefield.

"I *needed* this job credit for grad school," says Mia, clearly on the offensive following their inquisition with

Barb. "I was on track to graduate next May, but now that plan is shot to hell. So thanks for saddling me with another whole semester of tuition. Thanks a lot. I'm apparently minus a boyfriend now, too, but I guess I should be happy I'm still alive after whatever toxic cocktails you served."

"Oh, shut up, Mia! No one ever died from drinking a few lousy mini bottles of vodka."

"We all thought it tasted off."

"Like I said, it was probably just a strange chemical reaction from being inside the metal canteen. Maybe we just…had too much."

"The amount we had couldn't get a caterpillar drunk, let alone the four of us. Stop trying to deflect blame here."

"Oh, cut the crap, Mia. You made your own bed."

"As did you, evidently—with *my* guy."

"We made out, and then we passed out. End of story. But, ugh, don't remind me."

I'd love to keep eavesdropping, but they've been arguing long enough for me to realize I still have a way out. Mia and Ellen are standing at the front of the tent, but there is another zippered exit on the opposite side. I tiptoe over to it and, as gingerly as possible, unzip the back flaps.

"I need to pack my things now, so please excuse me," Ellen says in an icy tone, just as I scoot, unseen, through the back of the tent, evaporating from their midst like a drop of morning dew.

CHAPTER 13

This Falls Out Better Than I Could Devise

"Now I'll never make it back home in time to sing at the All-Star game," wails Titania. She's attempting to stuff her dismantled tent into its dust-coated sheath, pausing only to wipe the teary snot dripping from her nose. Rumor has spread through the camp like butter on biscuits, as Grandma used to say: we're headed back to Cinderblock City (a.k.a. base camp) so that the four counselors can officially be pink-slipped.

Nissa and Frances are sniveling in tandem, quietly rolling up Nissa's sleeping bag with all the somberness of flag bearers at a military funeral. Peabo whistles "Taps," and I hear Snout quietly humming along as he and Ronnie shuffle past me with their packs on their shoulders.

"Come on, guys," I say, trying to cheer them up. "It's not so bad. At least we can sleep in real beds and take hot showers, if we're lucky. That's a plus, in my book."

"Yeah, well your book *sucks*," Ronnie says, stopping in his tracks. "*You* don't care because *you* don't have anywhere to go." His voice is tight with anger, and he jams his index finger at me as though to emphasize each word. "Did you ever stop to think that maybe there are other people here who just want to finish their Stepping Stones and get back to their families? Fat chance that's happening anytime soon, now."

"Oh please, do you honestly think Barb can keep us in a holding pattern out here indefinitely?" Though my words are cocky, the pitch of my voice falters. Ever since I'd successfully swapped the incriminating canteens this morning, I'd been operating under the assumption that we'd all be sprung soon. After all, I'd unwittingly managed to bring Barb's entire operation to a screeching halt, and though I did feel bad that the counselors were collateral damage, I refuse to let that fact rain on my inner ticker tape parade. "No more counselors means no more DreamRoads. Doesn't it?" At my question, Snout wheezes laughter.

"Girl, for your supposed street smarts, you are all kinds of naive," says Frances. "Does Barb strike you as a quitter?"

"It could be weeks before she hires a new staff," says Quin, sounding about as worried as I feel. "So where does that leave us?"

"Limbo, kid," Peabo answers. "And I don't mean the party game you play with a stick."

"Which means that we now have to suffer for someone else's selfishness and stupidity." Saying this, Ronnie stares at me with eyes that could saw through bone.

"Well I, for one, feel awful for the counselors," says Nissa. "I mean, everyone makes mistakes, right?"

"No doubt," says Peabo. "The hike back to base camp with them is going to be, like, the longest walk of shame ever."

"I'm serious!" she says, flinging a ball of twine at him. "They've been cool with us. Probably nicer than we deserved. Who knows what our new crew will be like?"

"I don't even want to think about it," Frances says with an exaggerated shudder.

Worried that my very presence might tempt Ronnie to rat me out to the others, I retreat to the kitchen area on the other side of camp. Once again, without even trying, I've managed to make everyone hate me. The truth is, I agree with Nissa: I feel sorry for our counselors. But I also feel something else: a terrible, ugly guilt that is eating away at my insides like a school of hungry piranha. Deep down, I'm sickened at what my thoughtlessness has set in motion. I'm starting to wonder: is it the world, or is it me? Does everything always have to be so damn hard? Snatching dingy grey dishtowels off branches where they'd been hung to dry after breakfast, I stoop to retrieve one that's fallen to the ground. At eye level, I'm struck by the unexpected beauty of a cobweb that is strung between two lower branches of the shrubbery. Tiny droplets of water glisten there like small Swarovski crystals on a prom dress; intricate and frail, the web must have gotten caught in the downpour of this morning's washing of mess kits. It is is an ordered array of nested circles, an exquisite death trap. Caught within are the shriveled remains of an insect the size and color of a peppercorn. Its legs are curled in upon its body. I lean in for closer inspection and count eight tiny appendages. *Stupid thing*, I think. *What kind of spider gets stuck in its own web?*

I swipe at the web in frustration, and it clings to my fingers like a possessive ghost. Almost without thinking, I stand up and head back across the small clearing, shaking my hand wildly to free the web's hold on me as I stride with sudden purpose.

"Hey, where are you going?" Frances asks. I stop and stare back at her and the other kids, trying to turn my swirling thoughts into words that would make any kind of sense at all. It dawns on me that I don't quite have an answer to her question. I'm starting to lose it out here, but strangely enough, it's not an altogether-horrible sensation.

"Do you know how I got the name Puck?" I finally ask no one in particular. Seven pairs of eyes are trained on me, and though no one says a word, I continue. "It gets hard to memorize the house numbers, the phone numbers, after a while. All the places I've ever lived, different street names, subdivisions, school districts. And the rules. So many goddamn rules to learn—different ones for different people and places, and I'm always getting them wrong. *Always.* So what do they do? They slap me around from place to place like it's the social-welfare equivalent of the Stanley Freakin' Cup. So yeah, I'm hard. And slippery, too, just like a hockey puck. But I've had to be. That's who I am, now. And not even Paula could . . ." I trail off, not quite certain what to say on that account. "Well, bottom line, Ronnie's right. I *don't* have a place to go to from here, but you guys do. You probably don't think much of me at this point, and your instincts are right. Believe it or not, I'm sorry about that. I'm sorry, for everything, really, because after five weeks, I can honestly say you've become the closest thing to a real family I've maybe ever had. That probably sounds pathetic," I add, glancing, red-faced, at the ground, "but just know that you're not going to have to stay out here one minute longer than you have to on my account."

"Puck, wait," Quin calls out to me as I head toward Barb's tent, but I just keep walking. There's no looking back now.

* * *

I'd braced myself for pretty much anything, figuring no riot act Barb could read me would be too severe, humiliating, or explosive to withstand. What I never bargained on was this strange silence and that disappointment in her eyes. It's not just unnerving. It's unthinkable. Unbearable, even.

"Aren't you going to say anything?" I whisper, petrified and suffocating in the stale, warm air of her tent after I've made my confession.

"I'm sorry, Puck."

"Wha…what?"

"I'm sorry. You shouldn't be here. We should never have brought you in." She dabs at the corners of her eyes with her thumbs and sniffs, glancing upward and then back at me. "I told Paula I could help you, and honestly, I thought that I could. I *hoped* that I could. But I was wrong."

"What?" I can hardly believe my ears.

"People could have been seriously hurt, Puck. Worse, even."

"But it was just a flower," I say, protesting even though I know I have no right to.

"That flower you thought you'd 'play pharmacy' with? It's the Angel's Trumpet, otherwise known as *sacred datura* or 'the devil's weed.' It's a hallucinogen. Native Americans used to think it could help them commune with the dead, and indeed, it *did* allow some of them to commune with the dead—because guess what? They *died* from it! If it doesn't kill you, it can cause permanent psychosis and amnesia. The counselors are *lucky* they're only dealing with end-of-days hangovers and humiliation." I feel a chill go through my body. I pray she's just exaggerating all this to teach me a lesson, but something tells me she's being truthful.

"I didn't know," I say again, more quietly this time. "Are they going to be okay?"

"It depends on what you mean by 'okay.' I get the sense that you and I have two very different definitions of that word."

"So what happens now?"

"We need to find a better situation for you, that's all. I'm so sorry."

"*Stop* apologizing." My disbelief is morphing into something more like anger. "Why are *you* crying? Stop crying!"

"You're right; this is totally unprofessional of me. It's just that, last night, I thought maybe you were finally turning a corner. I got my hopes up…thought that maybe we were reaching you. But I should have looked closer. I should have seen."

"Seen what?"

She blinks the tears away, and a renewed hardness settles back into her expression. The tent shudders from a stronger-than-usual gust of wind. We both glance at the thick canvas, which snaps with hostility before finally subsiding back into calmness.

"There's no sense in discussing it now. It's clear that you don't want to be here, and I think, for once, we're finally in agreement on something. This isn't the place for you."

There is nothing left to say, or at least nothing I haven't already heard before. That's why I don't even bother to argue with her. Barb has reached the moment of truth, the moment when, despite their mantra of "being the change they want to see in the world," people finally give up on me once and for all. I thought I'd conceived of every possible punishment for what I did, but never in a million years did I expect her to give me exactly what I wanted: my freedom. Only it doesn't feel at all like I thought it would. I slowly exit the tent. If I weren't so numb, I could almost laugh at the irony of it all. Here I'd been thinking all this time that I'd have to trick or connive my way out of this camp, when all I ever needed to do was wait for the inevitable to happen…again. Barb is no formidable enemy. Turns out that she's just like all the others, which is even worse. I lift my gaze to the sky, which seems darker than before, even though the sun is shining. I stride back to where I'd left my campmates and march toward Frances, who's lacing up her hiking boots. She stands as I approach, my hand curling into a fist.

"You're wrong about Barb," I say. "She *is* a quitter." Then, without another word, I walk away.

CHAPTER 14

Methought a Serpent Ate My Heart Away

"A mild *flu*? Come on! She must think we're morons. Those four got boozed and *busy*, and nobody's convincing me otherwise," Peabo mumbles to me under his breath.

Guilty as I feel about my part in the whole mess, I'd like to defend the counselors, but I keep my mouth shut. We're supposed to be giving our undivided attention to Barb, who has just called an impromptu meeting to announce that there's been a change of plans. Instead of returning to base camp, we'll be staying put at this site for one more day and night to give the counselors a chance to recover from a "stomach bug." (Barb should mind her own lectures about honesty, though, to be fair, I suppose it's partly my butt she's covering for. I'm also relieved that the counselors are no longer on the chopping block, but I'm fairly certain that their having booze, whether they actually drank it or not, remains a pretty serious violation in Barb's book.)

"Tents go back up, people. We'll lay low today, then pick up again tomorrow with the last Stepping Stone, so conserve your energy—and no goofing off."

"Hallelujah!" Titanita interjects. "I'm coming for ya, Water Challenge, and after that, it's showtime! Though, honestly, I can't wait to get back to L.A. so I can start a juice cleanse. And get an In-N-Out burger." She shrugs her backpack off her shoulders and heaves it to the ground, beginning to undo the buckles and belts holding it together. Snout drops his pack, too, but he saunters over to a spot underneath a tree, where he removes both boots before lying back on a comfy-looking patch of high grass, hands clasped behind his head.

Shadows from fast-moving clouds darken the little clearing we've called home for the past few days. There's a renewed sense of normality, if not flat-out relief, that everyone but me seems to be feeling. I glance around uncertainly, wondering how I fit into the landscape. Where will I go from here now that I've been expelled from the program? Back to the Center? Yet another foster home?

No. I won't be tossed back into the spin cycle of the system. I'd rather live on the streets, if it comes to that. If I can survive out here with next to nothing, I can fend for myself in the big city. In her letter, Paula had made it perfectly clear that returning to her house was contingent upon my graduating from DreamRoads. After what I did —ruining her relationship with a man she loved—I can finally admit that it was pretty generous of her to even contemplate taking me back at all. But that's off the table now, so there's no point in thinking about it. Still, my thoughts drift to her condo: the Christmas lights she'd let me string up in my bedroom; the sag in the center of her living room sofa where she and I would bury our socked feet while watching marathons of *Aurora's Harbinger* (trash TV at its finest); the separate jar of peanut butter kept for me in the pantry so that I could eat from it directly with a spoon—my favorite evening snack. My brain is scrambling for a different train of thought to latch on to when a sharp tap on the shoulder stuns me back to reality. I pivot to find Barb, who motions at me to follow her for a convo several paces away from others.

"We'll get you back to base camp tomorrow for your discharge," she says in a lowered voice. "You'll remain with us tonight, and though you are not expected to participate in any more activities, I *do* expect you to abide by the rules of camp while you are here. Is that clear?"

I nod my head solemnly, unable to make eye contact with her.

"I don't want to create any further drama and gossip for the rest of the group, so we're going to handle this quietly, and—"

As if on cue, a shrill scream from the campsite reverberates through the canyon. Barb takes off in a sprint. Jogging behind her, I catch up to where Titania is cowering like a Hitchcock heroine. Using Nick as a human shield, she periodically peeks over his shoulders at what's on the dirt in front of them.

"Snaaaaaaake! Snaaaaake! Oh my god, Nick, it commandeered my sleeping bag. I swear, it practically lunged for my throat!"

Peabo and Quin are both crouched on the ground inspecting what appears to be a streamer-length piece of crumpled-up bubble wrap.

"Gnarly!" Peabo exclaims, lifting it with the end of a forked stick.

"Promise me you won't let it come near me, Nick!" Titania burrows her face into his back, clutching the tail of his red uniform shirt. He raises his arm aloft like the leader of a tactical SWAT team to silence her. His protective stance and hardened facial expression suggest a B-list performer in a low-budget action flick.

"There's nothing to fear. You're completely safe," Nick says in voice that's a bit more manly than the situation truly warrants. I can tell he's feeling gratified to be somebody's hero rather than Barb's pack mule for a change. Where once Titania ridiculed Nick, she now reveres him. Given my part in orchestrating their newfound kinship, I ought to find it comic—pathetic, even. Instead, it strikes me as slightly sweet. Nick gets to feel respected and admired, for once, and, unless she's a better actress than she is letting on, Titania seems to have developed a sincere affection for the big lug that extends beyond starry-eyed wonder at his so-called family connections.

"It's only a snakeskin," Barb says, snatching at the limp remnant, "though I'm not sure how it got in your bedroll."

"I don't care if it's dead or alive or...or, whatever!" Titania says in an inane huff. "Keep it far away from me unless it happens to be gracing a five-hundred-dollar pair of stilettos!"

I mosey over to where Ronnie is kicking the dirt with a barely concealed shit-eating grin on his face.

"Nice one," I say in a low voice.

"I don't know what you're talking about." He shrugs, but I see a devilish look in his deep brown eyes.

"Oh give it up. That is the work of a master." I flick my wrist in a circle and subtly tip my head, as if bowing to royalty. "Well played, sir."

"What did you tell Barb this morning in her tent?" he asks, changing the subject.

"The truth." *Though not the truth she was hoping for,* I think to myself. "I didn't want the rest of you to be screwed because of something I did, so I came clean about the hooch."

"What did *she* say?"

"She's booting me from the program. Which is what I wanted," I hasten to add, hoping to cover up the catch in my throat. "So it worked out okay. Better than okay, frankly."

"All's well that ends well."

"Yep." An awkward heaviness hangs in the air, and neither of us seems to have any clue what to say next. We trade looks of confusion and surprise when another cry sounds from just a few feet away.

"Snaaaaake! Snaaaake!" The words are familiar, but the voice is altogether new.

"Snout?" Ronnie says, and it's not clear if his perplexed tone is meant more for me or for our newly verbal campmate, who is attempting to crabwalk himself away from what I can only describe as a pile of bad news.

In the grass near Snout's scrambling bare feet is a coiled patchwork of tan and brown. The snake's midsection is as thick as my leg, and it's definitely getting all gangsta' up on our friend, lurching its triangular head toward Snout in fits and starts. A nubby tail quivers, accompanied by a strange high-frequency sound that reminds me of static from a badly tuned radio.

"Snout!" shouts Quin, who is a few yards away in the other direction. "Someone come, quick!" Within seconds, everyone in our camp is standing at attention, wanting to race forward to help but simultaneously held back by the obvious danger of the situation.

"Barb?" Snout says, shakily. His face crumples, but his eyes never leave the snake. "I'm scared!"

"I know," she answers. Her voice is calm. Resolute. "I know. Just be still. And *don't* say another word."

"But he just started speaking Human! That is, like, so ironic," Frances interjects.

"Shut up, Frances!" I say. My pronunciation of her name comes out in a hiss. Or was it actually coming from the snake still staring down Snout? Xander, Dimitri, Mia, and Ellen have emerged from their respective tents and are also watching the scene unfold in horror.

"Xander," Barb says quietly, "is that what I think it is?"

"I'm afraid it is. A western rattlesnake; one of the biggest I've ever seen."

"The one you warned us all about at orientation!" Titania exclaims, as if she finally got an answer right on *Jeopardy!* "The only snake out here with venom! Oh my gosh, is *that* what ditched its leftovers on my sleeping bag? I really *could* have died!" She gingerly steps her way around Nissa and Frances so that she's positioned safely behind Nick once more. Snout's wide eyes dart from the snake to Barb and back again.

"Wh-what did she just say?" he stammers. I'm not sure what's more surreal: the disturbing man-against-nature sequence playing out in front of me, or hearing Snout speak in actual words and sentences. "Am I going to die?!"

"Stop talking, Snout!" shouts Barb, stomping her boots on the ground like a bull getting ready to charge.

"What is she doing?" I say in a whisper.

"She's trying to distract it," answers Xander, who starts stomping his feet as well. "A snake can sense vibrations far better than it can see."

The rest of us stamp our feet and holler like all hell, but the serpent doesn't take its focus off the target directly in front of it. It's looking *no bueno* for Snout, as Ronnie would say, and I keep glancing at Barb, hoping and

227

expecting that she'll direct some of her legendary hellfire on a creature that actually deserves it, for a change. Instead, it is Ellen who finally stuns us all by storming over to a nearby tree, cracking off a leafy branch, and marching straight toward the spring-loaded reptile.

"Over here, Hissy-Hissy! Over here!" she taunts it, rattling her foliage like a mighty saber. The snake takes notice, rearing its head to face her, and for a moment, a wave of pity washes over me. The poor thing is scared as all hell and is only trying to defend itself. Still, I'm relieved when Barb shouts for Snout to get up and run— *now*.

By the time he joins us, panting and sobbing, the snake has slithered off to a brush-covered hillside. Ellen drops to her butt as if she's just had the wind knocked out of her. Mia runs to her, crouches down, and buries her head in her neck. The rest of us whoop out relieved cheers.

"That was the bravest damn thing I've ever seen," says Dmitri, who stares at Ellen, mystified. He checks himself when he realizes I've overheard. "*Darn*, that is," he corrects himself. "The bravest *darn* thing I've ever seen."

"Hey, man, you'll get no argument from me." I raise both hands in joint acknowledgement that Ellen is one badass chick. "The girl can charm a freakin' snake." *So why can't she charm you?* I'm tempted to add.

The rest of the kids are encircling Snout, smothering him with love.

"Welcome to the conversation, Snout," Barb finally interrupts. "What do you have to say for yourself?"

The group hug dissipates and everyone retreats a few steps, giving His Eloquency a chance to address us for the first time. Wiping the sweat from his face with the crook of his elbow, he cackles, and I wonder if he's about to lapse back into his weird, barnyard-catatonic state again.

"For starters," he says with a sigh, "what kind of ridiculous nickname is Snout? Do you people even *know* how much that has irritated me for the last month and a half? Just call me Tom, for the love of god!"

"*Tom?!*" Our group echoes the conventional name in unanimous surprise.

"No way. Not gonna happen, man," Peabo says. "It's way too late in the game for that. We have christened you Snout, and Snout you shall be."

"You don't even look like a Tom," says Frances.

"But that's my actual name."

"Not to us, it's not," Nissa says, crossing her arms over her chest. "Putting up with your quote-unquote lunacy for the last several weeks earns us the right to call you whatever we want."

While they're busting his chops for finally breaking his version of silence, Barb, Nick, and Xander are powwowing a few feet away. I inch closer to eavesdrop.

"I'm surprised to see one of those this time of day," Xander quietly tells his boss.

"Maybe it came out to sun itself," says Nick. Xander glances skyward and I follow his gaze, silently noting the thick blanket of angry-grey clouds that have shrouded the sun while we were all distracted by the pit viper.

"Or maybe it already knew what we're just discovering," says Barb. "A storm's heading our way."

* * *

The drumroll downpour on the canvas above our heads is loud and incessant. Nick and Barb's oversized tent is designed to sleep six, but right now, the eight of us kids are also crammed in like sardines as the afternoon dims into a bleak evening. I'm in one corner hugging my knees to my chest.

"Fine, you can call me Snout, but only if *you* tell me *your* real name."

"I'm not frontin'!"

"Liar. No self-respecting parents name their kid *Peabo*."

"He's some old R&B singer my mom loves. If I were a girl, I would have been Aretha."

"In case it's not official, I'm ready to call it: we all smell like we're decomposing," Ronnie reports, changing the subject. "Somebody open one of the window flaps so I can breathe."

"Are you kidding? The rain's coming at us sideways over here. I don't want to get drenched!" Frances says.

"Maybe this is Nature's not-so-subtle hint that we need a shower," says Nissa. She sniffs her own armpit tentatively and curls her lips in disgust. "Ew."

"Are you *sure* we're not all going to get electrocuted, Nick?" Titania asks. "We don't have thunder and lightning in Southern California, and the last thing I need is to get fried like bacon out here. They'd probably get some hack actress to play me in the story of my tragic demise. Though if it came to that, I *do* hope Elton John would compose a song for my memorial . . ."

"Nothing's happening to any of you on my watch," Nick says. "We're at the bottom of a canyon—there are few safer places to be, actually."

Barb is handing out Slim Jims and granola bars for our makeshift dinner, which is five-star eats in these parts.

The four counselors are all back in their tents, supposedly sleeping off their green-around-the-gills status.

"Scientifically speaking, the carbon fiber tent poles *could* conduct an electrical current," Quin says. The humidity in the tent is fogging up his glasses, so he removes them. "Still, the odds of lightning actually hitting the tent are astronomically small. Approximately one in twelve thousand over the course of a person's lifetime."

"I *almost* don't miss the Internet when you're around, Quin," says Nissa. He grins widely.

"What makes you all think Quin is the only boy genius around here?" says Snout. "I'm insulted."

"Well, clearly, you were holding out on us," says Ronnie. "I'm not sure whether faking idiocy is the stupidest thing I've ever seen or the work of a prodigy."

"What I can't understand is, why?" Peabo says. "What did you have to gain from it?"

Barb's keeping quiet over on her side of the tent, but I can tells she's tuned in to every word.

"It seemed like the easiest way to avoid having to talk to anyone," Snout says, pushing a dreadlock out of his face before perching his elbows on his jackknifed knees. "No offense, but I sized up the rest of you and thought, *What* a bunch of headcases. Then I figured, why not just take it one step further and go full straightjacket? I thought if I was convincing enough, they'd at least send me to a nice warm psych ward where I could sit around, play solitaire, and enjoy a cup of Jell-O every afternoon."

"You definitely had me convinced," Quin says.

"I feel like such a chump," Peabo adds. "Why didn't I think of it first?"

A flash of lightning illuminates the tent, and a few seconds later comes the stampeding sound of thunder. After a round of girly squeals (from the guys and girls, alike), Snout continues explaining himself.

"Anyway, it doesn't matter. Barb didn't seem to care that I was supposedly two fries short of a Happy Meal, so there you have it. Old fork tongue out there finally blew my cover."

"All that work for nothing," Ronnie says.

"Not necessarily. He's been able to dodge Campfire Confessional," Nissa rightly points out.

"Yes and no," Snout says.

"Meaning what?" asks Frances.

"Meaning almost every minute of every day felt like one of those campfires to me. I felt trapped in my own head," he says. "It's hard to explain, but the longer you go without speaking, the deeper and deeper you sink inside yourself. Weird, big questions lurk there, man. Heavy questions, like, What's the point of it all? Why am I even here?"

"What *should* we do with a drunken sailor?" Peabo says in faux contemplation. He elbows me in the ribs and whispers, "Or counselor?"

"Okay, man, whatever," Snout says, acknowledging the joke. "It just got to the point where I thought maybe I actually *was* going a little crazy. It was intense."

"People who live the monastic life often take vows of silence for that very reason," Barb says, finally poking her nose into the conversation. "It's a contemplative approach to spirituality."

"After a while, it just seemed too late to come clean, and I guess it's a little embarrassing, but it's a relief, now, to just talk. Not speaking for that long is one of the hardest things I've ever done. Maybe even harder than all the physical challenges. But I'm not sure I completely regret it, either. Everything is there in that silence: the demons are there, but so is the power to stop them."

In the past few minutes, the light has almost completely vanished. It's dumping water outside as we collectively retreat inside our respective heads. I cast off a shiver and drop my knees to my chin, curling into a sitting fetal position to keep warm. Then, with a faint click, there is light. Barb has turned on her lantern, and she passes it to the center, where it casts on the tent ceiling a bright white circle studded from behind with raindrops.

"Not exactly a campfire," she says, "but we can all still listen."

* * *

"Wait, what?" Ronnie declares. "You didn't get caught for *seven months?* You were living at your high school that whole time?"

"It's way easier than you'd think," says Snout. "Everyone just assumed I was *really* into extracurricular activities. I even joined the rhythmic gymnastics squad for a while because they were the only club that stayed past five on Thursday nights."

"Dear god, please let video footage of that exist," I say.

"The early evenings required a bit of ninja stealth," Snout continues, "but once the custodial crew left every night around nine o'clock, I was king of the castle. Turns out the school's surveillance cameras were just for show. That meant I could raid the caf for midnight snacks, surf the Internet at my leisure. I slept at night on a prop bed belonging to the drama department and washed my clothes in the Home Economics lab."

As Snout describes how he managed to live and sleep for the better part of a year in his high school, I take mental notes. Sounds like it would sure beat another foster home.

"Where did your parents think you were, since you never came home?" Quin asks.

"That was the beautiful part," says Snout. "Their divorce was so nasty they wouldn't speak to one another. I told Mom I was staying with Dad, and vice versa. It made it all so simple. They never even tried to verify it. And neither seemed to care that I was permanently out of their hair, either." He chews on his thumbnail, pensively. "I guess that's why they sent me here after I finally got caught by school officials. Maybe wanting to be rid of me is the one thing my parents have in common."

"How'd you get caught?" Titania wonders.

"It all unravelled after I had to call 911. I accidentally started a fire with a Bunsen burner trying to cook a cup of ramen."

"You pulled a Peabo, in other words," Ronnie laughs.

"Yeah, but it was totally an accident in my case," says Snout. "That's the one thing I never understood about you, bro." He glances over at Peabo, who is absentmindedly picking at his eyelashes. "Why torch all those things? Was it just an adrenaline rush?"

"Like I told you guys before, my dad's a total sphincter. He drinks too much. He even broke my mom's ribs, once."

"But why set fires?"

"Because I could." Peabo shrugs.

"That's not a logical answer," says Titania.

"So what?" he says, anger rising in his voice. "Why did you skip out on your bill at the fancy London hotel when you could afford to buy the whole place if you wanted to? Why did Nissa shoplift a three-dollar novelty keychain from a party-supply store? Why did Frances carve the word *Frisbee* on her thigh with a razor blade? Why do any of us do the moronic things we do?"

His volatile words set off a mini shitstorm within the tent, but Barb intervenes to restore order.

"Okay, everyone, I understand that he touched some nerves, but Peabo's raising a valid point. What I *think* he's trying to say can be summed up in one word: control. When we don't have it in our lives, we have a tendency to go looking for it, sometimes in all the wrong places. Whether it's the strike of a match or just incendiary words, lashing out can feel good—in the moment. But there's always, *always* a price, and it's usually quite high. Part of what you're all learning out here is that you *do* have the ability to control things, even when the rest of the world is going haywire. You just have to look within and know that you're strong enough."

The pelting of rain on the canvas tent downshifts to a gentle pitter-patter.

"Do you think it's letting up?" Nissa asks in a quiet voice.

"Not yet," Ronnie says. "But it seems like the worst may be over."

CHAPTER 15

The Course of True Love
Never Did Run Smooth

The next morning we detour from our typical landscape, trading the vast arena of ancient rust-colored sandstone for new terrain that's even more unworldly. The canyon gradually closes in on us, defying gravity as it curves upward and inward over our heads, like a skate park with ramps fit for giants. The hike isn't at all strenuous, perhaps because the winding trail makes a steady descent, or perhaps because it's easy to be distracted by the scenery's unexpected costume change. Ferns, grasses, and moss-covered boulders carpet the landscape in a million hues of green, and brightly colored tropical flowers grow straight out of cracks on the sheer sandstone cliffs. Though it's damp and shady here, it's also muggy, like the inside of a terrarium. We continue along the switchbacks that lead down toward the gently shushing of flowing water.

"What *is* this place?" Quin poses the question when we stop near a lookout twenty feet above the bottom of the canyon. Sunlight reflects off the river below us and casts dazzling patterns on cliff walls that are alive with vegetation and pint-sized waterfalls. I'll be damned if I didn't just land in Pixie Hollow.

"Welcome to Eden's Corridor," says Barb. "As you can see, we're in a unique microclimate. Many of the plants here can thrive without soil. See that clump of maidenhair fern, over to your left? It has taken root in small fissures in the cliff, where trickles of water seep out from the stone. You'll find examples of that everywhere, like hanging gardens. Life springs from this impervious rock, against all odds."

Titania twirls, gypsy-like, to visually soak in her surroundings. "My spirit home! I'm sooo shooting my next music video here. Nick, you can direct!"

"This must be where garden gnomes are born," says Peabo in amazement. "Puck," he adds, placing his hands squarely on my shoulders and stooping his tall frame so that his face is level with mine. "We've found your people, at long last!"

"Very funny," I say, not even bothering to hide my smirk.

"I told you guys you were going to love it," says Ronnie.

"Yeah, only I can't even take a stupid selfie to prove I was here," Frances laments. "*Completely* ironic.*"

Hiking a few hundred yards further to the water's edge, Xander points out various species of flowers: cliffrose and columbine, shooting stars and scarlet monkeyflowers, bluebells and false pennyroyal, and orchids that look like they belong in a rainforest. At last, we reach a spot where two large bright yellow rafts are moored to a metal hook that's been drilled into a giant boulder.

"The drink seems higher than the last time we were here," says Ronnie. Old hat at this, he is helping Dmitri and Xander pull helmets and life jackets from a DreamRoads-branded wooden crate that, along with the rafts, was placed here in advance.

"It's from the rain," says Barb. "I had Xander and Dmitri scout out the river this morning, and the good news is we shouldn't have to lug the rafts over dry sections of the riverbed like we did last session. All right, everyone, huddle up! Before we go over the finer points of this

Stepping Stone challenge, it's time to part ways with our friend Puck. This is where she leaves us."

The deflating sound of gasps mingles with a chorus of incredulous "Whats?" Even the four counselors appear confused, and I glance awkwardly at their stunned faces as Barb dances around the details of my sudden exit.

"Circumstances necessitate her leaving the program early," she continues. "Instead of joining us on the river, Nick will escort Puck back to base camp by way of the eastern trail. We'll say our goodbyes to her now. She will be in Arizona by the time the rest of us make it back."

This announcement leaves me with the feeling that I've just been trampled by wildebeests, though I'm not sure why. What could be wrong about finally getting to peel out of this joint? But everything's happening so damn fast, and the idea of having only a few minutes left with my brethren brats—the last I'll likely ever see of any of them—floors me.

"Puck, we will regret not having you with us for the graduation," Barb continues, "but I know I speak for everyone when I say we wish you the best life has to offer. I realize you didn't come here of your own volition, but I hope you can take something positive away from this experience, whether it's something you've learned about yourself or simply a new appreciation for the natural world." Her words are courteous, but her delivery is curt.

"But, I don't get it! Why's she leaving?" asks Frances.

"I do not accept this!" As she says this, Titania looks half-puzzled and half-outraged. "You can't just bail! You're my Dorothy! I *need* a Dorothy! Nick…?" She stares at him, hoping he'll somehow intervene. She and I both. But he only picks up my pack, which I'd dropped earlier, and helps me into it like I'm donning a jacket.

"I'm sure we can figure all that out," he says. "Right now let's just—" He searches for words. "Show Puck some love."

Snout, Peabo, Nissa, and Frances are the first to give me a succession of hugs, but I barely register their promises to stay in touch.

"Are you okay?" Quin whispers to me a few seconds later. I bite my lip, smile, and nod.

"When have I not been? You're going to be okay, too. Remember that. And don't let any of these other numbnuts boss you around."

"Right."

Titania is still off stewing about how I've ruined the show, but Ronnie finally approaches. His face is cast

243

downward, but he reaches his big brown fist toward my puny one.

"Over and out, Dangerbird."

"Umm...yeah. Bye, I guess." This can't be right. It's not supposed to happen this way. Once again, Barb is trying to bogart the reins to *my* life for no other reason than to prove she's top dog. I walk over to where she's scrutinizing her clipboard, having apparently already disposed of me in her mind.

"Can I talk to you?" I ask. "Privately?'" She and I walk behind a nearby boulder.

"We've got to make it downriver by sunset, Puck, so I don't have a lot of time. What is it?"

"Are you *letting* me leave, or are you *making* me leave?"

"I'm not following what you're asking."

"Because if you're *making* me leave, I get it. But the way you said it yesterday wasn't all that clear. So if you're just *letting* me leave, then I'd like to do the Water Challenge with everyone else." She eyes me like I'm up to something.

"I think at this point, it's better if you just—"

"Please. I want to stick with the others until we get back to base camp."

"Haven't you figured out how this works by now? You don't call the shots here."

"I know that, I really do. It's your decision. Look, I know I'm not going to graduate, but…just let me complete this last Stepping Stone. Let me say goodbye to them all on my own terms. I promise I won't cause any trouble."

I'm obviously a pro at telling adults what I think they want to hear in order to get my way, but these words spilling out of my mouth are accompanied by something strangely unfamiliar: sincerity. (I didn't even know I had that in me.) Barb slowly exhales, tapping her clipboard with the end of her pen.

"Puck, I don't think you even know what you're asking to get yourself into."

"Is that a yes?"

She sizes me up, trying to determine, no doubt, whether this is just another one of my stunts.

"You *want* to go on the river?" she asks. "Are you sure?"

"I'm sure." The universe seems suspended in a strange limbo as she considers my request. Though I can't read her gaze, I have an unsettled sense that my very life depends on her answer.

"Xander," she finally calls out over her shoulder, "can you grab another helmet and life jacket for Puck?"

*　*　*

Beggar's remorse has officially kicked in. Call me naive, but I thought we'd be riding down *in* the boat, buffered on all sides by the raft's big, cushiony gunwales. You know—the safe, logical way. Instead, all of our gear and packs are comfortably nestled there in drybags, secured by ropes and carabiners, while my butt is precariously balanced on the outer edge of the raft with absolutely nothing to hold on to except for an unwieldy T-shaped paddle. I'm the lightest person on the raft, which means if anyone else on this floating bounce house so much as sneezes, it's likely to catapult me through the air and into the…well, trust me when I say I hold up in water about as well as a papier-mâché piñata.

I wedge both of my feet deep into the crevice where the side of the tube I'm sitting on meets the bottom of the crosstube in front of me. The river's surface is mirror placid, but I'm not taking any chances.

"Puck, you've got to paddle in time with the rest of us if we're actually going to get anywhere," says Mia, who's sitting opposite me. Quin and Titania are paired up at the front of the raft, and directly behind us are Ronnie and Xander. Barb is perched on the back of the raft, stretching her oar behind her and occasionally shouting out instructions for the rest of us. Frances, Nissa, Peabo, Snout, Ellen, and Nick are in the second boat behind us, with Dmitri as their "coxswain" in back.

Before we'd even pushed off from the riverbank, Barb and Nick had spelled out a shit-ton of safety information. I tried to commit everything to memory, but the more they talked about what to do if things went terribly wrong, the more all of the guidelines seemed to escape my brain and settle chaotically in the pit of my stomach.

Careful not to fall in, I lean over the side of the raft to slice my paddle through the water. The late-morning sun glints off the wings of zigzagging dragonflies, and birds are chirping each other's ears off. I unclench my jaw and let gravity coax my shoulders downward, reminding myself that there is nothing to be worried about. Though I can never be fully relaxed, I eventually settle into a state that feels significantly less than spastic. The water is calm, the day is pretty, and it all feels gloriously lazy. *Life is but a dream*, I muse, thinking of a song from childhood. The moment seems suited to soaking it all in, which of course gives Betty Buzzkill another opportunity to ruin things with a lecture.

"There's a reason, beyond all this lovely sightseeing, that I brought you to this place," Barb says, projecting her voice so the second group of rafters can hear. "First, check out the flowers and plants surrounding us here. Pretty beautiful, huh?" Everyone grunts their assents. "Now, I want you to remember where you started on the DreamRoad. Think back to base camp. Can anyone remember what kind of plants are there?"

"Prickly pear," Peabo mutters. "Stuff that will bite you in the butt if you're not paying attention."

"Don't forget the giant mutant tumbleweeds," Frances adds.

"That's right," says Barb, twisting around to address them. "Only dry desert chaparral, black brush, and cactus as far as the eye can see."

"All of it butt-ugly, if you ask me," yells Titania from in front of me.

"That's one way to look at it," says Barb, "but here's how I see it: In a barren, arid climate, those plants are *survivors*. They're brittle. Scratchy. Hard. They've had to be, to weather tough conditions."

Our boat glides past a clump of cattails growing amidst the rushes. It reminds me of a story I learned a long time ago in Vacation Bible School: baby Moses, left in a basket by his mother among the reeds of the Nile. An

Egyptian princess discovered him there and raised him as her own. Lucky bastard.

"Now what about after we left base camp, all that strenuous hiking?" Barb continues. "How did the landscape change?"

"It just got more boring?" says Nissa. "It all seemed like one big blur to me."

"Oh, come on, Nissa—you, of all people, should remember the juniper bushes," says Ronnie, sarcastically. The rest of us stifle laughs remembering the time she thought Quin could magically conjure up gin. "And what were all those puny, Puck-sized pine trees called again?"

"*Pinyon pines*," I shoot back. "And don't start with me."

Seated directly behind me, Xander gently knocks his fist twice on my shoulder, a way-to-go for remembering his nature notes. Barb, meanwhile, is still caught up in the roundabout lesson she's trying to cram down our throats.

"And now, we end our journey among gorgeous flowers that are rooted in stone, flourishing against all odds," she continues. "Every plant we've encountered out here has learned to adapt. They've figured out how to grow strong, and even, in some cases, to blossom. I believe that can be true of people, too, and I think every one of you—"

"Sorry to interrupt, Barb, but you've got a strainer approaching at one o'clock," Dmitri calls from his boat. I glance ahead and see a large jumble of tree limbs extending out of the water on my side of the river about seventy yards in front of us. Though we're still moving at little more than a crawl, we're heading directly toward it. I glance right, then left, at the sheer vertical cliffs of the gorge hemming us in, slowly wising up to the fact that there's no riverbank to escape to here, no ledge of ground to scramble up to safety.

"Right forward, left back!" yells Barb, issuing the paddling command that will help us to steer around it. I match the movement of my oar to Titania's in front of me as we sweep through the water in unison. The boat shifts toward the left in plenty of time to skirt the brambles. Behind us, Dmitri and his crew manage to avoid the obstacle, too. Barb, who had reclined herself almost horizontally off the back of the boat with her paddle serving as the rudder, sits forward again.

"Nicely done, everyone," she says, and lucky for us, she seems to have forgotten about the metaphor she'd been trying to bang into our heads with all the delicacy of a sledgehammer. I take a deep breath and convince my galloping heart to slow down to a steadier pace. If this is the worst of it, maybe it won't be so bad.

We stop for lunch a few hours later in a wider section of the gorge that is carved out into a small gravel beach. It feels good to stretch our legs. Stooping to reapply sunscreen from the industrial-sized jug we have on hand, I notice Ellen and Dmitri nearby, standing at the river's rocky edge with their backs toward me. They are unaware that I'm so close; that is, I don't *think* they'd be having the discussion they're having if they knew I could overhear every word.

"Don't you get it? I'm trying to apologize. I was completely wrong about you," Dmitri says, placing his hand tenderly on Ellen's shoulder. She swipes it away.

"You need to stop whatever this is, right now."

"What if I said I wanted to kiss you?" He inches closer to her.

"I'd say that's incestuous considering you think of me *as your sister.* Or did you forget?"

"I didn't mean it like that."

"You wanted Mia. I'm not just some leftovers you can reheat the next day."

"Babe, I was confused. And stupid, I'll admit. But yesterday morning, when I realized that Xander and you had . . ."

"Don't even say it!" Her face reddens with a mixture of humiliation and horror.

"I'm not! What I mean is, maybe it made me a little…jealous. And then, when you took command with the snake, I saw you in a whole new—"

"You're wasting your breath," she interrupts, shoving him angrily in the chest to brush past him.

So there's irony for ya. My Angel's Trumpet cocktail helped do the unthinkable. It turned Dmitri on to Ellen, but now *she* wants absolutely nothing to do with *him*. And if that weren't enough, Xander and Mia—formerly the most adorable closeted couple on the planet—have been giving each other the freeze-out for the past twenty-four hours. What Cupid brings together with a bow and arrow, I destroy with a wrecking ball. The power to gum up other people's lives used to give me a charge, but now I just feel kind of awful about it. I can't undo the number that's been done on this unsuspecting foursome as a result of my stupid mistake, but there's got to be some way to fix it.

"Hey, Dmitri," I say, approaching. He glances back, startled to see me.

"Oh, hey, Puck. I didn't realize you were…um, what's up?"

"I'm sorting through some kind of heavy stuff. Do you have a minute?"

"Sure. Lay it on me."

"Well, I was thinking about my foster mom, Paula. Ever since I messed up her engagement, I've been pushing her farther and farther away, and I think I might finally know why."

"I'm listening."

"Maybe it's because I was scared. I'm not used to having anybody *want* me, at least, not since my grandma died. After I pulled that stunt with Ted, Paula wanted to try to resolve things, and I just turned into a pit bull. Chewed her out every second I got. It's not that I don't love her. I just don't know if I can trust her. It's easier to push her away than risk getting burned. Do you know what I mean?"

I study Dimitri's face intently to see if he is taking the bait, and I'm not at all sure that he is until he speaks.

"Yeah, actually," he says, glancing in the direction that Ellen had stormed off in. "I think I do. Do you suppose there's anything your foster mom could do to convince you that you can actually trust her?"

"I guess the most important thing would be to just... not give up on me."

The truth is, I'm certain I've botched it up too badly with Paula to salvage things with her, especially now that I'm officially a DreamRoads flunky. Seeing the light won't help me, personally, and I'm not certain that spilling my guts like this will bring Ellen and Dmitri together, either. But it wasn't so awful, giving him a brief peek at my closely guarded thoughts. Even if it amounts to nothing, trying to do the right thing feels strangely soothing.

CHAPTER 16

Down Topples She

"If you could live in the world of any TV show, what series would you pick?"

By this late in the afternoon, the novelty of our ride downstream has worn off, and though we're going through the motions of paddling, the current is finally doing most of the work for us, offering the chance to engage in absolutely mindless conversation.

"Easy. *Golden Girls*. Next question," says Ronnie. We all stare at him in disbelief. "What?" he shrugs, resting the handle of his paddle on his thighs. "I enjoy it in reruns. Betty White is the bomb, yo. My turn: Would you rather be a celebrity or a superhero?" At the front of the raft, an abrupt and boisterous "Ha!" escapes like a burp from Titania's mouth.

"Superhero, duh," she says. "They get the one thing I'll never have again for as long as I live: anonymity. I'd still need to be loaded, though, like Tony Stark or Batman. And I'd pretty much steal Wonder Woman's getup from head to toe. 'Fighting crime with cleavage and a smokin' hot bod!' Which I already have, so . . ."

"Your superhero name could be 'The Screech Owl.' The sound emitted by your vocal cords obliterates your archenemies."

"Careful, Ronnie," Barb interjects in a scolding tone.

"What? She's a singer! Wouldn't her power be her voice? Oh, nevermind."

"It would be cool to be able to save people I guess," says Quin, "but there's a trade-off. Superheroes are all so angsty and emo."

"Oh, yeah, and celebrities don't have *any* issues," says Titania, glancing back at the rest of us and rolling her eyes. "I'm only here because I hate indoor plumbing. Okay, new question: if you were an ice cream, what flavor would you be?"

"Rocky Road," says Ronnie.

"Way to strain your brain for that one," I say without looking at him.

"Oh, I'm sorry," he says. "What do you want me to say? Inner-city chip? Gangland crunch?"

"I'd be vanilla," interrupts Quin, glumly. "Safe and uninteresting."

"Don't knock it, Potter," says Ronnie. "Vanilla is the unsung hero of the frozen dessert world."

"I wish Nick were in our boat for this, because you just *know* his answer would be Ben & Jerry's Chunky Monkey," says Titania, with a smile and a giggle. "God, Barb…you're so lucky to be married to someone with such an incredible sense of humor. I've always thought it's one of the most attractive qualities in a man."

"Okay, I think we're getting a little off topic," Barb says, sounding mildly irritated. "Xander? Mia? Care to weigh in on the ice cream question?" Her attempt to bring the stone-faced counselors in on some of the fun fails. They're clearly still mega-miffed with one another about yesterday morning's game of musical tents.

"I'll pass," says Mia, the Sad Panda of her former enthusiastic self.

"I don't eat dairy," Xander responds. The uncharacteristic hollowness of their responses makes me restless and ill at ease.

"Ice cream flavors? Really? I cannot believe we're even devoting what little brain function we have, Quin excluded, to this," I say.

"And then you have Miss Popsicle," notes Ronnie. "Hard and cold, with a stick up her—"

"You better watch it, Buster." Barb reaches down and palms the top of his head with her hand.

"It was a joke! Okay, okay...*sorry*."

I'm not offended by Ronnie's insult; I'm still too preoccupied with knowing that Xander and Mia's maybe-someday-you-never-know babies might cease to exist because of me. I do *not* need that shit on my conscience on top of everything else.

"My turn to ask something," I say. "Mia, which do you think is harder: Forgiving someone, or asking for forgiveness?" From the front of the raft, Quin and Titania both slowly turn to look at me as if I am speaking in tongues. Titania crinkles her nose in disgust.

"Way to ruin a perfectly good conversation by going all 'Barb-arella' on us," she says. Even Mia appears mildly perplexed. She and Barb exchange dubious glances.

"What?" I say. "It's a legitimate question that I'm grappling with, personally. I'm just curious to hear what she thinks."

"Damn. DreamRoad transformation complete," says Ronnie. "Her brain has been washed, rinsed, and repeated." Mia smiles at me, hesitantly, but her gaze wanders past my shoulder, to where Xander is seated behind me. Target locked.

"It depends on the situation, but I guess I'd have to say they're both pretty difficult things to do," comes her faraway response.

"What do *you* think, Puck?" says Barb. Seizing at the loose thread I've just dangled, she's jumping at the chance to unravel the whole thing, but instead, she's just getting in my way. This isn't *about* me. I try to pick my words carefully.

"Both suck," I say, "but the alternative—staying mad and broken—that's worse. Forgiving someone doesn't mean you've been bested, just like asking for forgiveness doesn't make you weak. Don't you agree, Xander?" I glance back at him to gauge where his head's at.

"One hundred percent," he says. His eyes never waver from Mia's. "But sometimes…it's just hard to find the right words."

"That's so true," I say. "I suppose in a perfect world, if you had two people with two basically equal grudges against one another, then there's an easy out. 'She's sorry, he's sorry; she's mad, he's mad . . .' At that point, it's a draw." I'm rambling, my brain picking up speed to match the pace of our rafts, which are racing faster now, too. The sound of the water is amplified, and I feel the urge to raise my voice. "I'm not saying the offenses would cancel each other out, exactly, but if you took stubbornness out of the equation, I think 90 percent of the world's conflicts would be pretty easily resolved!"

I glance again at Mia, who purses her lips and raises her eyebrows as if conceding that I have a point. The corners of her mouth turn up ever so slightly, and she has yet to break eye contact with her former (and, I hope, future) sweetheart. I revel in what I hope is a modest victory, but the satisfaction doesn't last for long.

"Oh, no. Oh, no, no, no, no…is that?! *Shit!*" Barb stands up in the back of the raft to better glimpse what she's clearly decided is something worth breaking DreamRoads's cardinal no-cussing rule for. She turns to yell to the other boat, which is about fifty yards behind us. "Nick! Dmitri! There's white water up ahead—too much! Go around! Get them to the side! *NOW!*"

Dmitri immediately fires off instructions to his raft, and Barb whips back into her seat and digs her paddle into the water behind her with all her might. "Right, forward, left, back!" she screams at us.

"It's too strong!" Mia cries. "There's no detour!" Barb's face is ashen, and it terrifies me. I'm still staring at her when she locks eyes on me and, in a voice shaky and hoarse, shrieks, "Don't look at me! Turn around and paddle, damn it! Everyone, together now!"

Facing forward now, I see it: a giant boulder positioned in the center of the river, and about fifteen feet parallel to it, a scattering of smaller (but equally intimidating) rocks. The water there is being thrashed and flung, as if a school of aggro sharks are feeding just below the surface. Foamy, hostile rapids are funneling through this natural goalpost, and beyond that, I can't actually see where the river continues. It can mean only one thing: a drop. Titania screams, and Quin ducks down in anticipation of what he sees coming, through the eye of the needle. My limbs go numb, and I feel as though my bladder is failing me.

"Hang on, everyone!" Barb shouts. "Keep paddling through it! Whatever you do, don't stop paddling when we hit bottom!"

My stomach rises to my throat, and I instinctively hook my left foot through the bungees that are holding our backpacks in the boat.

The last thing I remember is the sound of Ronnie screaming, "Puck! Don't!" —and then silence as the bottom drops out. Xander body-slams me from behind at full force. We are crash-test dummies, a jolt of bone on bone. The hard handle of my paddle pops me in the chin, and I see nothing but glittering stardust. I expect the sensation of falling, but instead, I'm flung upward.

Sprouting wings, I soar, up-up-up, arcing in graceful flight as bodies to the front and left of me dive off the raft in all directions—a slow-motion sequence of synchronized swimmers. The last collision is the worst. I hit the water, and the massive rubber raft lands second, closing over me like the lid of a coffin.

Bubbles. Only the sound of bubbles—a battalion of them—glubbing and popping. What I once thought of as dainty and fragile are now frenzied and furious, bombarding me—wrestling me into submission. I've been here before. My eyes are open, but all I can see are light, shadows, and memories of being woken in my bed on that shocking start to my DreamRoad. I wave my arms and thrash my feet, but one of them is paralyzed. I'm being held against my will…it's happening all over again. *Why is she doing this? Why?* I'm confused and scared, and I thrash some more, only to be wound in endless circles— left, right, left—like the agitator post in a washing machine. With my legs above me, I struggle to curl my body up toward the underside of the raft, praying for a pocket of air. The current keeps yanking my head and arms back down, but my flotation device buoys me. I finally grab hold of one of the ropes of the raft, only to discover that the baggage still secured in the boat is blocking out any empty space above the water's surface that I might have found to breathe. *I wasn't supposed to survive that day*, I realize. *I was supposed to have gone with him. Death has come to finish what she started. My turn has come.*

I think back to all those petty payback fantasies—my hopes that something tragic would happen to me out here so that Paula would be destroyed with remorse; those foolish dreams have finally taken root. It's happening. *Paula...Barb...Mom...Shane.*

I have two choices now. Two means of escape. Light and darkness continue to ripple before my eyes, shapes of things past and things to come. My arms grab at my trapped leg, and I can feel where the bungee cord encircles it. There is some give when I yank. Letting go of the cord means letting go of everything, following Shane. I can feel his arm on my shoulder, tugging me hard—he's yanking with all of his three-year-old might. I know he can't be here, but it feels real. He needs me.

I could slip my confines—free my ankle from its bondage. Would that mean abandoning my brother? Would choosing to live be a betrayal? His hand grips me tighter, snatching at my sleeve like a briar, and my lungs are desperate to just inhale. I can't stay here in this limbo, waffling, for much longer. I have to choose. This world or that?

I see the image of my mom's face—the mug shot—an empty soul.

A murderer.

Her face morphs into Paula's face, and I know my mind is messing with me now. *They're all the same.* The sum total of my life is telling me what I need to do, but the words from Paula's letter are lobbying hard: *"You are loved. Come back to me."*

My brother is closer now. His limbs knock and flail against me just like they did that horrible day from my past. He doesn't feel like a child anymore, though. It's as if he's grown. Now, he's gripping my leg, too, and we're wrestling over the rope. He wants me to let the rope remain. He wants me to stay, but I wrench his hand free and shove him away.

Once I loosen the bungee from around my foot, both legs sink, and I strain to move myself, hand-over-hand, along the bottom of the raft. The current is fighting me, pushing me back toward the direction of my brother. I'm tempted to let it carry me back to him, but instead I grab hold of the large outer tubing at the front of the raft. *Goodbye,* I think, just before I dip my head below it. *Grandma's with you...you'll be okay.* I emerge on the other side, and my face breaks through to sky and

264

sunlight, blue and new. Incredibly new. I take my first gasp of air. Noise and chaos cracks the silence.

"Puck!" Ellen screams from the embankment. She tosses me a float that's attached to a rope, and I grab it, turning onto my back and melting into submission as they pull me to them, in stops and starts.

"I still don't see her!" That voice is Nick's, and I smile lazily at his foolishness. *Why, I'm right here! I'm right in front of you!*

Finally, I'm sprawled on rocky sand. Ronnie, Quin, Titania, and Xander form a dripping canopy over me. Their hair is wet. *Did they just go swimming?*

"She's not up yet!" Dmitri shouts.

"I'll get to it, all right?" I say, between uncontrollable coughs. "Man, just give me a sec!"

"I'm going in," says Nick.

"It's too risky, Nick," says Xander. "Puck got out… she will, too."

"She's been under too long!"

"She, *who?*" I say, propping myself up on my elbows and glancing around in alarm. In a quick survey, everyone is accounted for but one.

"Barb?" I ask. The world instantly comes into focus, a hazy nightmare coalescing into perfect clarity.

"There she is!" screams Ellen, pointing to the center of the river, where the raft is still bobbing in its violent vortex. Nearby, the bright orange of a personal flotation device glides on the river's surface, smooth and graceful. Barb's head is facedown in the water. Dmitri grabs the throw-bag they'd just used to rescue me. He runs further down the riverbank, then charges toward the water, attempting to time the trajectory of Barb's body as it swiftly sails past. *'Her body'...Oh, god.* Miraculously, he reaches her, but in lifting her lifeless head from the water, it's clear that his efforts may not be miracle enough. Nick and Xander frantically set about pulling them both back in.

I am shocked senseless, teeth chattering, but with strength enough to tug on the leg of Ronnie's pants.

"What's going on?" I ask.

"The boat flipped, and we all got tossed," he explains, "but you stayed under. I saw you hook your leg in the raft. She went back in to free you."

"I didn't know." Teardrops escape my eyes and roll heavy down my cheeks. I don't even attempt to blink them back. "I didn't know it was her."

CHAPTER 17

I Won Thy Love Doing Thee Injuries

I'm the small and crafty one. The bunny that escapes through the gap in the fence. The mosquito that spreads malaria. Puny, but powerful. Trivial, but tough. What I've never, ever been is helpless. Until now.

"Don't *do* this to me, Barbie! Don't you *dare* do this!" Nick is kneeling on the ground, bent over his wife, performing chest compressions. It's something I've only seen before on TV—actors going through motions. There's a ringing in my ears that makes me wonder, *Is any of this actually real?* Horror and hope are manifest on faces. Hands sealed over disbelieving mouths or clasped behind necks in dread and apprehension.

Ellen finally grabs Nick by the shoulders and persuades him to let Xander take over the work. Relenting, the wretched spouse curls to the ground, a shaking ball of quiet sobs. Titania hastens over and drops beside him, placing her hand gently upon his back as it rises and falls with his gasps. My chest aches and I feel woozy, but I rise to standing and walk toward Barb. Mia and Dmitri are kneeling at her head, caressing her forehead and ears. Xander continues to stamp his locked arms upon her sternum, hard and fast, and I notice that her face—the one I've always identified as severe and calculating—is pale, peaceful, and dewy with dampness. Her lips, parted slightly, are purple. I try to think of something I can do—anything—but I come up blank. Only one thought sounds in my brain like a chorus of jurors: *You did this, Puck. This is because of you.*

I see Barb's leg twitch and wonder if it's a sign that her body is shutting down, but then her right fist clenches and a sound like paper ripping emanates from her throat.

"Turn her head! Get her on her side!" Xander yells, sitting back on his heels. He helps the other staffers tilt her body, and she coughs, her whole body spasming from the force. Nick is back with her in an instant, his tears dripping onto her face as he brushes aside the hair that's plastered to her forehead. Gently cradling her, he pulls her up to seating. She opens weary eyes and collapses her cheek onto his shoulder.

"My girl," he cries, rocking her in his embrace. "My sweet girl! I thought I lost you!" He gazes toward heaven and shuts his eyes tight, sending even more tears spilling down his cheeks. Barb coughs a few more times and wipes her mouth on Nick's soaked shirt.

"I'm okay, my love. I'm not going anywhere," she whispers, managing to eke out a faint smile. "But what about . . ." She lifts her head off Nick's shoulder and locks eyes with him in a sudden panic. "Puck? Where's Puck?!"

"I'm right here," I say, stepping forward. She extends one of her hands to me. I clutch it, sinking to my knees next to her. I'm crying too hard to say anything more.

* * *

Forty minutes later, Barb and I sit together, still gazing at the river. The sun is hanging low, and its orangey-pink filter contributes to the sensation that none of this is actually real. Everyone else is busy setting up camp here for the night—we'll all hike out tomorrow, Water Challenge be damned—but Barb and I haven't moved from this spot on the banks. Her ankle is swollen to the size of a softball from where her foot got trapped among the rocks after she'd gone back in for me. She's resting it on one of the backpacks to keep it elevated. One semi-dry sleeping bag is flung upon both our backs. Maybe the fact that we're both still in a state of shock explains how we're sitting here trading thoughts as easily as we're sharing the sleeping bag.

"I should have predicted what all that rain would do. I should have scouted further down the river myself. We could have waited a day. We could have hiked around that section."

"I tied myself into the boat, the very thing you warned us never to do. It would have just been a good soak and a laugh, if I had only followed the rules for once."

"It's not your fault."

"Don't. People have been telling me that my whole life, and I refuse to accept it. It was my fault then, and it's my fault now. That *stupid* grape juice…why was I so clumsy?" I can't tell if it's from the chill in the air or from the avalanche of sorrow descending upon me, but my body is shaking so hard that the memories I've spent years tamping down are ready to tumble out.

"Puck? What is this about? What's going on?"

"I spilled it," I manage to choke out through tears. "She told me to be careful, and I spilled a full cup of grape juice all over the table, the floor, my little brother." The words come haltingly, hidden fiends softly tiptoeing into the open. "She got angry, then, and she threw Shane and me in the tub. Like, *literally* threw us."

I pause, and the rest of the story piles up into a verbal traffic jam. I'm crying so hard the words won't come, but Barb is quiet, giving me the space to finish my story. I'm not sure I will, or if I even can, but after I finally catch my breath, I do. "The water was scalding. Shane was already pitching a fit, and when my mom dumped shampoo on my head, it got in my eyes and burned, and I started screaming. And that just…put her over the edge, I guess." Barb gently puts her hand on mine as I struggle through trembling staccato breaths.

"I tried to stop her. I tried to pry her arms off him, but by the time she finally let go of him, he'd been under the water too long. He was already gone." Shaking my head in defeat, I place my forehead on the top of my knees, but blacking out my vision only makes those final images worse. There are some things I will never be able to convey. "She grabbed me next, and I knew fighting wouldn't help. Then it just…stopped. She let go of me. I'll never know why, just like I'll never forget the way she looked at me right after. The faucet was still dripping, and it was…over." I feel physically ill and strangely dizzy, so I lift my head and focus my concentration on the river. Oddly enough, it has a calming effect. "He was so little," I whisper. "He was just a baby."

"So were you." Barb waits for me to respond to this, but I don't. I pull my arm away from under her hand, but she grabs it again and adds, "She wasn't in her right mind, Puck."

"Sure. She's 'sick.' That's what Grandma used to say, like having a cold or some stomach bug makes you want to drown your kids in the tub. My mom's a psycho. I wished her dead, you know," I say, glancing hesitantly in Barb's direction. "So many times. Even out here, that's what I wrote in the Earth Challenge: that I'd kill her if I could."

"How did that make you feel?"
I clench and unclench my fists in frustration, not so much with her question (for once), but with the undeniable answer. "If I'm capable of feeling that way, then I'm just like her. It's written in my DNA."

"Puck, your mother is a drug addict. But who she is and what she did is not who *you* are."

Barb's mention of my mom's addiction makes it clear that, just as I suspected, she is clued in to every detail of my past. Somehow that knowledge comforts rather than embarrasses me, but I'm still not persuaded by her words.

"You can tell me I'm nothing like her. You can say it a billion times over, but how will I know for certain it's true and not just wishful thinking?"

"Because you have a choice. We all do."

"But *how*? How do I make the right choice?" My voice quavers with both insecurity and more sincerity than I've ever mustered. If only she had the answers I'm seeking, some secret instructions for overriding my own destiny. I turn to face her, and for once, I don't look away. This time it's real. It's as though I'm back underwater, and Barb is the only one in the world who can bring me back to the living.

"Life is not a labyrinth with only one right path," she says. Choices are something you make every day. Sometimes we mess up, and sometimes we do the right thing. If your intention is to make the right choices, more often than not, you will."

"How are you so sure? You've seen the destruction I'm capable of. What if I was just born that way?"

"You want some kind of proof?" she asks, although her voice sounds as though she's somewhere else, somewhere far away.

"I guess so."

"Well, you're looking at it." She places the palm of her hand on her chest to indicate herself. I'm dumbfounded, and I'm sure my expression shows it. "If you need proof that a person can triumph over a nasty

childhood and find her way to a life that's meaningful—
even happy—then I'm it."

"What do you mean?"

Barb gingerly readjusts her outstretched leg so that
she can turn to face me more squarely.

"It's extremely unprofessional for someone in my
position to share too much personal information, and I've
never wanted this to be about me. I haven't disclosed my
past to any of the campers before—*ever*—but since you
aren't *officially* in DreamRoads anymore, I'm going to
make an exception, just this once." I feel a sudden,
inexplicable urge to stop her confession. Everything is
shifting, and I'm not sure I'm ready for that. "For starters,
I want to show you how much I trust you and believe in
your innate ability to show good judgment. Secondly, I
have to take some responsibility for things that have gone
wrong over the last several weeks. I've made more than a
few mistakes. I had all the best intentions, but I was also
incredibly stubborn. I was rougher on everyone than I
needed to be at times, my own husband included. It's
something I was reluctant to admit to myself, yet it's true.
I can see that now. I guess the truth is, I saw myself in
you."

I look up at her, shocked. "You and I have a lot more
in common than you realize, Puck."

"Like what?"

"I'm not going to go into too many details, because I don't think that's relevant, but you know the cycle of violence they talk about in therapy?"

"Uh-huh," I nod.

"Well, I know it intimately, because I was born into it. Both my parents weren't only neglectful; they were downright abusive. I've come to a place of forgiveness with them as I learned more about their own childhoods. But more importantly, I've come to a place of forgiveness with myself. I've found a purpose, and no matter what happened in my past, I know that I have *earned* the life I have now, and I'm grateful for that."

"I want to do that, too. I really do." I can hear the desperation in my voice. "But where do I start?"

"You can start by allowing the people who care about you to help you. You don't have to do this alone."

"You mean Paula?"

"Yes, Puck. I mean Paula. And I mean me." Then Barb does the most surprising thing of all. She puts her arm around my shoulder for a hug, and I burst into tears. But this time, the tears aren't from frustration or grief; they're tears of relief and, for the first time ever, hope.

* * *

It's against camp protocol to set up our sleeping bags in a circle around the campfire, but not even Barb balks at the idea of falling asleep under the stars tonight. After the day we've had, it seems pointless to pitch tents. There's also an unspoken sense that no one is willing to retreat to his or her respective hidey-holes after what almost happened—what could have happened—during the Water Challenge. There's safety and comfort in being out here with everyone else. Just as we've shed the tents that were our barriers against nature, the invisible and meaningless barriers between us have vanished now, too. Under the twinkling expanse of the universe, all our sins, mistakes, and failings have made themselves scarce. Tonight, we're not the bad kids. We're just kids. Kids who need each other.

The sound of the nearby river coursing through the darkness doesn't unnerve me, nor does the brisk, black night. The fire is only embers now, and darkness has stolen almost all of my vision, save for the lights dotting the sky by the thousands. I rustle into a more comfortable position in my sleeping bag and gaze at them all, finally understanding what the word *starstruck* really means. I feel exposed, yet thrilled, and I take a deep breath of the fresh night air. It finally feels like there's room in my lungs to let my chest expand fully. I let my body rise and fall, calmly, and as the white noise of the rushing river floods my ears, a voice chimes in. It's soft at first, humming a tune that sounds familiar to me but that I can't quite place. Then, after a few bars, lyrics begin to drift skyward. The sound is pure—almost angelic—and I'm startled to realize that it's Titania I'm hearing, completely devoid of her self-indulgent swagger.

Sleep, my child, and peace attend thee,
All through the night.
Guardian angels God will send thee,
All through the night.

A memory of the song, buried deep in my past, surfaces. My birth mom is brushing my hair back from my face and looking into my eyes. Her expression is clear and sane, and it's filled with love.

Soft the drowsy hours are creeping,
Hill and dale in slumber sleeping,
I my loved ones' watch am keeping,
All through the night.

Is the memory real, or is it simply one my mind created for me? It almost doesn't matter. As Titania's lullaby gently wings its way through the night, an unfamiliar peace settles over me. I close my eyes and drift closer to my dreams, trailed by one small, sleepy spark of thought: Perhaps what I choose to hang on to can be just as important as everything I have been struggling to let go of.

CHAPTER 18

The True Beginning of Our End

So here we are, eight salvaged souls loitering on a dirt road that dead-ends around a bend half a mile down, at base camp. Nick joins us, walkie-talkie in hand. Its occasional static and crackle are fitting background noise for how we're all feeling: wired.

"I can't wait to go home and see my cats," says Frances, fanning dewy eyes with frantic fingers. "And my friends. And I know it's going to freak my Waspy mother the hell out when I see her in a few minutes, but I feel hugs coming on."

"I may just plant a big wet one on her. She sounds kind of foxy from all your descriptions."

"Don't be such a stain, Peabo!"

"Relax. I'm not hunting cougars today," he continues. "I fully expect that my girl Chastity is going to be down there to meet me."

"The quote-unquote girlfriend?" Snout says. "This ought to be good."

"How many times do I have to tell you people? She *exists!* Man, I liked you better when you were the mental equivalent of a meatball."

"My parents won't even recognize me," says Titania. "I'm sure I resemble the Bride of Sasquatch." Upon examining the dead ends of her tangled long white hair, she looks up and studies me just as thoughtfully.

"What are you looking at?" I say, perched on the edge of defensiveness.

"Nothing that concerns you," she replies, startled out of her reverie. "You know, you're lucky the DreamRoad has enlightened me, or I'd still be annoyed with you for abandoning the show. However, I've processed it, as Barb would say, and I've come to understand that not all of us are born for stardom." A garbled voice issues from amidst the static of Nick's walkie-talkie. He listens, rogers back, then addresses Titania.

"Speaking of showtime, Tonya, you're on," he says, motioning for her to proceed down the road.

"Me?"

"Yes, you! Start jogging, and don't stop till you get to the finish line!"

"I can't believe this is actually, finally happening!"
She offers the rest of us a catch-ya-later grin, spins on her
heels, and sets off in a run down the road.

"Nobody's ever going to believe I spent six weeks
with her," Quin says. We watch the celebrity disappear
from view where the road curves behind a hill, and then he
turns to face me. "Why *aren't* you doing the show,
anyway?"

"Have we really only been out here six weeks? Wow,
it seems like so much longer."

"Don't change the subject."

"It wouldn't seem right," I finally answer, shrugging.
"I'd feel like a sham being onstage with the rest of you
considering…well, I'm *leaving*, yes, but I'm not actually
graduating. I sort of got kicked out."
Quin's eyes widen in disbelief.

"You didn't do anything *that* bad out here. Did you?"

"I probably shouldn't get into it right now, but I'll tell
you all about it some day. I promise."

"I hear the big guy over there—" he gestures toward
Nick, "is going to be your understudy. It's one thing
having featherweight *you* stand on my back, but if he does
it, I am going to be the Yellow Brick Road with internal
hemorrhaging."

"Is that actual sarcasm coming out of your mouth? You know, you're, like, a *thousand* times cooler than you were when we first met, and I think I should get partial credit for that." We watch Nissa peel off from the group toward the rest of her life. Nick receives yet another update from base camp.

"Quin, you're up!" he says. Visibly tensing, Quin pushes his glasses higher up the bridge of his nose, exhales, and forces a smile.

"My uncle's here, I guess."

"Go on, then." I give him a hard slap on the shoulder, the way you'd start a horse running. Frances gets called a few minutes later, and then Snout. He takes off in a skip, flapping his arms like a chicken-strutting Mick Jagger.

"Tom, Snout…whatever his name is, I'm going to miss that nutjob," I tell Ronnie. He is reclining on the ground against a nearby tree. "Bet you can't wait to finally see your little brother again." He ignores my remark.

"Catch you on the flip side!" he yells to Peabo, who takes off following Snout.

"You better start limbering up," I say, prodding him with the toe of my hiking boot. He doesn't budge. "Why aren't you more excited? You finally made it!"
He shakes his head.

"Nope."

I eye him like he's nuts. "But you *did*," I say, leaning closer so that Nick won't hear us. "So what if you used a lighter to get your fire started? That's our secret."

"Not really. I came clean to Barb two days ago, after the rainstorm."

"God damn it, Ronnie!"

"Cool your freakin' jets; I didn't sell you out."

"That's not what I'm mad about! I don't care if she knows I used the lighter—I've already forfeited anyway."

"Then why are you getting so steamed?"

"You still think he'd be better off without you, don't you? Your little brother, I mean."

Ronnie scratches the side of his neck that's branded with the crown tattoo, then deliberately cracks his knuckles. "You chickened out," I continue. "You're a coward. Look, I understand that it can feel safer to stay out here. I'm scared about going back to the real world, too. But I'm not scared of *you*. You're not the sort of person who hurts people anymore. And how could you do this to Eddie? He needs you! I gave you that lighter so you could get back to him!"

"I can't get back to him, Puck. My auntie—his guardian—she's done with me. She's not having it anymore. I'm not allowed back, and I'm not allowed to see him. Letters, maybe. Phones calls? If I'm lucky."

"What?" I half gasp the word.

"I don't blame her. She took Eddie and me when we had nobody else, but I've messed up too much. Like I said, she's done, and she's requested that I keep my distance. When I leave here, I'm not sure where I'll end up —in the system like you, I guess."

I inhale again, sharply.

"The fact that I haven't graduated yet is a simple kindness on Barb's part, to keep me from . . ." He doesn't finish his thought. "Anyway, in four months, I turn eighteen. She says we'll reassess then. I try not to think about it."

We both stare at Peabo jogging away from us in the distance.

"Making us run to the finish line?" I scoff. "Stupid theatrics and metaphors, right up to the end."

"Not really," he says, shrugging. "I've witnessed plenty of graduation days before this one, Puck. It means something. When it's finally *my* turn, it's going to be *real*. And not because I conned the system."

"The lighter, you mean? Yeah," I sigh. "I guess I kind of wished I hadn't cheated."

"In the end, you didn't, though. The way you confessed to Barb about poisoning the counselors."

"That's an *extreme* way of describing what actually happened, but—"

"Whatever. The word *integrity* never meant much to me, until then. You didn't *have* to tell her. You never would have gotten caught."

"Watch it, dude," I say, beginning to catch his vibe. "I am *not* morality's poster child. If anything, I'm on its Most Wanted list." I'm about to blast him for being ridiculously sentimental—what is this, some sappy ABC Family series?—when Nick interrupts again.

"Puck!"

"Yeah?"

"You're up."

"Huh? No," I stammer. "I don't think Barb is cool with me doing the victory lap."

"I just heard from her—" He lifts the walkie-talkie in his fist. "And she says you're next. You know what she's like when she doesn't get her way, so help a guy out."

I look left, then right, seeking clarification from the desert weeds, if not from Nick or Ronnie. *Beats me*, Mother Nature seems to say. Okay, then. I contemplate the road ahead of me but turn back to Nick.

"I hear you're filling in for me tonight?" He nods an assent. "I hope I get to see it. I know you think you're better in supporting roles, but I am absolutely certain you will knock 'em dead."

"Oh, boy," he says, frowning. "Leaving kids' cadavers strewn all over the stage? I'd better tell Barb to up our liability insurance." He examines my face for any sign I might have appreciated the joke. "Aha—I saw it. You smiled; I saw it! Have I finally vanquished the great stone-faced one?!"

"I'll never be able to think about you without laughing. Wait, that came out wrong."

"I take it as the highest compliment," he says. Uncertain what else to say and feeling a touch embarrassed, I head off down the road at a trot.

I'm not a runner. I used to brat myself to the principal's office at Fifth Bell just to avoid having to do laps in gym class, which was kind of ridiculous, looking back. This whole running thing isn't really so bad. In fact, it's kind of exhilarating. Or maybe it's just that all the ditch-digging and hauling ass up and down mountains I've accomplished in the last two months has left me feeling like the end product in a *Rocky* training montage.

I shift my legs into second gear. The sun is warm, but the air is cool as it speeds past my face. The combination of these two sensations leaves me feeling pleasantly prickly, a phrase that reminds me of the camaraderie I've shared with my fellow campers. Maybe you'd expect a massive onslaught of positive feelings at the end of a journey like this, but that's not quite how I'd describe it. None of it is as pretty and perfect as all that. It more boils down to the fact that we know each other. We know how to get a laugh—or a rise—from one another. We've shed tears together, sometimes in legitimate pain, but far more often from crying with laughter over inside jokes spawned in hours of boredom. I can't wait to ditch them all, but I'm not sure how to live without them, either.

Spiky yucca plants border the dirt road like pom-poms lining a parade route. In the distance, to my left, the majestic plateau of rock and wilderness stands solid, and yet I can almost imagine it crumbling like a sandcastle as soon as it's out of my sight. It's an absurd thought, but one that leaves me irrationally wistful. Chatter—not from birds, but honest-to-god *human* chatter—sings on the breeze as I round the corner. Heading into the straightaway, I see a smattering of twenty-five or thirty people, which constitutes a mob scene to me these days. Everyone is clapping and pumping fists in the air, and with a faltering step, I turn to glance backward. This can't possibly be for me. Judging by all of their smiles and screams of encouragement, it's pretty obvious that Barb is ushering me out by way of the standard "rah-rah" ritual rather than having to explain me, the random saboteur who almost (accidentally) killed off her staff. This is

287

clearly a "spray-paint the dead grass green" sort of thing, and I guess I'm okay with that. After yesterday, I sort of owe my life to Barb. Going along with the gag is the least I can do for her.

Extending both arms horizontally, I slap obligatory high fives with the camp counselors, who are flanking me on both sides, a gesture that leaves me feeling like an Olympic sprinter finally crossing the finish line. But this is no finish line, and, in fact, it feels much more like a concrete wall when I almost collide with two familiar but unexpected faces.

"What's going on?" My tone could be mistaken for a casual, "Hey, what's up?" greeting, but I shuffle my feet backward, guarded. (When is anyone finally going to understand that I don't do well with surprises?)

"Hi, Puck," says Ted. His smile is tight and nervous. Next to him, Paula simply bursts into tears and rushes forward. I allow her to wrap her arms around the stone pillar of my body. Eventually releasing her lengthy squeeze, she draws back and grabs my face in both her hands to have a better look at me. My emotions are mobbing the exit doors of my psyche, and I don't think I'll be able to hold them back. I desperately scan the small crowd and am relieved to lock eyes with Barb, who is leaning on a pair of crutches.

"Hey, Barb! Nick wanted me to tell you something!" I spare one more awkward glance for Paula and Ted. "Will you guys wait right here for a sec?"

Barb and I powwow about ten feet away while everyone else drums up more congratulatory applause and hoots for the last camper heading for home: Ronnie.

"I don't get this. Why is she here? Why are *they* here?"

"Where else would they be?" Barb answers, appearing mystified.

"Doesn't she know that I'm not graduating?" I whisper. "She said I had to, if I wanted to come home."

"She's aware of the circumstances."

"But that was the condition, and now she's *here*."

"So what does that tell you? Even at your worst, you have worth. You are loved."

I shake off this comment, unwilling to accept it. "You shouldn't have made me jog in. It feels like getting one of those stupid 'participation' ribbons, when we both know I don't deserve any big honors."

"It was about celebrating the journey and how far you've come. In the end, maybe this program wasn't a good fit for you, but it doesn't mean you didn't accomplish things out here." I eye her dubiously, so she continues. "After all, you completed the Stepping Stones in your own *unique* way."

"Then there's me almost getting you and your staff killed."

"I'm not saying there weren't hiccups."

"Do you think they actually want me to come back and live with them?" Paula and Ted are eyeing us expectantly from fifteen feet away, like uber-fans waiting by the backstage door. "Do I have to? Do you think I should?"

"I can't write the future for you, Puck. Only you can do that. You should know that the outside world hasn't necessarily changed while you were away. Things won't magically be the way you might want them to be, and it would be naive to think that all is mended. But I think you *have* changed. You're stronger now. I can vouch for that."

"What if she ends up marrying Ted, and it's a total nightmare?"

"What do *you* think?" No conversation with Barb is complete until she turns the table on you.

"I can't control what other people do," I say hesitantly, "but I *can* control what *I* do—how I react to whatever life throws my way. So, I guess whether or not I would be okay is up to me."

"I can see that they're anxious to reconnect. Maybe this is something you should be talking with them about."

* * *

We're seated at folding tables covered in blue-and-white-checkered plastic tablecloths, and the conversations run the gamut from silly to stilted. I think we all feel, more or less, like we've just woken from a long, crazy dream. Certain things seem familiar, but so much feels different and rusty, and I'm grateful to still have the other kids nearby to help diffuse the general weirdness of being with Paula and Ted again. There are going to be some long and difficult conversations ahead of us, but right now, I'm trying to just enjoy the late-afternoon sunshine, the grilled hot dogs, and the potato chips—all we can eat.

Titania is seated across from me with her parents, who have exactly the sort of fake tans and veneer smiles I expected them to have. They're joined by her manager—a slight man with a receding hairline—who is filling her in on potential Hollywood opportunities.

"From a publicity standpoint, the All-Star game this weekend will be a favorable venue to reintroduce you. Sing the anthem, leave through the dugout, a 'no time for press' sort of thing," he says. "From there, we can get you back into the studio for some new sessions."

"What about acting? I told you six months ago it was something I wanted to pursue."

"Yeah, about that. I'm not exactly sure any studio would want to insure you at this point."

"I'll start with small cameo roles. You could video the show we're performing tonight as part of my reel; I don't care."

"Sweetheart," her mother says with a patronizing smile, "monetarily speaking, maybe we should just focus on your music. You're selling like gangbusters in Asia, so we thought maybe a Japanese-language album would—"

"I don't want to speak 'monetarily,' Mother! Or Japanese, either!" Though I can tell she doesn't want to, Titania is starting to lose her cool. I remember Barb's warning earlier, about how we may have changed, but the rest of the world hasn't. When Titania's mom decides to press the music issue, I grab a hot dog bun from the opened plastic bag in the middle of our table, set it against my plastic fork, and catapult it toward the pop star. The bun drops in a perfect thud on her plate. I glance at her parents and give them my attempt at an adorable grin.

"We've recently weaned Tonya back on to carbs," I say. They both look horrified, but Titania bursts into relief-tinged laughter.

"Puck," says Paula quietly, her voice bordering on disappointment.

"It's okay. Getting beaned with bread products is all a part of my recovery," Titania assures her. She picks up the bun and takes a bite, adding in muffled chews, "Mmm-mmm!"

At the table behind her, Peabo is seated with his parents and girlfriend. (He wasn't overplaying it. She looks like a model, and the way she's Velcroed herself to him, you could argue that love really *is* blind.) Next to them, Nissa and Snout's families are chatting it up, while Quin is deep in conversation with an older man who is greying at the temples. They look so much alike that I could be watching Quin talk to his future self.

"I really thought his mom and dad would have changed their minds," says Frances, who is watching Quin, too. She's seated at the end of our table with her mom and little brother, whose head has been buried in some handheld video game for most of the cookout. "I wish they'd have come."

"What's she talking about?" says Paula, leaning in for clarification.

"His parents didn't show," I explain.

"Oh, that poor thing," she says. "I can't imagine."

"He's okay," I assure her, hoping it's the truth. "His uncle looks like a nice guy, anyway."

Ronnie is helping Nick man the grill, and I'm glad he's being distracted from the fact that the rest of us have families to reconnect with.

"So, Puck, Ted and I need to talk with you about the wedding," Paula says when the rest of the table has emptied out. "I know I had asked you to be my maid of honor, but a couple of weeks ago, we made the decision to do something quick and easy at city hall."

"Wait, you mean you're already married? But you were so excited about the ceremony and a big reception," I say, confused at the strange blend of emotions I'm feeling. "What about your inspiration board? What about the dress you'd picked out?"

"We'll have a party at some point," Ted says, "but Polly and I thought maybe simpler would be better."

I can't believe how dense I am. Of course they wouldn't want me to stand at the altar with them in front of their friends and family after what I did. And in paying to send me here, how could they possibly afford it, anyway?

"Why are you here?" I finally ask, my voice quavering. "All I've ever done is ruin your lives. You shouldn't have come. You should just go be happy and start a perfect little family, without me. God, Ted, I don't know how you can even stand to look at me, let alone sit here acting all chipper, as if all is forgiven."

"I *do* forgive you, Puck."

"That's what families do," Paula adds gently.

"I'm not even your kid!" I say. "I'm faulty merchandise. You're allowed to return me, you know!"

"Return you? You're not some broken toaster, babe. You're the best thing that ever happened to me!" Paula's statement seems so illogical that I cannot even form a response to it.

"I didn't even know kids could get kicked out of a place like this—it's like getting kicked out of jail—but somehow, I managed. I couldn't even complete the program like you asked of me. That was your one condition."

"And you thought we would just abandon you if you didn't?" Paula says, sounding incredulous. "Puck, we love you—unconditionally. I'll admit, the last year has been a challenging one, and I was disheartened when Barb phoned us a few days ago to tell us it wasn't working out here with you. I had really hoped this place would help you, and frankly, I think maybe I was a little misguided. What could a group of strangers give you that I couldn't? I should have known this wouldn't be right for you, so we'll just keep trying to—"

"It's not like that," I say. "This experience is exactly what I needed. You sacrificed so much—more than I deserved—for this. I fought it every step of the way, and I'd be lying if I said it wasn't hard. It was horrific, really, but I wouldn't trade a minute of it. Yeah, I botched things, big-time, but being out here has opened my eyes to…well, everything, I guess. I've left ghosts out there—" I jab my finger in the air, pointing to the landscape surrounding us. "And I know this all probably sounds like a load of…well, it probably seems like I'm only saying what I think you want to hear. If you're willing to give me another chance —if a kid like me could really be so lucky—then I'll make it up to you both. I promise you, that's the truth. I don't want to be a liar anymore."

Before they can actually respond to my heartfelt proclamation, Nissa and Frances are by my side, hoisting me off the folding chair.

"Girl, you are never going to believe your eyes," says Nissa. "You've got to come see what Titania just did!"

CHAPTER 19

Is All Our Company Here?

Entering the bunk room of Cinderblock City, I clasp my hand over my mouth.

"Holy crud, what did you *do*?!" I ask.

Holding a pair of scissors—god only knows how she obtained them—Titania runs her hands through her hair. Or, I should say, what's left of it.

"Like it?"

"Your parents are going to freak."

"I know." She raises her brows and grins. "It's my new look. A pixie cut, but more messy and bed-heady. Like yours!"

Short, feathery tufts of platinum stand at attention on her head, growing from roots of dishwater brown where the color has grown out.

"It's different," I say, at a loss for any more-inspired adjective.

"Exactly. They think they can reinvent me? Well, I'll reinvent myself, on my *own* terms." She picks at a few spiky wisps on her forehead. "I can already see what you're thinking: Trainwreck Titania is back. Don't worry; it's just a haircut. Only, I sort of feel like I can handle anything with this hair. It gives me strength. It's my way of saying, 'PUCK YOU!' to anyone who tries to stand in my way."

"I love it. I really do." I'm not quite sure this is the truth, but a quick gut-check tells me it's the right thing to say. And though she looks, in part, like she lost an epic battle with head lice, her features are thrown into sharp relief on her face. Her eyes are self-possessed and certain. There's not a trace of high-maintenance bimbo left in the girl.

"I need those scissors back, T," Ronnie interrupts, poking his head around the doorway. When he sees her, his mouth gapes. "What the...? You look a dandelion that's gone to seed."

"Do you want me to hand these to you or throw them at you?" she asks, holding up the scissors.

"I didn't say I didn't like it," he says. Uncharacteristically, Ronnie can't seem to look Titania squarely in the face. "It's just that I'm pretty sure the last

298

thing somebody like you needs is a reminder of how gorgeous she is."

"Well, thank you for the ego check, but *I'm* pretty sure that's the last thing *you'd* ever tell me."

"I don't say a lot of things." He shrugs, eyes cast downward. "That doesn't mean I don't think them."

Slowly, Titania hands him the scissors, visibly flustered.

"Why do you have a toilet-lid cover, Ronnie?" I ask. He's clutching a circular piece of bath-mat material in a color any department store would likely describe as "Goldenrod."

"It's part of my costume," he says, setting to work cutting the bulky fabric.

Quin enters the room with the yellow-rug counterpart to Ronnie's potty cozy pinned to the front of his torso.

"Found the garbage bags," he says, tossing the small box to Titania. "Nick says it's ten minutes to showtime."

"I didn't get to meet your uncle yet, but he looks pretty nice," I tell Quin.

"Uncle?" he says, perplexed. "Oh, that's right," he continues. "You missed it, because you came in after me. That's not my uncle; that's my dad!"

"Seriously? I thought your folks were hitting the delete button on you."

"Me, too. Apparently Barb called and lobbied them on my behalf. My mom's not here because she had to take my sister to a recital this weekend. Or so Dad says; I'm not sure I really buy it. But *he's* here, anyway. And I get to go home."

"That's great. I'm glad he reconsidered," I say.

"Yeah. You could too, you know. About doing the show, I mean. There are still approximately nine minutes and thirteen seconds before showtime."

"Approximately," I say, mocking him. "I've already told you; it wouldn't feel right. I'm not graduating."

"Neither am I," Ronnie interrupts, glancing up from crafting his costume, "and this is my third show."

"Yeah, but you're still technically in the program; I'm not. It's different. Besides, I think Nick is really excited about filling in for me. Who am I to take that away from him?"

Titania has started unspooling black plastic trash bags from the roll when Nick enters the room, followed by Nissa, Snout, and Frances.

"Is everybody here?" he asks. "Where's our Scarecrow?"

"He probably can't tear himself away from that girlfriend of his," I say. "I'll go out and let him know he's being paged. Break a leg, everyone! I can't wait to see the show!"

* * *

Paula, Ted, and I are sitting in the second row of an improvised mini amphitheater outfitted with folding chairs and picnic benches. I'll start by saying that, minus the five-o'clock shadow he's sporting, Nick is hardly less believable onstage playing a wholesome fifteen-year-old girl from Kansas than I would have been. Having fashioned a dress, of sorts, from one of the blue-and-white-checkered tablecloths leftover from the cookout, he's also got two long white-blonde braids (Titania's "Locks of Love") affixed to his bushy brown hair by way of clothespins.

"*C'mon, boy! Good dog!*" he exclaims onstage in a comic falsetto voice. Snout lurches forward and sniffs him, letting Nick tousle his hair appreciatively. "*My, what a lovely day in Middle America!*" he adds, gaping at the sky.

They are sitting in front of a large box fan, and offstage, Quin plugs the ends of two extension cords together to set the machine whirring. "*Strike that*," yells Nick. "*A twister! It's a twister!*" He and Snout stand up, spinning and swaying in an outlandish interpretive dance that seems to go on forever. Nick finally motions for Quin to cut power to the fan. When the rotary blades drone to a stop, Dorothy and Toto jump once, in unison, landing on their feet in a dramatic thud.

"*Toto,*" Nick says, surveying the faces in the audience with exaggerated uncertainty. "*I* don't *think we're in Kansas anymore.*" The line elicits soft chuckles from those seated around me.

"Judy Garland, eat your heart out," Ted whispers. I nod, smiling. (Okay, sure, he can be a little dorky, but what Dad-type isn't when you really think about it?)

Running in from stage right, Quin awkwardly attempts a headfirst slide, skidding on his stomach in front of Dorothy and her dog. He remains perfectly still on the ground when Titania appears in a witch's costume made entirely of trash bags, including a flowing cape and one tied with dramatic flair on her head like a turban. Joining her is Frances, who has sprouted wings jimmy-rigged from posterboard. She is standing in profile to the stage, holding a banana in one hand and a flashlight in the other.

"*Interloper!*" Titania screams, approaching Dorothy. Nick cowers dramatically, Snout barks like he's rabid, and Frances brandishes her banana at him, screeching.

"Oh, dear," murmurs Paula. "I take it she's a flying monkey?"

"Yep. But just wait," I whisper. A moment later, Frances jumps one hundred and eighty degrees to face Titania. She throws her banana offstage and flips on her flashlight, which is now in her upstage hand.

"Line!" she calls out, looking slightly stumped. From the floor, Quin cranes his neck toward her.

"Back off, you shrew," he prompts her. (Quin has everyone's lines memorized, naturally.)

"That's right! *Back off, you shrew!*" she tells the Wicked Witch in a folksy twang. Inching backward toward Nick, she accidentally bumps him in the face with her cardboard wings. "*This sweet young child is in Oz under my protection.*" She waves her flashlight around his face in concentric circles, prompting Nick's eyes to blink manically.

"I don't get it," says Paula under her breath. "Why is the flying monkey talking?"

"She's Glinda, too," I whisper.

"Okaaay."

As cornball a production as this is, Titania owns the stage as she squares off with Frances. "*This is* my *'hood, you vapid beauty queen,*" she proclaims in the sort of high-and-mighty tone she used to have at camp. "*Now give me the shoes!*"

"*Puh-leeease, girl,*" sighs Frances. "*Dorothy ain't got time for fancy footwear! She just wants to go home; don't you get it? Get out of here, before somebody drops a house on you!*"

"*Aaaack! Airborne real estate!*" Titania flinches and glances above her head as she says this, then cackles and zooms offstage with the broom she'd borrowed from the supply closet.

"*See ya! Wouldn't want to be ya!*" Frances shouts after her, before turning to Dorothy and offering her a hammy wink.

"*Thank you, beautiful fairy lady!*" says Nick, looking more oafish than naive.

"*Not a prob,*" she replies. "*Now, to get home, you could use GPS, but it'll just take you the long route. I suggest you follow this yellow brick road, instead.*" With her foot, she kicks Quin, and he barrel-rolls from his stomach to his back, exposing the yellow bathroom rug pinned to his front. Collective "aaahs" sound from the audience.

* * *

In Act Two, Dorothy and Toto meet up with the Scarecrow and Tin Man. Peabo has stuffed some fire kindling up the sleeves of his shirt and has the words *Highly Flammable* written in black marker on a swath of masking tape running across his shirt. Nissa appears wearing a metal spaghetti strainer on her head and holding spatulas for hands.

"Can you help me find my way home, Scarecrow?" Dorothy asks.

"No can do," Peabo shrugs. *"I don't have a brain."*

"Nonsense! Those are horrible words with which to describe yourself. Pathological self-criticism is not the answer."

"If you're looking for answers, you're asking the wrong heap o' hay, lady. I'm so dumb, I fail public-opinion surveys." He pauses, waiting for the audience's laughter to subside. *"I'm so dumb, I submitted a patent for non-stick glue. I'm so dumb, I brought a ladder to my first day of high school."* When this last line fails to get a chuckle from the audience, Peabo breaks character and addresses Nick. "I told you no one would get that one."

"Your IQ woes are trivial, Straw Man," interrupts Nissa. *"What about my issues? I am doomed to a life of loneliness. I will rust away like some old bucket of bolts with only cats for company, all because of a faulty ticker."*

She taps her chest, and Ronnie advances onstage, growling and snarling with the latch-hook toilet-lid cover encircling his face like a mane. "*See*," Nissa continues, gesturing to him. "*This feral cat probably senses how desperate and dateless I am. It's happening already.*"

"*This is no cat. It's a brutish, horrible lion!*" says Nick in his girly voice.

"*Dang straight, I am!*" Ronnie roars (pretty believably, in fact) and flexes his muscles.

"*But I am in no way afraid of it,*" Dorothy adds.

"*You're not? Oh, snap!*" Ronnie sinks to his heels in defeat. "*It's been this way ever since I was neutered! Please don't hurt me or spray me with a squirt bottle!*" Dorothy sighs and tosses up her hands.

"*In terms of self-esteem issues, you three are real pieces of work*," Nick says, "*but if you want to come along with me, I'm trying to find my way home. What do ya say?*"

Linking arms, they skip offstage together, with Toto following behind. Quin lifts his head from the ground and yells, "Intermission!"

"Well?" I say, turning to Paula and Ted.

"They're very impassioned," says Ted, tactfully, "though Dorothy could probably use a shave."

"I kept really wanting to laugh, but I wasn't always sure if I was supposed to," Paula says.

"It's not Shakespeare," I assure her. Behind us Mia, Xander, Dmitri, and Ellen are sitting on the picnic table, their feet resting on its attached bench seat as if they're hanging out in the bleachers. They look chatty and happy —no hint of the angsty aloofness that was on display twenty-four hours ago, and I've got to wonder if my efforts yesterday helped smooth some of their romantic wrinkles. (Not that I'm banking on a double wedding in their future, or anything. I'm not *that* good.)

Act Three hurries toward the play's conclusion in typical bizarre and bumbling fashion. I'm half-relieved and half-disappointed that I'm not part of the theatrical train wreck in progress, but there's no denying that Nick can charm an audience. And even though I know all the gags and funny lines ahead of time, there's something almost magical about watching it play out for real as giddy moths swoop and circle in the stage light. Mingled among the laughter, there's a solemnity here, too, a distilled sense of perspective beneath the backdrop of a watchful moon. I feel a sense of excitement building with the knowledge that Titania's pivotal death scene is about to occur.

Nick tosses a bucket of "water" (ripped-up pieces of paper) on her, and I wait for her to shriek and slowly shrivel to the floor as she'd done a million times before in rehearsals. Instead, she just stands there with her hands on her hips, glaring at him. Quin is still lying on the ground. He's watching Titania as if this unexpected detour is no big surprise.

"*Imposter!*" Titania screams. Ronnie and Nissa step forward and unhook the clothespins holding Nick's braids in place. They display them to the audience, gasping in shock. "*This is not Dorothy,*" Titania continues, circling him accusingly. Peabo divests Nick of his blue gingham tablecloth dress, which comes off in one yank, revealing his regular camp clothes underneath. Titania points the business end of her broom at Nick and makes sounds like a laser gun. Nick clutches his throat and spins in a circle, his eyes bulging from their sockets.

"*Alas! Alas! Alas!*" he cries. "*You have discovered my ruse! I am not who I claimed to be, despite having portrayed the role in a most credible and inspired fashion!*"

The audience is laughing, but I'm just confused. This wasn't at all like we'd been practicing for the last few weeks. Frances jumps around the stage in her wings, bellowing like a monkey, then finally throws her banana straight at Nick's head. He falls to the ground and convulses on the floor for several minutes as the audience continues to lap up his over-the-top antics.

"*He's dead,*" says Peabo. He nudges Nick with the toe of his boot, which sends the great goofus gyrating across the floor in a few more seconds of his comic swan song. He finally comes to a rest on his back, his face turned to the audience to reveal his crossed eyes and his tongue dangling from the side of his mouth.

"Now *he's dead,*" Peabo clarifies. I would laugh, if I weren't still totally baffled by this unexpected turn of events.

"*But where is our* real *Dorothy?*" Frances pans her flashlight across the audience, searchingly. The audience waits and wonders expectantly as the light dances over faces in the crowd, until finally it lands directly upon me.

"*There she is!*" shout all of the players onstage in unison.

My heart is racing, but before I have a chance to react, Titania and Ronnie are standing right in front of me, tugging gently on both my arms.

"No. I can't," I say. Though I'm protesting, I rise to my feet, casting my eyes about uncertainly until they finally land on Barb, who's sitting a few rows away. She smiles at me and raises her eyebrows expectantly. *It's up to you,* she seems to say. Making my way to center stage feels like sleepwalking. It's not clear what is happening as Titania and Ronnie position me on my mark. I glance at them and the other kids, confused.

"I don't know what to say."

"It doesn't matter," answers Titania. "You're one of us."

"But we're completely off-script," I stammer, turning to Quin for guidance. He shrugs.

"So what?" says Ronnie. "You're supposed to be here."

I turn and face the audience, which is backlit by the floodlight shining from the side porch of Cinderblock City —the one that's illuminating the stage. As a result, I can't really see any faces in the crowd, only a quiet, collective anonymity that's waiting for me to set the world spinning once more. In the gentle, familiar sounds of night I sense a calm but unrelenting whisper. *He's right,* it says. *Ronnie is absolutely right.* A shiver washes over me. I fold my arms over my chest and speak.

"I'm not an actress," I say, addressing the darkened silhouettes. "Not like Titania or 'Dead Dorothy,' here." I point to Nick, who's still sprawled on the floor. His eyelids are closed all but a sliver. "Even Toto—some of you may know him as Tom; we affectionately refer to him as Snout—trust me when I say this kid deserves an

Oscar." The other kids onstage laugh knowingly as I continue. "I used to be pretty good at pretending to be someone, playing a shadow of myself projected big and dark on a wall. I acted like I didn't care, like I wasn't afraid of anything. That was all a lie. See, I may not be an actress, but I'm a *really* good liar."

The audience is silent, suspended in front of me. "I thought that by lying, I could make my life what I wanted it to be, but when you live that way, it's like living a dream. We all know it's impossible to control your dreams once you fall asleep. Or your nightmares, for that matter. If you want to tell your own story, you've got to wake up." I'm trying to remember what my actual lines are—the ones we rehearsed for weeks—but my mouth seems to be working independently of my brain.

"I used to hate Glinda for making Dorothy go through all those trials in Oz instead of just telling her from the get-go that she could tap her heels and go home. It seemed like such a con job. I see it differently now. For years, I've searched for the shortcut, some instant heel-click to happiness. The world owed me that much, I thought, especially after everything it took from me."

I can feel my chin start to tremble and want nothing more than to just run offstage and keep running, back into the safety and simplicity of the wilderness. But then I

311

think of Paula watching me, and it gives me the strength to continue. "I'm so happy to have a home that I can go back to, with two people who, against all common sense, are willing to give me another chance. It's more than I could ever ask for. I only wish I had earned it the right way, by doing the work and fixing what's wrong inside me— what's *still* so broken. But second chances are hard to come by in life, and I know it's too late for a do-over. Still, I'd give anything to rewind this summer journey—all of it —and take advantage of the help so many people have been trying to offer me. To all those people, and you know who you are, I'm sorry. If I could do it all again, I know I'd do it right."

I quietly walk back into the audience and take my seat on the picnic bench between Paula and Ted, and Paula digs through her purse and hands me a tissue. I gratefully accept it, and when she places her arm around my shoulder and squeezes me toward her, I am comforted, but scared. Scared that I will never actually deserve it.

CHAPTER 20

If You Pardon, We Will Mend

I can't think of any rite of passage in the world more boring than a graduation ceremony, which is why I'm relieved that Nick and Barb have dispensed with the formalities in honoring the six campers who have successfully completed the program. Apart from the flimsy paper diploma they each accept as they stride across the same stage we used for the play, it's really not ceremonial at all. Instead, Barb, Nick, and the four counselors take turns sharing their favorite memories and anecdotes of their time with the graduates, prompting cackles of knowing laughter (and frequent clarifications) from the campers in question.

"I asked Barb for an *emery board*, not a nail file," explains Titania, her cheeks turning pink. "Why is that so funny? I thought she'd have one in the first aid kit. It was a nail emergency!"

It's like one of those reunion shows at the conclusion of a reality series, but without all the name-calling and hostility. We finally discover that Quin—not his tent mate, Snout, as we'd all assumed—was responsible for snoring every night like an asthmatic warthog. Following repeated pleas, Peabo demonstrates the weird extremes of his double-jointedness for old time's sake, and Frances rattles off her names for the multiple cuss-word rocks she accumulated over the course of the journey. (Snug, Randy, Tinker, Mojo, Jasper, and Frisco McGillicuddy.)

Sitting in the audience, Ronnie and I occasionally chime in, too, never being made to feel like what we actually are: the two duds who didn't quite make it. Though part of me feels content sandwiched between Paula and Ted on the front-row bench, there's definitely a huge part of me that wishes I were up onstage with everybody else. Still, I'm happy for them. This is their time. Eventually Barb signals for us all to quiet down so that the ceremony can conclude.

"To finish off this extraordinary evening, we have an unusual treat," she says. "Though you might not recognize her, we have a very talented young singer in our midst. She's been on the Billboard One-Hundred chart more than any other young artist in the last decade. That didn't mean a whole lot to me, when I first met her—" Barb turns to give Titania a wink. "But after getting to know her over these past few weeks, I've realized that she is also a beautiful human being in all the ways that really count. Titania, are you ready?"

I've never seen Titania appear anything resembling shy, but at this moment she's almost humble. Stepping forward, she clears her throat and accepts the guitar that Xander presents. She puts the strap over her head and adjusts it before looking up to address the audience. Nick carries over a tall wooden stool, and she gracefully balances on the edge of it.

"Call me Tonya," she says, nervously reintroducing herself. "I'd like to play something I've been working on while I was out here. It's called 'Starting Over.' It will be the first song on my new album and, more importantly, the first song in my new life."

She checks the tuning on the guitar one more time and, after a few false starts, begins strumming a few simple chords. Initially, her voice is so soft that we have to strain to hear it, but by the end of the first stanza it has become strong and confident, and the lyrics hold all the hope and promise of a better future, the kind all of us are now striving for. Unlike all her over-produced pop songs (the ones that make her sound like a tarted-up cyborg), the sound of her voice is tender and transcendent in its simplicity. I had no idea she had been composing an original song over these past few weeks, and it makes me proud to be her friend. Not because the whole world knows her, but because I finally know her. The *real* her. And she is incredibly talented.

When she finishes the final chorus, everyone applauds enthusiastically, but I can barely see anything because my vision blurs over like a window on a rainy day. I'm happy, but sad at the same time. What good is starting over when you have to say goodbye to some of the truest friends you've ever had? Once again, Barb motions for quiet, but this time it takes several minutes for the cheers and whistles to subside.

"Thank you, Tonya," she begins. "That was lovely. I'm glad you all enjoyed the song, and I hope the rest of the world enjoys it just as much, because Tonya has offered to donate any profits from the 'Starting Over' single to DreamRoads." More clapping follows this proclamation, which seems to take everyone but Barb and Nick by surprise.

"I was disappearing under the weight of other people's expectations before I landed here," Titania explains. "I mean, I actually *landed* here in a helicopter. How obnoxious is that? I realized over these past few weeks that the only image of myself that really matters is the one I see in the mirror, which is why I want to give back to this place, so it can make a difference in someone else's life, the way it did for all of us." She glances at her fellow graduates, who are standing arm in arm on the stage, smiling at her supportively.

"We'll be using the funds to launch our first-ever DreamRoads scholarship," Nick explains, stepping forward, "and we hope the inaugural recipient will be willing to give this place another go." He looks directly at me as he says this, and I realize that, once again, I'm a few steps behind.

"Puck," Barb says, "You told us all that you want a second chance. Well, we'd like to offer you one. If you choose to accept it, you will be our first DreamRoads Scholarship recipient. You know by now that DreamRoads isn't a punishment, it's an opportunity, but this isn't just a freebie either; it's something you've earned. You made mistakes, but you are not the sum of them."

"If *I* can change, anyone can," Titania adds encouragingly.

"Me, too," says Peabo.

"And us," Frances and Nissa say together.

"Arf," adds Snout, cracking everyone up. (Everyone but me, that is.)

My body tenses and my pulse pounds in that way it always does before I lose my cool. I don't like being put on the spot, and this makes it twice in the course of an hour that it's happened. Barb actually believed I was being sincere up onstage when I spoke about the regrets I had. *Did I mean it?* Now that I'm being given the opportunity to back up my words with action, my heart sinks. Push has come to shove, and all I really want to do is back out, to go back to Flagstaff and the creature comforts of civilization with my head hung low. As much as I believed what I said in front of everyone, in hindsight, it has the familiar ring of classic Puck b.s. I look over at Paula and Ted to see if my staying here for another session is okay with them. They both nod and smile. Crap. Six more weeks of crouching to pee? Six more weeks of sleeping on the cold, hard ground? Six more weeks of flavorless food, throbbing feet, and firestarting fails?

"I need another 'old-timer' around here," Ronnie says encouragingly. "Somebody who will scare the new recruits more than I do for a change."

"What do you say, Puck?" Quin asks. He can read me better than anyone else here, and the doubtful expression on his face mirrors how I'm feeling at this moment. I take a deep breath and let my shoulders sink down my neck, sensing an invisible set of hands bearing down on me once again. I can't bring myself to look at Barb, Nick, or anyone else onstage, so I focus on their shadows, which seem to have a life all their own in the backdrop of the harsh stage light. I think of my own shadow, too, remembering my first dinner here, when I caused all hell to break loose. That familiar spark has resided in me for a long time, and I'm not completely certain it will ever go away, or if it even should. It has wreaked plenty of havoc, but it's kept me strong, too.

"Do you think she'll stay?" I hear someone behind me whisper. I'm overwhelmed by a crush of feelings, but the shadow dances across my face and finally materializes in a smirk. Tonight's party is finally wrapping up, but nothing's ending here. As a matter of fact, I have a sneaking suspicion it's only just beginning.

"Will I stay?" I repeat the question. I know what I'm about to say may offend people, but that's who I am, for worse (and, I hope) for better. Here goes nothing. "Puck yeah!"

9 780998 161303